# THE ENGLISH EARL

## THE EARLS OF MERCIA
### BOOK SEVEN

## MJ PORTER

MJ PUBLISHING

*Copyright notice*
*Porter, M J*
*The English Earl*
*Copyright ©2018, Porter, M.J, Amazon edition*
*All characters and events in this publication, other than those clearly in the public domain, are fictitious and any resemblance to actual persons, living or dead, is purely coincidental.*

ALL RIGHTS RESERVED. No part of this publication may be reproduced, stored in a retrieval system or transmitted in any form or by any means without the prior written permission of the author, nor be otherwise circulated in any form of binding or cover other than that in which it is published and without a similar condition being imposed on the subsequent buyer.

Cover design by MJ Porter

Cover image by Illustration 66509238 © Mr1805 - Dreamstime.com

ISBN: 978-1-914332-13-5 (ebook)

ISBN: 978-1717854582 (paperback)

ISBN: 978-1-914332-56-2 (hardback/large print)

✽ Created with Vellum

*For my Mum, on what should have been her 70$^{th}$ birthday.*

*We miss you.*

# CONTENTS

| | | |
|---|---|---|
| | Preface | 7 |
| | The Story So Far… | 9 |
| | Prologue | 11 |
| 1. | November AD1035 | 21 |
| 2. | AD1035 | 39 |
| 3. | Oxford, December AD1035 | 49 |
| 4. | AD1035 | 74 |
| 5. | AD1035 | 88 |
| | The Anglo Saxon Chronicle Entry for 1035 | 105 |
| 6. | London, AD1036 | 106 |
| | *London* | |
| 7. | AD1036 | 120 |
| 8. | AD1036 | 139 |
| 9. | Summer AD1036 | 149 |
| 10. | Outside London, AD1036 | 167 |
| 11. | AD1036 | 179 |
| 12. | AD1036 | 190 |
| 13. | AD1036, Ælfgar | 196 |
| 14. | Late AD1036 | 205 |
| 15. | AD1036 | 221 |
| | The Anglo Saxon Chronicle Entry for 1037 | 229 |
| 16. | Early AD1037 | 230 |
| 17. | AD1037 | 249 |
| 18. | AD1037 | 258 |
| | The Anglo Saxon Chronicle Entry for 1037 | 269 |
| | Cast of Characters | 271 |
| | Historical Notes | 277 |
| | About the Author | 283 |
| | Books by MJ Porter (in series reading order) | 285 |

# PREFACE

(Note – there are a number of characters with identical names in this book – all historically attested – both a Lord Harald (Cnut's son) and a Lord Harold (Thorkell's son) and an Earl Godwine of Wessex (of the Godwinessons) and a Lord Godwine (Leofric's brother), as such I have given Lord Godwine the Norse sounding surname of Godwine Leofwinesson to differentiate them, and to prevent repetition of 'of House Leofwine').

# THE STORY SO FAR...

King Cnut has finally named Earl Leofric as the Earl of Mercia. England is peaceful, following a small altercation with the kingdom of the Scots, and Cnut has spent the intervening years in England since his pilgrimage to Rome in 1031 – his two sons hold power outside England. Harthacnut, his son with Lady Emma, is in Denmark, where his influential Aunt, Lady Estrid (Cnut's sister) assists the seventeen-year-old, whereas Swein, his son with Lady Ælfgifu, is Regent or King of Norway, at the age of twenty-one alongside his mother.

Harald, his remaining son with Lady Ælfgifu, is being fostered by Earl Leofric within Mercia, and has just turned nineteen. Earl Godwine holds Wessex, and Earl Siward, Northumbria, where he's married the Earl of Bamburgh's daughter, uniting his right to rule with the House of Bamburgh's hereditary one.

Gunnhilda, Cnut's daughter with Lady Emma, is just fifteen years old but has long lived with her future husband in the lands of Conrad, the Holy Roman Emperor.

The Danish Earl, Hrani remains in England ruling his lands in Herefordshire, Mercia, and Lady Gunnhildr, the widow of Earl Hakon

(Regent in Norway before Swein), is also still ruling his lands in Worcestershire, also in Mercia. Earl Eilifr, who once held lands in Gloucestershire yet lives, but is in exile from England and no longer an ally of King Cnut's, following his brother's death for treason in Denmark, where he was married to Lady Estrid, Cnut's sister.

England is peaceful, as shown by the dearth of entries in the Anglo-Saxon Chronicle, where only the deaths of churchmen are mentioned in the years 1032, 1033 and 1034.

# PROLOGUE
## SUMMER AD1035

He found the King outside, gazing at the royal horses that frolicked in the early summer sun, some rolling onto their backs, hooves all over the place as they enjoyed the comfort of having their backs caressed by the lush undergrowth. Yet others were content to nibble at the grass lying thick on the ground.

So engrossed in the animals was Cnut, that Leofric was sure the King didn't notice his presence, and so he stood quietly, just off to one side, content to enjoy the spectacle.

He didn't know why the King had summoned him, but it had been a strangely personal message, delivered by Brithmær in a perplexed voice, asking, not demanding his presence, and so Leofric had come, in all haste, to find the King at Shrewsbury Abbey. Even the meeting place was unusual. Cnut favoured Oxford, or occasionally Winchester, where Queen Emma preferred to live, but it seemed he was alone at Shrewsbury Abbey, his wife elsewhere.

Or so it seemed. Little pomp and ceremony had greeted him, and the monks had offered nothing, their silence as worrying as the message delivered by Brithmær. Orkning, his only companion had turned a puzzled frown Leofric's way, but all he could offer was a shrug. He had no answers but knew they'd be given shortly.

Leofric blanked his mind. There was no point in trying to determine the reason for the King's unusual behaviour. He would know soon enough. He'd worried throughout the journey here, undertaken with more haste than usual, Orkning allowing his horse the freedom to speed, as he wanted. Now that he would find out the truth of the King's wishes, he felt strangely loath to know the truth.

He assumed the request must be to do with his son, Harald, Leofric's foster-son, but even there he couldn't be sure. Despite everything, Cnut had failed to build a good relationship with Harald, and the summons had not included his son. It had been personally addressed to Leofric, and only to be heard by him. It upset Leofric that even after all this time, Cnut didn't see his son as worth knowing.

As a parent, he felt Cnut should have tried far harder to maintain close contact with his children. Instead, he saw them all as political pawns to be moved about at his command. Leofric knew he could never be as callous with his one and only son, or even with his nieces and nephews who looked to him as the head of the House of Leofwine.

The silence stretched, broken only by the nickering of the horses and the occasional irritating fly. The sun felt warm on his face, as he tilted his head backwards.

"I often wonder whether the horses know how ridiculous they look when they do that?" Cnut spoke softly, his voice filled with warm amusement, and still, Leofric jumped. He hadn't realised that the King had been aware of his approach, and he too had allowed his watchfulness to fall as he watched the animals frolic in the summer heat. He knew of no creature, man, woman or beast that didn't revel in the heat from the sun when summer finally arrived in all its glory.

"My thanks for accepting my invitation," the King continued, his voice barely above a whisper, still not turning to look at Leofric, his attention fixed on the animals. One of them was standing aloof from the others, and if Leofric hadn't known better, he'd have said the animal disdained the others.

His coat was well oiled, brushed to perfection, his long midnight nose somehow held a little higher in the air than all the others. He was a horse aware of his superior position.

"Is that Blue?" Leofric asked, pointing toward the horse he watched, and Cnut nodded.

"Yes, he's always a bit strange when the summer arrives. Give him some time, he'll throw himself to the ground as well and forget that a king rides him. I always like to observe this moment. The daft beast. I'll miss this next year," the King ended wistfully, and Leofric felt his heart contract as Cnut finally turned to look at him.

His King, his sometime friend, and erstwhile enemy had aged beyond all counting in the short month since they'd last met. Cnut's handsome face was sunken, his expression gaunt, and his clothes seemed to cascade from him in a vast expanse, as though made for a giant and now festooned around a dwarf. His warrior's stance and gait had melted away, just like a candle that burns too hot in the breeze from a stray draft. Only half of him still remained. The rest had sloughed away.

Cnut smiled with gentle mocking and bowed scornfully. "Yes, I'm all gone. Well, almost all gone. I linger yet."

"My Lord King," Leofric gasped, and Cnut strode the short space between them and unexpectedly flung his arms around him. Caught unaware, it took Leofric a few moments to reciprocate and when he did all he could feel was the fluttering heartbeat of a bird in the once colossal chest of Cnut, the embrace from Cnut feeling as though he were caressed and not overpowered by a man who knew his immense strength well.

"Yes, I'm dying," Cnut when he finally released his grip and stepped away again, his eyes straying back to his horse with longing. Blue still stood alone amongst the rest of the horses.

"I've some time, but not very much. I'll not be here to see this next year, or even to see the beginning of next year. Don't offer sympathy. I don't need it." A harsh edge had turned Cnut's voice to the iron of the warrior Leofric had long known, and Leofric understood why the Queen was not with her husband. Her sympathy and concern would be unwanted for a man more used to dealing death with a sharp blade than watching life recede away through illness.

"I understand," Leofric said, his voice gruff with emotion, hating the fact he could say nothing else, but understanding Cnut's wishes all the same. He'd watched his father, and Wulfstan, fail. He knew the honour of a warrior's death should come in battle and not like this.

"I must make plans before I die. My son..." he paused. "My son Swein, Regent in Norway, has failed. I'm sure you know. What you won't know is that he's dead. Killed on his way to Denmark. The young King Magnus and his Regents now claim Norway, and those Regents have killed my son and threaten the rest of my Empire. Harthacnut is embattled, Lady Ælfgifu returning to England swaddled in grief and failure, with the remaining ship-army that escorted them."

Leofric held his tongue, watching Blue, not Cnut. Secretly he was pleased that Cnut had masterminded their meeting in such a way that neither need see the sadness of the other. The news of Cnut's death was somehow far more important than events in lands far to the north that Leofric knew more by name than experience. But he was sad to hear about Swein. The news, given so callously, was new to him. He would have to inform Harald. It would not go well.

"She's unharmed?" Leofric finally thought to ask, and Cnut nodded, or so a swift glance at the profile of his King showed him as he asked after Lady Ælfgifu.

"She's well. Distressed, of course, as am I. It's not right that I'll never see my son again, but then, I've so little time, it's possible I might never have seen him again anyway, even if he had held Norway." There was a harder edge to Cnut's voice now. It was as though he were bitterly disappointed by Swein's failure to hold the Norwegian kingdom, but also deeply saddened by the loss of Swein, named for his grandfather, Swein Forkbeard, when the grief of King Swein's sudden death had plunged England into chaos once more, twenty years ago. Leofric remembered it too well.

Cnut's relationship with his elder sons had always been complicated. It seemed Cnut might be regretting that now that one was dead, and his own death loomed uncomfortably close on the horizon.

"England?" Leofric asked, understanding that this was where Cnut's thoughts had tumbled away to as he lapsed into silence once more. It was almost as though talking was exhausting, let alone standing and watching the horses.

"Can't be left without someone to rule her."

"Of course not," Leofric agreed, his own worries for the future seeming to matter little in the wake of Cnut's foreshortened life. Cnut had once spoken of dividing his Empire between his sons, as though he couldn't imagine anyone ever wielding as much power as he did. As though building an empire was something only he could have done. Leofric wondered if that had now changed.

"My wife, the Queen," Cnut swallowed thickly, "believes the kingdom should fall to Harthacnut, but of course, he faces war in Denmark, and he knows his duty to the House of Gorm. Denmark first, England is but second to the House of Gorm, but not to others. I understand that too." Cnut spoke with the experience of a man who'd spent his adult life juggling twin responsibilities – to the land of his birthright and the land he'd conquered in battle, subjugated to his will by the sheer power of his magnetism and determination.

"Then who, my Lord King?"

"The 'who' rather depends on my Earls; you, Siward and Godwine, and of course those of my former Earls who still hold some power in Mercia – Hrani, and Hakon's widow and her new husband. Earl Godwine will want Harthacnut. He's little respect for Harald, in that he thinks like the Queen." Bitterness tinged Cnut's voice when he spoke of Earl Godwine. They'd long been friends and allies until Godwine had overstepped the mark some years before. It seemed that in the crisis of his death Cnut realised just how much Godwine's power was dependent on him.

No doubt Godwine, with his usual tact, had made it very clear to his King. No doubt there had been a revelation for Cnut in that knowledge – kings were rarely loved for who they were but rather for the advantages they could provide to their loyal followers.

Leofric had once thought the King would deprive Godwine of all his power and possessions. It was a constant disappointment that Godwine still held the King's ear when he didn't deserve it. Some friendships were always blind to the weaknesses of the other, and it seemed that in some respects Cnut was a victim of the same criticisms that had been levied against King Æthelred II.

Leofric ran Cnut's words back through his head as he tried to follow his line of reasoning. He was pleased Cnut mentioned Earl Hrani and Lady Gunnhilda, Earl Hakon's widow, but he also thought there was a slight censor there. Cnut's Danish Earls had not proven popular in Mercia. They might once have trampled over his father's position of power as Ealdorman of the Hwicce and Mercia as a whole, but most, even Hrani and Lady Gunnhilda, accepted that Leofric represented the whole of Mercia now. They had a voice, and he listened to it when he could, but he was Earl of Mercia, they were merely honoured members of the nobility, and few would ever add the word 'Earl' before their name now – not even the royal scribes when they transcribed the King's wishes for future reference in the charters they labouriously wrote out.

But the King's thoughts were on Godwine and Siward now, his Earls of Wessex and Northumbria.

"I believe Earl Siward will welcome continuity and good leadership, but I see him so rarely it's hard to tell."

Ah, Leofric was finally unravelling the conversation. There were warnings here, and also something else. Cnut was accepting, despite everything, that his wishes might not be followed upon his death, primarily by those he'd long thought of as his closest and most loyal advisors. He was also warning Leofric that the future of England's kingship rested in the hands of himself and Earl Godwine, for all that they were mere earls and not kings. Or even members of the King's complicated and elongated family, that stretched from England, to Denmark, to Norway and Sweden, even to the lands of the Holy Roman Empire.

Leofric accepted the compliment, as awkwardly as it was offered.

"Many will assume the Queen and Earl Godwine will be the people to lead England until Harthacnut can extract himself from Denmark."

"But I'm not the many?" Leofric asked softly, a caution to his voice now. He and the King had long had a problematic relationship. It seemed it might end on a similar note.

"You're not the many," Cnut agreed with finality, turning to gaze at Leofric again. Blue still stood aloof, alone, a reflection of Cnut's position now.

"I'd die happier knowing that my other son is not abandoned, that he'll at least have some consideration upon my death. He does deserve that. I could only wish that Swein were not dead already."

"Then you should make your wishes known, have a will drawn up that reflects your desires," Leofric spoke harshly, the weight of the King's onerous task already pressing down on him. The King had talked of this before but had never acted on it, and now it seemed there wouldn't be time for him to implement those wishes for after his death.

"I should yes, but I will not, and cannot. I ask this of you instead. It might well cause 'problems', but I trust you to handle them with your usual effectiveness." Cnut spoke calmly, as though it were a simple matter, and yet he knew that his request was not as easy as the words made it seem.

"You would pitch me against the Queen and Earl Godwine?" Leofric said, just for clarity and just to ensure he understood the King's demand on him.

"I would have you do what you've always done, no matter what."

"And what exactly is that?" Leofric probed. His sadness was being replaced by a slow-burning rage.

Cnut had never stopped demanding the impossible from his family, and it seemed he wasn't about to start now, even though Leofric was the foster-father of Harald, his son.

"You have always done the 'right' thing, just as your father before you, and often despite your own personal preferences. You're a rare man, Earl Leofric, a very rare man. Few can put the good of the kingdom, and others above the good of themselves. Few would even consider it necessary, especially amongst the nobility."

"A back-handed compliment, if ever I heard one," Leofric grumbled, and Cnut surprised him again.

"It's the highest compliment I can give a man. I only wish I'd known more men like yourself. I was always a warrior who wanted to be king, never a king who wanted to be a warrior: a strange distinction but one I'll make all the same. Warriors seek personal gain and treasure, the funds to raid once more, to destroy others, to profit from that destruction. A King should only do that when there's no other option. In another life, Leofric, you would have been an excellent ruler, but not in this life. In this life, you've helped me try and be a better man, and as such, a better King."

Leofric was surprised by the vehemence in Cnut's voice.

"Your father swore an oath to my father to make me King, and he did so even though he was already oath sworn to King Æthelred, and somehow, he managed to honour all of his pledges. I would lay the same on you. Harthacnut must be King after me, but he will not be for some time, maybe not even during your lifetime. But Harald can be King in his place, you can make that happen, and all without me enduring the final months of what life I have left listening to Earl Godwine and Queen Emma persuading me otherwise. I trust you with this."

As he spoke, Cnut's lower lip trembled with emotion, and Leofric swallowed thickly, pleased to be distracted by Blue finally lowering himself to the floor, and letting his hooves fly as he scratched his long, sinuous back on the undergrowth.

"Stupid bloody horse," Cnut choked on tears, as Leofric held his tongue.

The horse rolled from side to side, his hooves high and mobile, and when he stumbled upright once more, all haughtiness was gone from his stance, and he happily joined some of the other animals, grazing on the green grass and enjoying the warmth of the sun on their back.

"In the end," Cnut said, his voice soft and filled with emotion, "we're all the same and crave only to be welcomed and accepted by everyone, even Kings. And in the end, even Kings are only men, and they will die and leave a tarnished legacy without the aid of their friends and allies to ensure everything is as it should be."

With that, Cnut turned and began to walk back toward the Abbey building, shining under the warm sun in an array of deep golden browns reminiscent of the vast Mercian forests the wood had been felled from, and which Leofric maintained with deep pride, and the aid of his commended men and woodspeople.

"You have my oath," Leofric called, and Cnut paused in his laboured steps, and Leofric thought he'd let the moment pass without saying anything else.

"My thanks, old friend. England needs an Earl of her own," Cnut said, without turning around. Then he resumed his walk and Leofric watched him go with tears leaking from his eyes, while Blue grazed without a care in the world.

# 1

## NOVEMBER AD1035

Once more Earl Leofric gazed upon the dead body of a man he'd only recently called King.

Cnut, young, even by Leofric's own standards, was dead.

Unbidden, images of King Swein, King Æthelred, and King Edmund's deaths entered his mind, and he was, once more a youth, not a man grown, with his own son to his name. He was once more unsure, and unwilling to accept what had happened, and he was fearful as well. The death of the King would bring about a monumental shift in the politics of England, and he knew, from experience, just how destructive that could be.

King Swein's death had been sudden and unexpected, to all but his own father, Ealdorman Leofwine, who seemed to have been preparing for it. King Æthelred's death had been a little more expected, because of his age, but then the worst of all, the death of young King Edmund, from wounds gained in a battle against Cnut. He'd been a young man, with an entire life to rule England, and a young son to rule after him too.

Leofric shook his head at the tricks of fate. He'd hoped to serve King Cnut for far longer than he had. Cnut hadn't even celebrated his fortieth birthday. If he'd died in battle, it might have been easier to accept, but instead, disease had stolen his strength and then his life as well.

Earl Leofric tried to be stoic in the face of his sorrow, but he knew, perhaps better than many within that frigid room in the Old Minster at Winchester, how difficult the coming days would be.

The death of the King was no light matter, especially when that King's death was somewhat unexpected and his 'chosen' heir far from England's shore. England might be at peace, but there was no assurance that status quo would continue.

Harthacnut, the English born son of the Danish King and his wife, Emma of Normandy, was in Denmark. He was already King in all but name in Denmark, and now he'd be named King of the country from which Swein and Cnut had originated, and where their family line had long ruled as the House of Gorm. Gorm had been a bully, and an ogre to his son, or so rumour had it, and yet it was his name that would ring through the ages as he'd fathered the great Swein Forkbeard, and he in his turn, Cnut, King of Denmark, England, Norway and Sweden. What happened next lay in the hands of a very young man, only seventeen years old.

Yet Harthacnut should have been in England, taking the acclaim of the earls and thegns, holy men and women on his father's death, not in Denmark, where his succession was already assured, by his birthright and also because of the support of his aunt and cousins. Leofric knew this would cause nothing but trouble in the coming days, for Cnut had more than one son.

Once he'd had three sons. Swein, his eldest son with his first wife, had died earlier in the year, having failed to hold Norway against the pretensions of others who also wished to be named King. Cnut had lived long enough to learn of his death, and Leofric knew that it had saddened him, adding to his own distress at his impending death.

This situation, with two sons, from two different wives, with only one of them in England, would make the future rule of England problematic, and that was without even considering the oath that Cnut had extracted from Leofric before his death, and without his obligations as foster-father to one of those sons, Harald.

Already Leofric could feel the scrutiny of Earl Godwine in the cold little room. The man was a consummate political animal, and Leofric knew he'd be busy deciding on the best steps to take following Cnut's death. One of those steps seemed to be watching and shepherding those who'd come to pay their respects to their dead King before his burial.

Leofric knew he should be doing the same, but instead he felt lost, as he had done when each of the three previous Kings had unexpectedly died. No matter his warning from the King himself, to know something, and to see something come to fruition were two entirely different things.

He'd never been as quick thinking as his father, but he believed that the situation was unwinnable, especially given his loyalty to Lady Ælfgifu and her surviving son. He'd be tested now. He knew that, and even Cnut had ensured the next few months, or years, would be especially difficult for him. Lady Ælfgifu was an exacting ally. She'd expect him to declare for her son and it seemed that Cnut wanted him to do the same.

The irony wasn't lost on him that for the first time, ever, Cnut and his first wife seemed to be in agreement on something that concerned their children.

But, it would involve a confrontation with Earl Godwine and the Queen Dowager, and Leofric would much prefer to avoid such a thing. Should he fail, the endeavours of he and his father would all be for nothing, and his family would face the same, slow decline that other noble families had endured over time. Those families remained, hovering on the periphery, just hoping for an opportunity to redeem themselves in the eyes of a new King, keen to take advantage of any indiscretion or mistake made by those currently in favour.

He suppressed a sigh, as he tried to clear his mind.

His King was dead, that should be all he thought about.

"Has word been sent to Denmark?" Leofric thought to ask softly, turning to face Earl Godwine, who seemed to stand as a guard over the body of his King and ally. Earl Godwine's face was gaunt, but his beard and moustache were well-oiled, his clothing chosen for warmth in the frozen room in the Old Minster. Leofric knew Godwine would watch all who came and went that day, and then he'd begin to plot and seek out new allies and new enemies.

Earl Godwine's face was calculating, and Leofric considered him all over again. They weren't outright enemies. It was difficult to be that and retain the support of the King, but they could never be called allies. Leofric hoped that Earl Godwine had not made Cnut's final breaths too difficult, but he thought the hope might be a vain one.

"It's winter. The North Sea is like a tempest. Word will be sent when we find someone skilled enough to tackle the waves, or deluded enough to think they can. Until then the knowledge that King Cnut is dead is known throughout England, and not much further. Well, not the confirmation of his death." Earl Godwine paused in his answer, licking his lips as his eyes followed those who bowed and prayed before the King's coffin.

"I understand that Cnut sent word to Harthacnut warning him that he'd die soon, and offering instructions to his Aunt Estrid on how they should proceed." Earl Leofric considered the words. There was no malice in them, just simple facts for all that they sounded cold from someone many considered Cnut's greatest friend and ally.

Leofric would almost say that Earl Godwine was displeased with Cnut. But then Cnut had chosen a terrible time to die.

"Word has been sent to Harald?" Earl Godwine asked now, but he already knew the answer, just as Leofric had known the answer to his question about Harthacnut. Leofric's loyalty to Lady Ælfgifu and her sons was well known, as was his place as Harald's foster-father in recent years. "Do you know when he'll arrive?" Godwine probed.

"No, I've received no firm details from him, but it won't be long.

I'm sure of that. He knows the funeral is tomorrow. And the Queen Dowager, Lady Emma, she's in Winchester?"

The King had died at Shaftesbury Abbey, the final place where Leofric had seen him, but his body, as he'd wished, had been transported to Winchester so that it could be interred within the Old Minster.

"She accompanied the King's cortege," Earl Godwine confirmed, a hint of irritation in his voice at the conversation and the persistent questions. Leofric both nodded and waved his hand to indicate he meant no offence.

"Apologies, Lord Godwine. It's difficult to order everything."

"Yes it is," was the terse response he got, and Leofric decided it was best to leave the enclosed room within the Old Minster to Godwine and his haughty if wounded, eyes. He didn't wish to intrude on either the man's grief, or his political plots, or even his anger that Cnut had died and inconvenienced the Earl so bloody much.

Before he left, he took a final glance at the King. Cnut lay in state in his royal coffin, his body embalmed so that all that could be seen was his head, not yet covered by the holy shroud that would cover him for eternity, in imitation of Christ. His crown had been placed over his blond curls, and a crucifix lay on his chest. Other than that, only the shroud showed.

Herbs littered the room, to drive away any corruption from the body, but it was cold, winter, and the body, just as those who came to bow jerkily before it, was frozen, just about solid, ice particles having to be cleared from the dead eyes of the King each morning before others were allowed to see him.

Leofric, an irreverent mood taking him, was pleased they wouldn't have to find wood enough to offer a traditional Viking sea burial. He doubted they'd be able to create enough heat to warm the king's solid body, let alone burn it to ash that could be scattered on the waves.

He strode from the room, resolved to be gone from his strange thoughts, and out into the more open space of the main chancel of the Old Minster. It wasn't his favourite church, he much preferred the more elaborate New Minster next door, but the King's final wishes were being followed, at least in this one regard, so Leofric tempered his unease at being inside the ancient building.

It seemed to whisper of secrets and deceits, not at all a source of comfort for Leofric. So many dead lay interred within its confines that Leofric always expected to turn a corner and be faced with the entreaties from a long-dead king or prince of the long-standing House of Wessex; someone who had unfinished business with the current ruler and nobility.

Leofric breathed deeply, content to find a chair to sit on, away from everyone else who queued in an orderly line to see the dead King, and just think of the future.

The Old Minster was busy, and Cnut's household warriors lined the room where his body lay, determined that no one should despoil their dead lord.

There was near silence, apart from the near continual soft murmur of prayer coming from the monks and holy men of the Old Minster. They knelt close to the altar, braziers driving the cold from around them so that they could pray all day and all night without suffering the deep pangs of winter's icy fingers.

It could almost be termed restful and orderly, despite the sorrow of the event, and Leofric supposed that was the point of all the pomp and ceremony that surrounded the death of any loved one.

Cnut had been dead for ten days. He'd been in Shaftesbury when he'd met his premature death, but Leofric had received word only two days later. In the last eight days, Earl Godwine had had time to act and set his own agenda in motion. But it seemed he hadn't, or so Leofric had determined so far, from his conversation with Earl Godwine, and from the generally depressed mood within Winchester itself.

There were no furtive meetings taken place. No one even seemed to use the terrible weather as a cover for rushing through the streets with their hoods pulled tight around their ears to plot in the shadowy recesses of smoke-filled halls.

It had taken time for the King's body to be prepared for transportation, and longer yet for the actual journey to Winchester, along storm-ravaged roads, filled with icy puddles and thick mud both. As such Leofric had had ample time to send messengers to his foster-son Harald in Northampton. They had been concerned with the future of England and had sought news about his foster-son's mother.

Lady Ælfgifu's journey home to England had been much delayed due to Swein's death in Denmark, but Harald had sent word that his mother had finally returned some weeks before. It was a double-edged sword to have her return to England at such a disturbing time. While Leofric was pleased she's arrived, it would mean that she was free to meddle and meddle she would.

"Father," his son spoke to him, worry in his voice, and Leofric turned to look up into his young son's concerned face. The lad was the very image of his own father, and sometimes he forgot his youth and almost asked him for the advice that his father would have so readily given him. Today, he remembered with the words already forming on his lips and bit back the comment.

"Ælfgar," he responded, keen to allay his fears.

"You're well?" the youth asked, and Leofric nodded absently.

"Yes, yes. It's just," and here he paused to think of the right words. "Difficult to gaze upon the face of a man who's now dead, when last he was alive."

"Ah," Ælfgar said, seemingly consoled by that knowledge. For a moment Leofric pondered the possibility that his son had thought him about to drop dead, as Cnut had, and he spared a thought for upsetting him.

"Do you wish to pay your respects to the King?" he asked his son, but Ælfgar was already shaking his head. His face had turned pale at the mention of a dead body, and Leofric took pity on him. Ælfgar had been raised in a different time to him. He had little experience of dead bodies and battle. Leofric thought back to his experiences at the same age and then dismissed them. There was simply no comparison. Ælfgar and his cousins had taken part in a brief skirmish with the Scottish some years before. It had been over quickly, and now the borders were safe. Or so they appeared to be under the careful watch of Earl Siward and the House of Bamburgh.

He was pleased his son had known peace and security. He wished he'd enjoyed the same experience.

"Come on, let's get some air. I know it's cold enough to freeze your balls off outside, but it's to be preferred to being in here." Leofric raised his hands to indicate the high-sided building and began to make his way to the door. It was tightly closed against the raging storm outside, and Leofric had to force his way outside, using his shoulder to open the large wooden door into the howling wind.

Immediately the wind stole his breath, and he hastily turned his back to the gusting sheets of rain and hunkered down into his great cloak. His son tumbled outside, slamming the door behind them, and mirroring his father's actions.

Those who'd made it to the Old Minster were lingering inside, not out of respect, but because the thought of facing the tempest was so unwelcoming.

Together they made their way along the twisting pathway to the gate that led out from the Benedictine Monastery and into Winchester itself.

It was no time of year to be out and about, let alone traipsing through the countryside to attend a funeral. Leofric grimaced. It was no time of year to be worrying about the future either.

The harvest was in, wood and kindling gathered to ward off the winter snows, and hay and grasses gathered for the animals lucky enough to live through the winter. Indeed there was little that anyone should be doing but eating and drinking, dreaming of the long-awaited summer, and listening to the stories of ancestors and brave warriors while the women took the opportunity to repair clothing and make new clothes, in the limited light of the dark days.

Winchester itself was sparsely populated when they exited the gate from the Old Minster. A few hardy souls braved the wind and rain to rush from shop front to shop front, avoiding the ever-growing puddles as they huddled inside their own cloaks. Not that many shop fronts looked open for business. Most had kept their shutters down, not wishing to allow their goods to become water damaged. There were no horses in the street, and Leofric thought Winchester as forlorn as he felt.

Hastily they made their way to the house they were staying within. Once, Coelric had presided over it, but now his daughter owned the house, and yet she was still happy to offer a roof over their head for him and his son, and any other family members who chose to journey to Winchester. Leofric was grateful for their hospitality. Cnut had much preferred Oxford as the place to meet his members of the Witan, but Winchester was the traditional capital of Wessex, and therefore England. That was why it retained its importance and Cnut had chosen to be buried within the Old Minster, with past members of the House of Wessex.

For a moment, Leofric wondered why he'd not chosen to be buried with his father, at Gainsborough, or even why he'd not asked to have his body returned to Denmark. Perhaps Cnut had given it only a glancing thought. After all, who liked to think of their death when they were still alive?

Once inside the well-maintained hall, Leofric discarded his cloak and settled beside the blazing hearth fire, gratefully curving his hands around the warmed wine-filled goblet he was offered by one of the household servants.

Ælfgar followed suit, joining his father beside the hearth and neither of them spoke while they considered what they'd just experienced in the Old Minster. Leofric found comfort in the dancing flames, but Ælfgar shuffled with unease.

"Lady Ælfgifu will expect Harald to become King or at least regent in Harthacnut's absence, won't she?" his son probed, and Leofric nodded. They'd had this conversation endlessly since news of

Cnut's death had reached them. Still, it did no harm to revisit the possibilities. And Leofric had chosen not to share the content of his last interview with any member of his family. His actions would be telling enough, in due time.

"Yes, she will."

"But Queen Dowager Emma will want to be regent until Harthacnut arrives?"

"Yes, she will."

"And Earl Godwine will support her?"

"Yes, again. He was Cnut's firmest ally. He'll do all he can to ensure Cnut's wishes are adhered to." Leofric winced to speak of Cnut in the past but knew he needed to get used to it.

"Lady Emma has never accepted Lady Ælfgifu's position?"

"No, she hasn't. The King was prepared and happy to use his children from the marriage to accomplish his goals but Lady Emma has never been tolerant, and she won't be now. She wants her son to be King after his father. Only Harthacnut is embroiled in a war in Denmark. I can't imagine that Harthacnut, raised in the Danish court for so long, even thinks of England as his home."

"You think he won't want to rule here then?" Ælfgar queried, and Leofric sighed deeply and considered his answer.

"I think he'll see Denmark as a greater challenge, a way to prove he's worthy of being a member of the House of Gorm, or the House of Swein Forkbeard, as some call it. But England is wealthy, and Harthacnut needs that wealth to fund his war with Norway and Sweden. He'll rely on his mother and Earl Godwine to hold the kingdom for him, but in doing so, he'll be making a grave error. The English are not the most ... patient."

"While Cnut ruled, England and the English felt that it was the more important kingdom to him, but really, he was away for much of his reign, relying on others to hold England securely for him. Harthacnut doesn't have the same connection with the English. He hasn't won the support of the English in battle, and neither has he stopped the constant raids that bedevilled English shores while

Æthelred was King. He only has his father's reputation – for the time being."

Ælfgar was listening intently, as he always did, trying to determine the best way forward but Leofric knew it was far from as simple as his son wanted it to be.

"It's an unholy mess," Leofric muttered, feeling the strain of the future as a weight on his shoulders. He believed that England was in for a difficult time while the sons of Cnut fought over their inheritance. He considered the possibility, as little as he wanted to, that despite all of Cnut's achievements, he was most likely to be remembered for having two sons, with two different women, who both wanted to rule his Empire, rather than for winning that Empire through conquest.

It seemed wrong that a King should be remembered more for having sex with two different women than for his actual achievements in war, politics and religious matters.

He was reminded of Cnut's words to him, about his legacy and those who determined what was and what wasn't remembered.

Who would write Cnut's legacy? His second wife? His first wife? His older son? His younger son? Or would it be someone else? A monk in his scriptorium who'd never even met Cnut, who wrote what he was told? Would it even be something written now, or something written fifty years from now, when all the protagonists were long dead?

In reality, Leofric thought that Lord Harald would be content with England if only King Harthacnut would be happy with Denmark. But he knew it was unlikely. Harthacnut and his mother would have no intention of allowing the older brother, Lord Harald, to preside over anything. No doubt, Harthacnut held the same view of his half-brother as his mother did. It would be to his advantage to do so, and he'd always been a clever little sod.

If the Queen Dowager could erase the inconvenience of Cnut's first marriage, then she would do so. Not that she'd ever threatened the existence of the two sons, not like the mother, but Leofric understood that she'd been overjoyed by Swein's failure to keep Norway secure. She'd ordered no official mourning for his subsequent death, and Cnut had, as ever, let her have her way and mourned his son silently, as he awaited his own death.

Leofric would have expected more from Cnut, after all, he'd been a warrior, and made his name with his sword and shield. It seemed age and sickness had dimmed him more than Leofric would have thought possible.

The Queen Dowager was a woman of the court, a Queen of England for over thirty years, and she knew how to rule and govern. She'd always understood just how far she could force the issue before having to back down, and she'd recognised her value to the King as well.

It was she who'd helped him secure England, after the hub-bub of the battles, swords and shields, moves and counter-moves had died down nearly twenty years ago. It was she who'd been the continuity the English had demanded to stop supporting the sons of their former king, Æthelred II, and accept Cnut instead. She'd never left Cnut forget that, despite all of his other achievements. He won England with his sword, but he kept her through the machinations of his second wife.

Once more Leofric sighed and rubbed his head in frustration. Only a knock at the door prevented him from tumbling once more into despair at the future, and the oath his King had extracted from him when they'd last spoken.

It was Ælfgar who answered the door, and Leofric could hear muted voices before Ælfgar allowed whoever it was to enter. Leofric thought he recognised the timbre of the voice and was unsurprised when Lord Harald materialised before him.

Hastily Leofric stood to welcome his foster-son, as Ælfgar took away his sodden cloak, and hung it near the raging hearth to dry. It was saturated and black with rain, the weather outside foul, and the colour of his cloak when dry, impossible to gauge.

Lord Harald shook his head disagreeably, disgorging water from his hair and moustache, and Leofric held back the observation that he looked hound-like.

"Good day Lord Harald, disgusting weather," he began, and Harald growled with suppressed annoyance.

"Bloody awful," he confirmed, reaching out to greet Leofric with a clasp of his forearm, and a smack on the back. "It's good to see you, foster-father," he began, "despite the circumstances." Leofric held his amusement in place. Harald didn't like to be reminded he was a lord, but he did like to remind Leofric of their closer tie.

"The roads were passable?" Leofric asked.

"With care. Typical of my father to die in the bloody winter. He'll be laughing about it now."

Lord Harald and Cnut had always enjoyed a complicated relationship. Even now Leofric couldn't determine if they'd genuinely felt any affection for each other, but they'd been keen to acknowledge their relationship because of the advantages it garnered them both.

Not that any, but Lady Emma, would ever refute it. Harald had much of the look of his father, and grandfather about him. He looked, despite his mother being a woman of England, distinctly Danish, with his shock of blond hair, and his warrior's stance, gained under the guidance of the stringent teachings of Orkning. At any moment, Leofric was sure that Harald would simply begin speaking in Danish and never stop.

When Harald spoke English, it was with care, as though considering each word because it was not his native language, even though it was. He was almost more Danish than his father had been.

"Have you visited your father?" Leofric thought to ask, unsure how long Lord Harald had been in Winchester, but the younger man shook his head once more, stray raindrops tumbling from his head as he did so, to land on the floorboards and reflect darkly in the candlelight. Leofric swallowed down his premonition of blood splatters at the sight of the dark water.

Behind them, Leofric could see another six men had entered the hall, no doubt Harald's closest adherents and personal body-guard, and Leofric was pleased to see it. Now that Cnut was dead, he had no idea of the extremes that the Queen Dowager and Earl Godwine would stoop to keep the kingdom safe for Harthacnut. Or rather, he knew exactly what they'd stoop to and knew it was wise for Harald to take precautions.

"No, not yet. Bloody Earl Godwine is in constant attendance and he 'declined' to let me enter."

"On what grounds?" Leofric demanded before he could stop himself, but he waved the question aside irritably. 'On sheer bloody stubborn-mindedness' was the only answer for such behaviour. Lord Harald had become pragmatic about Earl Godwine and the power his father had allowed him to amass, no doubt spending his time considering his revenge against him, should the opportunity ever present itself. Leofric knew that Harald had pitied his father for being unable to banish Earl Godwine, even when the true extent of his treachery had been revealed. Leofric, however, had feared something more sinister

Leofric, though, worried more about Earl Godwine's future. He and his wife, Gytha, had been blessed with so many children, compared to only one for Leofric and his wife, that he knew he'd need to bring his nieces and nephews to the fore in order to ward off their growth, should it come, as he feared it would should Harthacnut rule England.

The family might originate from Wessex, but Leofric doubted that Earl Godwine would object to being given command anywhere within England, or even Denmark, from where his wife heralded.

He held a wry smirk in place. With Lord Harald, it was unlikely to be anytime soon.

"I'll try again when I leave here. Should Earl Godwine still be there, and denying my entry, I may have to make use of my men."

Lord Harald spoke casually of possible violence. Again, like his father, he had no problem with using force to ensure he got his way.

Cnut had always used violence first and words later, as was the Viking way.

"I could appeal to Bishop Beorhtheah on your behalf," Leofric offered. As a holy man, Beorhtheah's intervention would be less open to being misconstrued by Earl Godwine. The Bishop of Winchester could be seen to intervene for those wishing to pray within his diocese.

"No, no, leave Bishop Beorhtheah alone. Earl Godwine knows I have as much right to be there as anyone else. He'll let me pass when he feels he's made his point, that he holds more political clout than I." Harald laughed dismissively as he spoke.

"Has your mother stayed by her resolve to remain in Northampton?" Leofric asked, more quietly now, noticing Harald's wince.

Again, he spoke of another problematic relationship. Lady Ælfgifu had, more or less, abandoned her younger son in England, into Leofric's care, so keen was she to see her oldest son king of Norway.

Leofric knew that her recent return to England had not yet brought about any great reconciliation between her and her son. Yet Lady Ælfgifu was Harald's greatest supporter. But then, he imagined it would be easy enough to accomplish provided they never laid eyes on each other, and while she felt she could exert a force on him to carry out her wishes. It was a balancing act, for both of them, and also for him, stuck as he was between the pair of them.

"She'll not risk an altercation in Winchester. Instead, she meddles in my affairs from Northampton. She's both an asset and a liability." Lord Harald sighed on his words, rubbing his hand over his road-stained face and turning to Leofric. The fact that he confirmed Leofric's thoughts was no comfort.

"I take it you've seen Earl Godwine?"

"Yes, unfortunately. I learnt little but that Harthacnut hasn't yet been informed of your father's actual death, and that he's unlikely to be because of the winter storms at sea. Of course, your father wrote and warned him of his impending death, so he half knows."

A low growl rumbled from Lord Harald's chest as he stood and paced around the room. The three sons of Cnut had never been allies. Only time would tell how much they were enemies, but Leofric already thought he knew the answer to that.

"Still, there's to be a meeting at Oxford, of the Witan, and then all men will speak their minds," Leofric tried to assure, but Lord Harald only grimaced again, his young face lined with annoyance.

"My half-brother has Denmark, my full brother had Norway, until he lost it," a faint smile played around his lips. Again, a complicated relationship. Even the two full-blood brothers had never much liked each other, for all their loyalty to each other if another threatened them.

"I never found him the most brilliant of men. I imagine father wished Earl Hakon hadn't perished at sea, and then he wouldn't have needed to send my brother to replace him as his Regent. Still, he chose him, rather than me. I hope he learned to rue that mistake. But I believe it's time that England was mine, no matter what others might say. I think it time the English were ruled by an English King." A rare smile touched Harald's cheeks as he spoke.

Leofric had been expecting this. In fact, as the summer had waned and Cnut had descended ever closer to his death, there were few who'd not anticipated such a move by Harald, even if they thought it doomed to failure because of Earl Godwine and the Queen Dowager's support for Harthacnut.

In order to counter Harald's ambitions, Cnut would have needed to summon Harthacnut back to England. At the very least, he'd have needed to reach out to Harald and warn him against such actions. The King had done neither of those things, and Leofric knew why, even if others were confused by his inactivity, Harald included.

Cnut hadn't even summoned Harald to him to speak of his death, somehow deciding it was the role of his foster-father.

"My mother has approached the nobility of Northampton, and those to the north of her stronghold. She's sent for Earl Siward on his journey south, and of course, you've been summoned from Mercia.

I've spoken with the King's ship-army, at London for the winter, and they'll support my kingship as well. My mother was escorted home by the remnants of the force sent to Norway with my brother. They've joined with the rest of the ship-army, and she's assured their loyalty to me on her journey home. I don't believe that a combined showing of the Queen Dowager and Earl Godwine will rouse similar support for Harthacnut."

"Stories of his exploits reach far and wide, and none can be too keen to have him back in England, apart from his own mother. It would be better to send her to him, in Denmark. She's never been there. I'm sure she'd enjoy it." Harald spoke flippantly, but his words masked a wave of anger that Leofric knew well, and also understood.

Queen Dowager Emma had done nothing but sow discord between Cnut and his older sons. With Cnut dead, and Harthacnut in Denmark, she now had no one to protect her, and Leofric was sure that young Harald would delight in taking advantage of that. It would be far easier if Earl Godwine were not in the way but he would support the King's dying wishes, or at least, what he thought were Cnut's wishes, provided they chimed with his own.

"You intend to claim the kingship then?" Leofric was sure he would, but a slight doubt remained. His foster-son could be easily swayed by others, and some few had spoken against the idea.

"I intend to," Harald announced, but even he seemed to sense the question in his answer.

"I'll support you," Leofric confirmed. "You're Cnut's English son, my foster-son, and England should be ruled by an Englishman. I've little interest in Denmark or Norway. The Kings of Denmark, Norway and Sweden might well have called on my father and myself as their allies, but they've never done us any great favours." As he spoke, he fingered the cuffs of his shirt where the two-headed emblem of his eagles was stitched. Well, perhaps he spoke too harshly. One King of Norway had once gifted him this, as well as his sword that Leofric carried.

Leofric had considered the problem of the future carefully over the summer, relieved when Cnut had extracted no further oath from him, other than to do what he could for Harald. It had been an oath from King Swein to his father, Ealdorman Leofwine that had caused his family its greatest harm. Leofric was pleased that Cnut had chosen to remember that instance and leave Leofric more open to making his own decision about the future. Not that he was without encumbrance. Far from it, in fact. But he knew what he needed to do, and he had no problem with carrying out his intentions.

Lord Harald fixed Leofric with a steely stare.

"My thanks, Lord Leofric. Your words mean a great deal to me and I know you can be relied upon. In my turn, I assure you that I'll do all I can for the House of Leofwine. I barely remember your father, but his reputation is vast, and of course, I can claim you as family as well." As he spoke, Lord Harald stopped his pacing and looked at Leofric.

He didn't smile. Such oaths were not laughing matters. Instead, he held his arm out, and Leofric grasped it, man to man, standing as he did so. As they clasped each other's forearms and shook, Leofric knew that his decision was the right one. If not, he might just have created enormous problems for the future.

# 2

## AD1035

The funeral was a sombre affair, as it should be, but the atmosphere was so strained within the magnificent Old Minster, that Leofric fancied it had taken visible form, and meandered through the cloister clogging throats and making eyes stream.

Queen Dowager Emma was resplendent in her mourning clothes, a thick cloak around her shoulders to drive the chill away from her.

Leofric, for all his difficult prior relationship, pitied her.

She was twice a widow, and yet none of her children was truly destined to rule the country that had been her home since her youth. Neither were any of them here to support her now. She was a mother and a widow, but she could just as easily have grieved for her children as she did her husband.

She was alone. Always alone.

Leofric's father had escorted her to England, kept her from Swein's clutches on the perilous sea journey, and then handed her over. Æthelred had been not so much an old man by the time he married his second wife, but rather a much older man compared to his wife. And worse, he'd not only been mired in a wave of Viking attacks, but he'd also already had grown children to his name, some older even than his wife; some had even thought Emma would be a bride to one of them.

Queen Dowager Emma, so his father had told him, had made a good marriage with Æthelred, or as best as she could, and her two sons and daughter from the marriage proved that her duties to him had been fulfilled.

Yet, against all the odds, it had been with Cnut that she'd known true happiness. While Leofric couldn't begrudge her that, her marriage to Cnut had only served to cause more difficulties for his own family, and had served to make her both weaker and stronger than he would have liked.

Still, he knew the love she'd had for her often absent husband and felt pity for her grief. Cnut had not yet been forty on his death, she a hand-span of years older, but it was unlikely she'd marry again, and yet she might still have many years of life left to her.

He wondered if she could even have imagined a time that she'd not be the queen of England. In her wildest dreams, did she imagine she'd be married once more to a future king of England, or did she accept that she could now only ever be the mother of the next king?

She stood almost alone at the front of the Old Minster, escorted only by her ladies-in-waiting, his sister amongst them, as Cnut's coffin was brought from the side chapel, and laid to rest in its new position, under the altar.

Leofric couldn't see her face, but he could see her bowed head and her shoulders, which shook with sorrow. Her greying hair was the starkest reminder if any was needed that no one can outrun death and his own thoughts turned to his brother.

Northman, his older brother, had died at the instructions of Cnut. His life had been forever cut short, and yet the House of Leofwine had been left with little choice but to reconcile with the king. With Cnut gone, forever, Leofric considered that now was the time to mount a fitting memorial to his brother, perhaps in the Church at Deerhurst.

He would give it some thought.

In the past, it had been necessary to play down Northman's death, simply because of the ignominy of the household serving a king who'd ordered his death. Despite Ealdorman Leofwine's most stringent attempts to have the history of the time period recorded in such a way that his association with Eadric didn't stain Northman, it had been badly done. His nephews had been forced to downplay who their father had been. Hopefully, that time had now passed, and Leofric hoped the two boys could become firm allies and supporters of his own son.

The words of the bishop, Beorhtheah washed over him, the funeral mass one he felt he'd already heard too many times, and at his side, his wife shivered in the biting air. There were braziers to try and dispel the cold air, but it was November, a time of ice and winds, and nothing would entirely drive the iciness away other than the arrival of summer.

He reached over and took her hand, trying to rub some warmth back into her blue fingers, considering why she'd not worn her gloves. She met his eyes for just a moment, and once more he was mesmerised by the beauty that had forced him to marry her when they'd been little more than children.

On his other side, Ælfgar stood carefully, his two older cousins beside him, Wulfstan and Ælfwine, while Leofric's own brother, Eadwine and Godwine were also in attendance.

He'd decided, after his meeting with Lord Harald, that it would be better if his entire family showed their grief for the death of the king, and as such their unity at the troubled times going forward.

Lady Godgifu had not welcomed the summons, but she'd come to Winchester anyway, cared for by her son and her nephews so that she'd arrived less out of sorts than he'd thought she would.

After the funeral, Lady Godgifu would be able to seek out Queen Dowager Emma, and Leofric was sure that her reception would be smoother than his own. It was an open secret that Godgifu and Lady Ælfgifu were allies, but somehow Emma often managed to overlook his wife's split loyalties. He doubted she'd be so kind with his own.

Bishop Beorhtheah was bringing the service to a conclusion, with as much decorum as possible, but even his breath was pooling in the frozen air, as though he spoke the words and Cnut ascended to heaven on the cloud his breath produced. There was a time for obeisance, but it was not in the Old Minster in the heart of winter.

Outside a blizzard stormed, the streets of Winchester coated with more than a foot of snow, and yet people still stood out there to honour their king. When Cnut became king, Leofric could never have imagined that his death would be received with such sorrow. Neither, he knew had Cnut.

What had started as a reign of terror and war had ended on mournful sorrow. Many felt that Cnut had done a great deal for England, driving the Viking raiders from her shores. Sadly, Leofric did not foresee that opinion lasting for long. Not if Cnut's sons had a say in the matter.

Leofric hoped that someone had thought to provide warm food and drink for those who yet lined the street. If not, he knew many would soon be suffering from their sodden clothes and hair. He only hoped that his family were not marooned in Winchester while the snow raged outside.

He wanted to be home, by his own hearth, warming his feet and watching his hounds frolic with boredom. In fact, he craved some boredom. But he knew it would be in short supply. Already some were threatening to leave Winchester that afternoon and make their way to Oxford to convene the Witan. Leofric hoped that some lingered on a while. As keen as he was to know that England had a secure king after the death of Cnut, he was just as eager to put off the actual decision-making process for as long as possible.

Finally, Leofric realised that Bishop Beorhtheah had spoken the last words of the ceremony and that some were already scampering to the sides to the welcome warmth of the braziers, or even outside so that they could escape to the heat of Winchester Palace or their own accommodations.

His family moved away, and Leofric watched them go without censure. He yet felt the need to pray for Cnut but knew his wife and son, nephews and brothers, were keen to make their way to Winchester Palace as soon as possible. A feast of remembrance would be held for the king, and despite the late season, there would be ample warm food and, more importantly, drink to oil the conversations that allowed men and women to speak too openly of their future plans.

He met his son's eye as he escorted his mother from the Old Minster, a warning to see to her care, but then he resumed his seat, his head bowed low in prayer.

The Old Minster was slowly emptying, soon there would be few left, aside from the Queen Dowager, Earl Godwine and Earl Siward, and of course, the house-carls who had served King Cnut in a personal capacity as his guards. They, more than anyone, knew the sort of man Cnut had been for they'd travelled with him from Norway to Rome, spending far more time with him than the Queen Dowager, or even Cnut's sons ever had.

Leofric raised his head slightly, looking for a glimpse of Lord Harald, but the younger man had escaped the confines of the Old Minster as well. Leofric wasn't surprised. This was a perfect opportunity for him to make new allies, gather supporters from the heartland of Wessex, and further his cause to claim the kingdom of England as his own to rule.

Leofric tried to pray, his head bowed low, but instead of prayer his mind filled only with memories of his time with Cnut. He thought of all that had befallen the two families, intertwined due to King Swein's ambitions, and more, an attack on a little-deserted island to the far north of England. That had seen his father and King Swein caught in a tangled web that had wound its way tightly, not only around their own lives but also those of their children.

No matter how he remembered his youth, Leofric could never

think of it without considering the influence the House of Gorm had had on it. He doubted it would be any different for his son, although he hoped that outright war could be avoided.

Only slowly did the words of the others remaining in the Old Minster permeate his hearing, and then he wished they hadn't.

The two earls and the Queen Dowager clearly thought themselves alone, and as such, they spoke openly of plans for the future.

Stuck, Leofric knew no way to improve his situation. Should he move now, they'd think him an eavesdropper on the conversation that had passed, and should he remain, only then to be discovered, they'd also know that he'd been listening all along.

Instead, he tried to seek the oblivion of memories and prayers, failing utterly as his hearing too easily picked up the words between the other major players on the political front.

"Harthacnut will come as soon as he's able," Leofric heard the Queen Dowager speak querulously. It seemed the conversation wasn't much to her liking.

"That may be, but until then someone must rule England." Earl Siward tried to placate. He too was an old ally of Cnut's. He'd earned his position of power through bloodshed and loyalty, as all good Danish seemed to do, but the gift of Northumbria had been a double-edged sword.

It had, so far, required all of his attention and so his time with Cnut, little of it though Cnut had spent in England, had been even more shortened. His allegiance was to England, not the House of Gorm or the House of Wessex. He simply needed peace or the borderlands with the kingdom of the Scots might well erupt once more, as they had only a few years before.

"I'll rule England. I'm the king's mother. I've ruled for Cnut in the past, and so too has Earl Godwine. I think you worry needlessly, and pointlessly. After all, this is the day of the king's funeral, not the Witan."

The Queen Dowager sounded far from pleased with Earl Siward's line of enquiry.

"I think you need to be aware that others don't share your thoughts," he tried to caution, and Leofric, his head down low, heard an annoyed sigh from the Queen Dowager.

"You should remember who made you the man you are today, and you should reward that loyalty now that he's no longer here, and Harthacnut faces challenges in Denmark." Heat turned her words to thrown daggers, and Leofric winced at the fury he heard.

"That, Queen Dowager," and Earl Siward stressed the word Dowager, "is exactly what I'm doing. Earl Godwine might be offering you his support and reassurance, but he's doing you no favours. Lady Ælfgifu is keen to take advantage of Harthacnut's absence, and she won't be the only one to think Lord Harald's claim just as strong as Harthacnut's."

Leofric heard Lady Emma's whip-sharp inhalation and kept his head firmly down. Now would not be the time to be noticed.

"As always, Earl Leofric will contain Lady Ælfgifu, and you, Earl Siward, are reminded that the woman's name is not to be mentioned in my presence, and neither is that of her sons. I've always tried to keep my criticism of the king and his other woman away from the ears of any who would spread salacious gossip, but in that 'encounter' he erred. In promoting Swein to Norway, he erred. I will not make those mistakes. I will give the other son no place at the king's court, and Harthacnut will thank me for that when he returns to England." Her voice was icier than the storm that raged outside, and Leofric reconsidered his opinion of Earl Siward. He was a brave man to speak so bluntly with her.

He had none of Leofric's twisted relationship with the queen dowager to protect him, and certainly not the memory of a much loved, and missed friend and father in the shape of Ealdorman Leofwine.

"Then, Queen Dowager, I fear you've already lost this battle," Earl Siward snapped. Leofric heard the stomp of boots over the wooden floorboards of the Old Minster and hunched into himself even further.

He'd not taken a position at the front of the Old Minster before the ceremony began, preferring instead to escort his wife to a position she'd found near a warming brazier. It seemed the other two earls and the queen dowager had not missed him, and he hoped to keep it that way.

Only when the sound of angry footsteps had trailed away, did the conversation resume.

"He's no right to threaten me with Harald," Emma complained, her voice high, her sorrow evident to hear, her screech on Harald's name showing her utter contempt for him.

"No, he doesn't," Earl Godwine agreed, and then the pair apparently decided to end their conversation, and also made their way to the back of the Old Minster. Leofric stayed hunched in place, his eyes closed, his lips reciting prayers. Even if he were seen, there was some hope that they might think he'd not heard their snatches of conversation.

Only when the Old Minster was once more silent, did Leofric risk standing. He felt frozen, and standing was an effort, but one he persevered with. He'd never get warm unless he left the Old Minster.

Cnut's coffin had been laid to rest beneath the altar of the Old Minster, always his preferred religious establishment within Winchester. Leofric found the situation a little perverse; two minsters in such close proximity to each other that the service in one could be heard in the other. Why the House of Wessex had thought it necessary to build the New Minster so close he'd never know.

Yet, Cnut had closer ties with the Old Minster rather than the New, preferring to be buried with the more ancient members of the House of Wessex. No doubt it had been a conscious decision on his part, to distance himself as much as possible from the more recent members of the House of Wessex. Perhaps he'd also hoped that Winchester, the capital of Wessex, would retain its position for all time, and his achievements would never be forgotten about. Yet, even Cnut had preferred Oxford to Winchester.

Either that or he knew he needed such intervention from his God to enter Heaven. No man with two wives could hope for a comfortable passage into Heaven.

At the front of the Old Minster, Leofric took to his knees, leaning forward so that his head touched the wooden boards. Only then could he truly turn his mind to prayer.

He'd hoped to pray for Cnut when he'd visited his coffin before his burial, but the lurking presence of Earl Godwine had made it impossible. And now he felt his mind filled with the Queen Dowager's words so that once more his intentions were hard to fulfil.

Perhaps, or so he considered, it was because he'd yet to make his peace with Cnut. Maybe, there was still too much between them that would never now be resolved.

Angrily, he sat back on his heels, becoming aware that he was not alone within the Old Minster. Bishop Beorhtheah stood to the side of his altar, his ceremonial clothing discarded and instead, a thick black fur cloak around his shoulders, a hood covering his straggling hair.

"Apologies Lord Leofric, I thought all had gone." His breath plumed before him as he spoke, and Leofric couldn't suppress his own shudder of cold.

"I'd hoped to offer more prayers, but it's too damn cold," he stumbled to his feet, accepting the hand of the bishop when he almost lost his balance as his foot had grown numb.

"There will be warmer days in the future," the bishop consoled, and Leofric nodded. His sorrow for the king's death was heavily tinged with too many muddled feelings for him to yet give voice to them all.

"There will be. Come, we should make our way to the feast before my men freeze in place outside, and all the food is eaten."

Bishop Beorhtheah smiled at Leofric's attempt to lighten the oppressive mood of the Old Minster.

"Yes, we shall leave my monks to pray for King Cnut's soul, and they'll bring the braziers closer so that they don't shiver as much as we do. Even the work of God can't be conducted under such conditions," the bishop spoke as though sharing a great secret, and Leofric allowed a tight smile to strain his face. He and Beorhtheah had never been allies, but then, neither had they been outright enemies.

In what now amounted to the final years of the king's reign, England had benefited from a reasonable sense of political calm amongst those who ruled her for the king and with the king. The factionalism that might have marred previous king's reigns had been held at bay. Leofric doubted it would be for long, not now Earl Godwine was released from any bonds that might have tempered his ambitions.

Together, the two men stepped into the street, where snow now climbed higher than ever on the metalled road, and the sky looked so full that Leofric knew the temporary lull in the downpour would be short.

None but the horse of Leofric and Beorhtheah still waited in the snow, those hardy individuals who might have remained to lay eyes on the great earls and the queen dowager, long returned to their home.

Leofric shivered once more and offered an apology to the two men who'd guarded his horse for him, tethered out of the way of the Old Minster, and as far from the crowd as had been possible.

With frozen limbs, he mounted his horse and turned to ride away. As he did so a flutter of cloth caught his eye, and he stifled a groan.

His eavesdropping, as unintentional as it had been, had not gone without notice. No doubt, Earl Godwine would soon know that he'd lingered within the Old Minster and overheard what the queen dowager had thought a private conversation. He could only hope he managed to avoid the domineering woman at the feast in honour of Cnut. He didn't wish to make his choices well known before the convening of the Witan at Oxford.

# 3
# OXFORD, DECEMBER AD1035

Snow clung to the ground, the stark whiteness causing Leofric's eyes to tear even in the dull gloom of the late afternoon.

His family had lingered only an additional day in Winchester after Cnut's funeral, preferring to push for their properties in Oxfordshire. Leofric had spent a week at one of his properties close to Oxford, savouring the warmth and comfort, while his brother had pressed on to his lands in Bloxham and Adderbury. Only with trepidation had Leofric summoned his energy to make the short journey to Oxford itself, deciding, despite it all, that it was better, at least on this occasion, to leave his wife behind.

She'd done what she could for their family in Winchester, seeking out the eye of the Queen Dowager at the feast given to celebrate Cnut's life, but Emma had been less than forthcoming. Her expectation that the House of Leofwine would support her and Harthacnut had grated on Lady Godgifu's nerves. His wife had quickly made her excuses before she could say anything that might have further injured her family.

Leofric was thankful for her quick thinking. A stalwart of Mercian nobility, his wife, was content to hold influence within

Mercia. Her eyes rarely sought out any from Wessex, and she wasn't enamoured with the Queen Dowager at the best of times, and the situation had only deteriorated when Leofric had been chosen to be Lord Harald's foster-father. The relationship that Ealdorman Leofwine had shared with Lady Emma was often the only thing that kept Leofric's interaction with Emma from souring; that and his sister's almost constant intercession on the family's behalf.

Leofric already knew that Lady Emma expected Ealdgyth to remain with her during her widowhood, but his sister was unsure. She'd confided as much to her brother after the funeral. She had a long-standing loyalty to Emma, but it had been tested in the past, and Leofric could only think that it would be in the future. It was perhaps long over time that she turned her attention to Deerhurst and left Lady Emma's side.

Only one of his brothers, Eadwine, had chosen to attend the Witan. Godwine Leofwinesson was more than content to let his brothers speak for the family. He had little interest in the politics of England, as with Lady Godgifu, his eyes were more focused on the family interests within Mercia, and specifically within the ancient kingdom of the Hwicce, where he also oversaw the affairs of their sister, Ealdgyth at Deerhurst, while she was away serving Lady Emma.

The journey was short from his property, and Leofric knew that they'd reach Oxford that night. The only question was whether or not it would be before full dark or not.

At his side, his hound, Hund, loped along beside the horses. Of them all, she was enjoying the jaunt through the countryside more than the others. Her pure delight at such a turn of speed was enough to raise even a smile on his strained lips, especially when she darted after the odd small animal, trying its luck in the thick snow. So far, she'd caught nothing, but she'd come very close once or twice, and it was only a matter of time before she was successful.

His son chuntered onto Eadwine, and Leofric allowed them their conversation without feeling the need to join in. He was content with his horse, his hound and his thoughts.

Lord Harald had sought him out at the funeral feast, content to make their alliance well known, or at least to remind people of their close links. Harald was virtually unknown in Wessex, and many a whisper had followed them, asking who he was. Leofric thought it ridiculous. Cnut should have ensured his son with Lady Ælfgifu was as well known in England as Harthacnut had once been.

When he and Earl Godwine had spoken at the feast, briefly, and only to complain about the weather and share a memory of their King, he was sure that the Earl had been trying to peer into his mind, determine his ambitions for the future. Leofric hoped he'd given nothing away, but it was difficult to tell. Earl Godwine seemed to understand the twisted loyalties of men far too well, as he should. Those who were experts at manipulation and deceit often sought it in others, or so Leofric had decided.

Earl Godwine had no problem with exploiting any situation that presented itself to him. He'd done it before, and he'd do it again. Even now, Leofric was confused by Earl Godwine's survival at Cnut's Court. He'd bribed the Queen about her terrible secret, and still, Cnut had been unable to dislodge him. Leofric knew there had to be more to Cnut and Earl Godwine's relationship than he'd ever been told.

Within sight of Oxford, Leofric called his son and brother to his side. He couldn't see how Ælfgar, with his similarities to his own father, could possibly make a wrong step at the Witan. His brother was another matter entirely, and the older of the two perhaps listened more closely than the young, and inexperienced Ælfgar, as Leofric offered his warnings.

"This will be difficult going. Keep your thoughts from showing, and don't speak to any you don't wholly trust. I know neither of you would intend to, never think that, I speak only to caution myself more than anything."

"But the decision is made," Ælfgar sought clarity, and Leofric nodded.

"Yes, as a family we've decided to support Lord Harald, your foster-brother. No matter what else happens, we do only what Harald does. Should he decide to support Harthacnut instead, or anything else unexpected occur, we'll follow his lead. It'll not harm us for the other Earls and the Queen Dowager to understand our breed of loyalty."

"Agreed," Godwine Leofwinesson rumbled, his voice rich and thick. For a moment Leofric wondered what it would be like if his older brother had lived, and he, rather than Leofric held responsibility for the future of their family. Would he have made the same decision? He was sure the answer was yes, but then, his brother had been gone a long time, and Cnut had changed much in that time. Maybe he wouldn't have done.

"Then we travel to our house there and tomorrow we face the men and women of the Witan, the Queen Dowager and Lord Harald. It will be," Leofric thought furiously of the correct word to use, only for Ælfgar to speak.

"Interesting," he interspersed, and Godwine Leofwinesson barked a laugh of agreement, that swaddled all three of them in a plume of hot air.

Ælfgar smirked at his Uncle, and Leofric reached out to cuff him around the head. His son might well be foster-brother to the future regent, but Harald and Ælfgar had not always been friends, Harald too rough and brash for Ælfgar's liking when they'd been young. No, Ælfgar had much preferred Harthacnut as a playmate. But that had been many years ago, before Leofric and his family had been banished because of Earl Godwine's manipulations, before Harthacnut had ruled Denmark and before Swein had been sent as regent to Norway.

Much had changed, and also not a great deal. Leofric smirked at his son and brother. This would be a real test. For all of them.

. . .

The snow fell once more during the night so that when the morning came, Leofric's men were forced to dig their way out of the house where the snow had piled, almost thigh high around the door and reaching almost to the overhanging roof. A bitter wind raced through Oxford, driving everyone who didn't need to be outdoors, indoors.

"Will this damn stuff never cease," the servant grumbled, tasked to escort Leofric to the stables, and Leofric shook his head under his deep fur cloak, the hood pulled tight so that only his nose was exposed to the driving wind and snow.

His servant moved snow to the one side with a wide shovel, and Leofric stepped gingerly behind him. He would have helped, but he was swathed in his best clothes and wanted to arrive at the Witan looking like an Earl.

"It might be the coldest winter for many years," he agreed with the man. "A time for warm beds, not the death of kings." He spoke a little flippantly, his rancour with the situation perhaps unwarranted, but the servant gurgled with laughter. He was used to his Lord's dry humour.

"Well said, My Lord," the servant concurred and then they were within the earthy warmth of the stables, the sweet smell of hay mingling with the odour of horse manure. Leofric's horse was sluggish to move, content with his own warm bed, and in the end, they left the house later than Leofric wanted, and his mood had soured. It didn't help that Ælfgar and Godwine Leofwinesson's horses had been keen to escape their warm beds and that they'd teased him until his temper had almost snapped with his grumpy animal.

He'd been keen to arrive early, to watch others enter the vast church of St Michael's at the North Gate. Now he feared to be one of the last.

His horse walked proudly through the near-deserted roadway, his temper clear to see in the angry swishing of his tail, and desire to walk anywhere but where his master and rider commanded him. There was little noise, rather the smell of smoke escaping through thatched roofs swirled around them, enticing Leofric to want to return to his own home, and making him feel as though they were the only people alive within Oxford.

Every house within Oxford was closed up tightly. Here and there a spill of servants organised by the Reeve was working to clear essential walkways and thoroughfares, their grumbling catching his ears when the wind occasionally stilled. He pitied them all, and once more cursed Cnut for his untimely death. His mood was foul, he knew it, and his brother and son spoke quietly amongst themselves, as Hund once more bounded through the thick layers of snow.

Leofric knew the grand church of St Michael's at the North Gate would be cold. It was cold even at the height of summer. But he'd taken precautions, and wore two cloaks instead of one, and intended on keeping his gloves with him as well. He'd insulated his leather boots with scraps of fur, and inside his cloak, he carried a water bottle, insulated and filled with boiling water to rest his hands on, should the need arise. Even then, he knew it wouldn't be enough.

He couldn't imagine the Witan would be over quickly. Far from it. He hoped that there would at least be regular breaks, with warm food and drink, and the opportunity to force heat back into frozen limbs and digits. He shivered just to think of it.

Only when the church finally came into sight emerging out of the gloom and through the haze of fragrant wood smoke, did they come across any other individuals braving the snowy conditions. Hooded, as everyone was against the snow, it was impossible to determine who walked amongst them, who rode and who strode, head down, into the welcoming maw of the lit church. All sound was muted, and Leofric held his tongue as well. It was impossible to know who would overhear his speech and whether sound would travel with the gusts, no matter how quietly they spoke.

Now was a time for caution, and holding back, just as he'd warned his son and brother.

Leaving his horse in the stable for the attached monastery, the bad-tempered beast outraged to have been forced outside just for a short ride, Leofric hunkered down to travel the short distance by foot. His boots crunched over thick snow, the pathways barely clear, and refilling with snow as soon as they could be trampled over. He shivered once more, before ducking his head and entering the echoing space of the church. Sound welled around him, and he winced against the sudden onslaught to his ears as he stamped his boots to clear them of as much snow as possible at the entrance way. He didn't wish to sit in a pool of spreading water throughout the Witan. He shook his outer-cloak as well – the action dislodging more snow than he'd thought could possibly have fallen in the short distance.

Others did the same, and servants for the monastery had been tasked with mop and bucket to try and dry the wooden floorboards, although it seemed a fruitless task.

It was busy within the church, as he'd worried. As he lifted his hands to push his hood down, he became aware of how many others were doing the same. He might be late to the Witan, but not as late as he'd feared.

Hastily he gathered Ælfgar and Godwine Leofwinesson to him, and they made their way to the front of the church. Along the way, he caught glimpses of others who sought to catch his eye, but he kept his head down. The time for such open declarations of support still lay in the future. There was no need for him to be seen smiling at Osgot Clapa, Earl Hrani, Lord Harald or any of Lady Ælfgifu's adherents.

As he neared the altar, he glimpsed a sight of Earls Godwine and Siward and the Dowager Queen. Even he did a double take as he took in Emma's clothing. Despite the deep snow and even deeper cold, she wore a cloth of gold gown and no cloak. Around her exposed neck she wore a golden cross, studded with precious gems, and that was all that Leofric could see clearly. No doubt, the cross would prove to be more ornate when he was close enough to see all of it. It was a bold statement by the dead King's wife and Harthacnut's mother.

Queen Dowager Emma was staking her claim on behalf of her son for all to see.

Beside her, there was a spare seat, but the one next to that was occupied by Lord Harald, almost as well dressed as his father's widowed wife, only with the addition of a thick white, fur cloak. Leofric nodded his approval. It seemed that two could play the same game, and Harald was well prepared to out-do the still elegant appearance of the Queen Dowager and do it without risking his health by shivering throughout the discussions that would start shortly.

Behind the two of them, the holiest men of England had staked their claim. Æthelnoth, Archbishop of Canterbury would lead the Witan, in his role as the senior churchman. Ælfric, Archbishop of York, was seated next to him, the statuesque appearance of the man dwarfing those around him. For a moment Leofric pitied whoever was unfortunate enough to have to sit behind the tall man. They'd see very little of the action, although they would, of course, be able to hear everything clearly.

The familiar face of Bishop Athelstan of Hereford was the next Leofric saw, and he nodded a welcome. They knew each other well, and Leofric, while not exactly liking the slightly rotund man, found him to be an excellent conversationalist, even when they didn't agree. Athelstan held a sharp stare that matched his chiselled nose, and Leofric was never happier than when his attention was directed at someone other than himself.

Before he could further examine the holy men in attendance, the women as well, for the abbesses played an essential part in the Witan too, Æthelnoth took to the floor, his own rich winter cloak sweeping along the floor as he bowed before the Queen Dowager and also, without even a pause, to Lord Harald. Archbishop Æthelnoth was famed for his diplomacy, but he was also an ally of the Queen Dowager. Or rather, he'd been an ally to Cnut, and it was assumed, as with Earl Godwine, that he'd now support the Queen Dowager. But Leofric knew assumptions could be wrong. He waited to be surprised, or not. The minds of the men and women of the Witan could be contrary beasts.

"Good men and women of England," Archbishop Æthelnoth began, his voice, like all men of the church, able to penetrate even the darkest reaches of a lofty building, as the church was. "I would bid you welcome to Oxford, even in this terrible weather. Your assiduous attention to the duties you owe the kingdom are to be applauded, and it's to be hoped that this meeting will be short, and hopefully swift. The church, as many know, is not always a warm and inviting place, even when snow doesn't blanket the ground. But still, we meet here so that the Lord, Our God and Saviour, will witness our decisions, and they'll be taken as holy, as well as royal writ."

Leofric was impressed with Archbishop Æthelnoth's outspoken warning. It seemed that even he wasn't prepared to sit through a lengthy debate. However, Leofric thought the optimism misplaced. There was little chance of this meeting ending quickly, or to the happiness of everyone who attended.

"King Cnut, may he rest in peace, has made his wishes for the future clear. His son Harthacnut even now rules as King in Denmark, and Cnut desired that he rule England as well, a continuation of Cnut's great Northern Empire."

As the Archbishop spoke, Leofric tried to relax onto the hard wooden chair he'd been gifted. Beside him his son sat attentively, his face filled with wonder to be witnessing something as monumental as a Witan choosing a new king for England, his elbows on his knees so that his face rested on his hands as he listened attentively. Leofric already knew his patience would be tested that day for he had no ability to sit as quietly as his son. Rather, his bones ached with the deep chill, despite all of his precautions, and he wished himself back in bed.

Yet still, the Archbishop spoke.

"Regrettably, it's deep winter, the sea to Denmark impassable and so King Harthacnut doesn't yet know of his father's passing, or that he's needed here as King of the English. His Danish subjects need him there to drive back the threat from the Norwegians. The situation then, unfortunately, is not as clear-cut as King Cnut might have wished it to be."

Even Leofric heard the Queen Dowager's hiss of outrage at those words, but Archbishop Æthelnoth continued as though Lady Emma had given no reaction to his neat summation of the current situation.

"Plans must be made for the future of England, to safeguard her from those who would undo the many years of peace we've lived through, and also to hold the kingdom for when King Harthacnut, is able to take up his position, whenever that may be. Events in Norway, as many of us know, can be unpredictable."

With the position made clear, the Archbishop ceased speaking, while a rumble of conversation washed through the church at his words. It was highly likely that this was the first some had heard of Harthacnut's detainment in Denmark, and also perhaps the first time some had appreciated that without Cnut there was a real danger for England from Norway and even from Sweden. Those two countries, long coveted by Cnut, had proved difficult to tame to his ways, and Jakob Anund, with his distant family connections to Cnut, had perhaps proved the most difficult of all.

Skane was gone, once more, and Denmark, without Norway, was vulnerable.

Before Archbishop Æthelnoth could return to his seat, Lord Harald had taken his place before everyone. He was not a familiar face at the King's Court, as the feast after Cnut's funeral had proved, but there was no mistaking his lineage for those who took the time to look. It was almost as though old King Swein stood before them, for those old enough to remember him, and for those who weren't, he had only to tilt his head to the right, and he looked the very essence of his father, only younger, much younger.

"Good men and women of England," he began, his voice almost more English sounding than Bishop Æthelnoth's, for once, and then he lapsed into silence. Leofric admired his bravery in standing before them all, but more than that, it seemed that Lord Harald had fixed

Earl Godwine with a fiery stare and that was what caused the elongated silence.

For a moment Leofric considered. He wondered when Earl Godwine had last seen Cnut's middle son? Had he perhaps known more about the strange fate of the King's first marriage than Cnut had shared even with Ealdorman Leofwine? Did Earl Godwine know much more than Leofric did, or was he simply trying to outwit the young man before he could even make his case, so desperate was he for Harthacnut to become King of England.

When the spell was broken, Harald seemed none the worse but turned to gaze at Earl Godwine from a slight angle, Leofric could see that the other statesman looked shocked. Clearly, Earl Godwine had not seen Harald for a very long time. It was as though he faced the Cnut from his young adulthood all over again. Did it make him reconsider the future? Leofric doubted it.

"I'm Cnut's son, Harald, for those of you who don't know me. My brother, Swein, served my father, in Norway, until he lost his life, and my father, despite what some may think, has never denied that he was, indeed, my father, and indeed, legally wed to my mother. She escorted my brother to Norway, to act as his Regent. She has now returned to England." Lord Harald kept his eyes focused on the lines of men and women further back in the church, although Leofric thought it took a great deal of effort for him.

He stood proudly, his cloak thrown back so that all could see the wealth around his neck, a huge golden cross swinging proudly as he spoke, studded with flashing stones, a darker piece of jewellery contrasting with it; the hammer of Thor and a proud Danish emblem even now the country was mostly Christian.

Lord Harald had suffered greatly at the hands of Lady Emma, and it seemed he couldn't stop himself from reminding her of that.

"In the current situation, occasioned by the much-lamented death of my dear father, I would demand that the governance of England be passed into my own hands, until such time as my half-brother, Harthacnut, can return from his warrior's commitments in Denmark."

Unsurprisingly, the end of Lord Harald's words occasioned a huff of conversation to filter through the air that had grown thick with the clouded fog of intermingled breath, and yet, there was no outraged denial, from anyone. Well, apart from the Queen Dowager.

Perhaps unknowingly, she'd risen from her seat to face Lord Harald, and from where he sat, Leofric could see that wrath had descended on her, in almost as deep a layer as the snow lay outside.

She shimmered inside her cloth of gold clothing, the jewellery around her neck reflecting the hundreds of candles lined across the altar, that gave light, but only the fake mockery of heat.

He shivered inside his deep cloaks, almost holding his breath to see what would happen next.

No matter the Queen Dowager's thoughts on the issue, Harald had only spoken of facts. Leofric didn't think she could offer anything that would counter those words. But he was wrong to underestimate her stubbornness.

"You're not Cnut's son," Emma hissed, her outraged voice reaching Leofric's ears, and he cursed. This once more. Lord Harald raised an eyebrow at the snake-like attack from his father's wife but otherwise seemed unmoved by her accusation.

"You will not rule for Cnut's rightful heir, King Harthacnut." This time she spoke louder, and Leofric knew that at any moment she would turn to her husband's earls and ask them to speak for her son.

"I have a great deal of support," Lord Harald countered sedately. In contrast to the Queen Dowager, his face was devoid of all emotion, still holding the remains of the blue of cold from outside. Emma was flushed with royal purple, and Leofric could feel no pity for her rage, or for embarrassing herself so much in front of people who would never, ever, deny Lord Harald's parentage, himself included in that number.

Earl Siward had tried to warn her on the day of the funeral, but not only had she refused to heed that cautioning, she was unable to rein in her anger now.

"Cnut's ship-army support my claim, just as it once supported Cnut's own claim to rule England, after my grandfather's death, King Swein. My mother, Lady Ælfgifu, the King's wife, has ensured that."

The shock of the revelation was etched into Lady Emma's face, showing as a twitch to her cheek and a frantic look at Earl Godwine, where he sat directly before her. As much as she hated to be reminded that Cnut had fathered children outside their marriage, her true rage was always directed at Lady Ælfgifu. She wouldn't have her name mentioned in her presence, or so Leofric's sister had cautioned him.

Even now his sister sat within the church, ostensibly a member of the Queen Dowager's entourage, but he doubted she would be after today. She'd sent word that she was content to leave her position, as soon as Leofric made the position of his family clear.

"And my mother, foster-father and their allies in Mercia also support my right to rule, on behalf of Harthacnut, until he can be excused from his current duties to return to England."

Leofric nodded as Harald continued. He'd just formally named him as an ally, but it took a moment longer for him to feel the fury of Lady Emma's gaze, as the realisation of her son's peril finally revealed itself.

He steeled himself for the moment, anticipating that her anger would at least warm him.

"Is this true?" Earl Godwine spoke first, now standing as well, and Leofric saw that he'd not yet fully recovered from his first sight of Lord Harald for many years. His face was bleached of colour, two bright spots of red showing on his cheeks. His words, when he spoke echoed within the church, but they were harder to catch than usual. His ordinarily calm façade was falling away as he pulled his cloak tighter, as though a shield from any more physical blows to his understanding of who would rule after Cnut.

"I support Lord Harald, as Regent for Harthacnut. He shares the same blood as Harthacnut, they are half-brothers, no matter who denies it. They share a father, a father who was our King." At that Leofric knew Lady Emma whipped her face around to glare at him, but he ignored it. He spoke nothing but the truth.

"The King never denied his parentage of his older children or his marriage to Lady Ælfgifu. Everyone here knows that. England needs a ruler who can rule in more than the name of another, it needs a ruler who has the same political clout as the other, the same feared reputation as Cnut. Lord Harald has every right to claim the regency. His claim is stronger than that of the Queen Dowager's."

"King Cnut wanted his son to rule after him," Earl Godwine spluttered. His own face showed not the ire of the Queen Dowager, but rather confusion. He had, after all, known Leofric's father, Leofwine, for many years before his death, and had, like the Queen Dowager, expected him to honour what he understood to be Cnut's final wishes, as Leofwine would have done. Leofric was amused how quickly people forgot he'd been Lord Harald's foster-father, as though it meant nothing, that his loyalties had been tried and tested many times before.

Ealdorman Leofwine had been regarded as the ultimate man of honour, respected by many kings, even when those kings were enemies. Leofric wasn't as honourable or as respected, but none of that had been his own doing. He'd been tested by Cnut, most severely, from the killing of his older brother to the terrible treatment of his father when Cnut had become King to his own banishment, and then his return to the embrace of the King's warm wishes when Godwine's treachery had been discovered, and he'd been named as Harald's foster-father.

Even after all that, the King had forced one more disagreeable task upon Leofric's loyalty. But Earl Godwine and the Queen Dowager were not to know that in speaking as he did he followed Cnut's wishes more than even they did.

"And his son will rule after him. When he's here, and if he comes to England. Reports suggest that the war with Magnus of Norway, or rather with the young King's Regents may last many years. England can't wait for a new King. Not again. England must come before Denmark. Most of us remember the confusion and suffering at the end of King Æthelred's rule when rival claimants ripped England apart. That can't happen again. Not to the kingdom we are all sworn to protect." Leofric turned away from the blazing eyes of the Queen Dowager and looked at those in the audience behind him.

The breath of so many obscured the room, almost as though a fire raged at its centre, sending out icy tendrils of smoke to wrap around the faces of all within. He hoped to see some support for his words, and what eventually emerged from the gloom cheered him. Few looked ruinously disgusted by his suggestion. In fact, many were nodding, especially any who called Mercia, Northumbria or East Anglia their home, and his eye was caught by Earl Hrani in particular, sitting on the row behind him.

"Think of it, should, and I hardly wish to think the words, let alone speak them out loud, should King Harthacnut not triumph in Denmark, where will King Magnus turn next? It could well be England. We simply can't allow England to be of secondary importance. We have wives and children to protect, farmers and nuns, monks and traders: the glorious wealth of our prosperous nation. We don't want to go to war again. Not for the sake of a simple compromise. We need strong leadership, from Cnut's son, from Cnut's son who resides in England and calls her his home."

Leofric spoke with passion, almost surprising himself with the fervour of his words. However, he also knew that he was right to do so. The Queen Dowager and Earl Godwine were deluding themselves if they thought they could hold England while King Harthacnut was absent.

Only Cnut had freed England from the Second Viking Age, and only Cnut could have kept it free from attack should King Magnus, and his Regents turn their eye toward Cnut's most profitable domain. But Cnut was dead, and in his place, they had Harthacnut and Harald. Harthacnut was more Danish than English. He had been for many years. Harald was English, and always would be. If neither of them had their father's battle prowess, that was the fault of the father. He had brought peace to England, and almost to Denmark.

Given the options, and the possible outcome of Harthacnut and Magnus' battlefront in Denmark, he knew Harald was the safer alternative, and Cnut had realised that as well.

And Cnut had realised that many years before when he'd first planned to leave each of his sons their own kingdom to rule. Only the machinations of the Queen Dowager and Earl Godwine had changed Cnut's mind. That and his impending death. Cnut had, put simply, run out of time to dictate the future as he'd wanted to.

Leofric turned back to face those who disagreed with him, knowing as he did so that others were standing to show their support. Cries of agreement were reaching the front of the church, but he kept any triumph from his face, as did Lord Harald. Yet their eyes met, and in Harald's eyes, Leofric detected even greater respect for his foster-father.

He was nowhere near the old man his father had come to be, revered and respected as though he were the greatest of augurs, but Lord Harald was still his junior by many years, and Leofric appeared to have earned a new status in his eyes. First, he'd been his foster-father, and now he was his prime supporter.

Mercifully, the Queen Dowager remained silent, turning instead to Earl Godwine to plead with him to speak on her behalf. Fury still coloured her cheeks, and Leofric imagined she was too incensed to speak further, but what would Earl Godwine do?

"King Cnut, may he rest in peace, pledged his support for his son, Harthacnut, to rule in Denmark and England upon his death. It's Harthacnut that I support." Earl Godwine spoke bluntly and with belligerence, his features contorted by the unexpected strain of the situation. Leofric knew he wouldn't be the only one to notice that he spoke of supporting Harthacnut, without denouncing Lord Harald's scheme for the interim.

All eyes now focused on Earl Siward, well those who could tear them away from the figure of the Queen Dowager, who still stood, her cheeks stained with her outrage. For all her years, Leofric thought, somewhat irreverently, that she was a truly beautiful woman, as she literally glimmered with rage.

He could see why men had made fools of themselves for her. He wondered, once more, if she'd truly been intended for Æthelred's oldest son, Athelstan, as some said, only for King Æthelred to take her as his own wife on seeing her fresh-faced beauty.

Earl Siward was a Danish warrior through and through. Leofric liked the burly man, often surprised by the menace he could portray with just a stare. He was truly, one of Cnut's own men. He'd fought battles on the sea, in Denmark, Norway or wherever there'd been an enemy to fight, even exploring the lands of the Rus. And now he wrestled along the borderlands with the kingdom of the Scots, having tamed the House of Bamburgh with his marriage to the Earl's daughter. He never shied away from any form of altercation, and this was not to be the day he broke that custom.

He stood, his long hair slowly walking its way along the top of his head, his beard a bountiful creature that he found difficult to tame, and he bobbed his head to the Queen Dowager.

As one of Cnut's allies it would be expected that he knew the Queen well, but he'd been a warrior fighting for his King, and then he'd been shipped off to the far north. The King had recognised in Siward the particular skill needed to rule the half Norse, half English hinterland of Northern England. He'd known Lady Emma more by reputation than any real contact.

That his loyalty to Cnut had been absolute was without doubt. Cnut had trusted few men with the North who weren't intimately connected to him through ties of family, and those who had commanded the North had needed to be strong-willed enough to resist the guile of Lady Ælfgifu in Northampton. She'd never let an opportunity pass to remind Cnut's warriors and trusted friends of his betrayal of her, of the sort of man that made him, of how he'd lied and murdered his way to England's crown.

Leofric pitied Lady Ælfgifu now that she was a widow, but knew that she was finally free from the stigma of being Cnut's first wife, the woman he'd promised to make a queen only to renege on that promise.

It was a terrible tragedy that Swein, her oldest son, hadn't lived long enough to stand in Harald's place now. But then, he'd been given an opportunity to rule in Norway, and had failed, spectacularly. He'd proved unpopular with the men and women of Trondheim. And Leofric, with only a brief acquaintance considered how that had even been possible. He'd met hard men there, keen to claim kingdoms for himself, but none of them would have failed to recognise a good and strong-willed regent or King, as they'd called Swein. Swein had merely been too pig-headed for the position, his mother unable to control him. It had long been the same within England before Cnut had ordered Swein and Lady Ælfgifu to Norway. Lord Harald had once been the same, but Leofric knew that his time as his foster-son had shorn away many of his sharper edges, made him a man worthy of ruling England. Should he get the chance.

"I'm the Earl of Northumbria," Earl Siward began, his deep voice, heavily-accented still, filling the rafters of the church and perhaps permeating to the exterior of the building as well. "I swore my oath to King Cnut, to fight and die for him, to govern this realm for him. It was my honour to do so." His head dipped low as he spoke, as though reminded of a conversation with Cnut, perhaps even the moment when he was made Earl, as his clenched fist beat against his breast.

Leofric observed him. He knew that it was possible Siward would be conflicted by the choices open to him, especially with the intervention of Lady Ælfgifu as he'd travelled to Winchester to mourn his King.

"King Cnut made it clear that his magnificent Northern Empire, akin to that of Emperor Conrad on mainland Europe, the Holy Roman Emperor, was to remain in place after his death. He dreamed of uniting England, Denmark, Norway and Sweden for much of his life. After all, the Vikings have always been so keen to come to England," he spoke with a lilt to his voice, enjoying the suppressed irony of his words.

"What better than to be united under one King? This movement I supported and respected, and will continue to do so. England is vital to that Empire. It will remain in the hands of Cnut and his heirs. I'm sure of that. But, England is also vulnerable at the moment, and alas, as has been pointed out, King Harthacnut is far from England, and likely to be so for some time."

Abruptly he stopped speaking, his brow furrowing as though struck by a new thought or surprised by what he'd said. When he continued, he spoke hesitantly.

"In the meantime, England must be kept secure. A Regent must be appointed, but," and here he looked to the Queen Dowager and Lord Harald with some trepidation, "it need not be just one Regent."

Ah, Leofric thought, he'd wondered about this when he'd spoken to Lord Harald in the last few weeks. He'd not named it as an option to Harald. He'd not wanted to upset his foster-son's careful planning.

"England is a large kingdom, the South and the North very different and a vast distance apart. I think it should be ruled by two Regents, not one." Earl Siward puffed his cheeks out as he spoke, as though relieved to have put a voice to his words, and in doing so, he failed to notice the furious glare of the Queen Dowager or the calculating look on Earl Godwine's face. Leofric saw them both and then turned to face Lord Harald.

Harald wanted to be a King, Leofric knew that, but he first had to win the support of the Southern kingdoms of England, something he might never do. But, if he ruled in Mercia, Northumbria and East Anglia first, it would be possible for him to have the prestige to win over their support. It might not be what he wanted from this meeting, but it would be a good start.

Cnut had, by necessity, kept his son far from the central hub of the Wessex Court at Oxford and Winchester. That had worked in Queen Dowager Emma's favour as she'd been able to convince many that Swein and Harald weren't truly the King's sons, despite his favouritism toward them. Many times Leofric had been asked why Cnut had sent Swein, an almost unknown entity, to rule in Norway, by the men and women of Wessex. Few from the South had truly understood, and even fewer had believed his reply, that he was the King's eldest son.

But if Harald was Regent in the North, he might stand a better chance of becoming King of all of England, especially should Harthacnut meet his death in battle, or decide to remain only as King of Denmark.

There was another consideration as well, and one that Leofric thought few considered when they thought of the future. The Queen Dowager Emma, while championing the cause of Harthacnut, her son with Cnut, had other children, from her first marriage, Alfred and Edward, her daughter as well, Lady Godgifu, married to the Count of Vexin and with almost grown sons of her own.

Should no agreement be reached on the governance of the realm, Leofric knew it wouldn't be long until someone remembered their existence and they were summoned back into the royal fold. Or even, so rumour had it before the other grandson of Æthelred was recalled to England. Born after the death of his father, King Edmund, in 1016, the young boy had lived all of his life in exile. He might have no knowledge of England, but none would deny his parentage, or that he had a right to rule in England should all of Cnut's heirs fall away.

After all, he was a surviving member of the House of Wessex, the family that had ruled since before the First Viking Age, only to be usurped by the House of Swein Forkbeard. Leofric thought few would refuse a return to the status quo of the House of Wessex should the sons of Cnut fail to act together and in the interests of England.

As Leofric considered the alternatives, he was aware of a general rumble of conversation around him. Earl Siward might have spoken as he thought, but it seemed others were interested in his idea.

The Wessex heartland, led by Queen Dowager Emma, didn't

welcome Lord Harald as their Regent, but the North, led by Lord Harald, didn't welcome the Queen Dowager Emma as their regent either.

"The idea has little merit," Lady Emma called, finally finding her voice, and managing to speak the words clearly. Her face had finally lost its furious expression, but the colour of her cheeks was far from indicative of the cold church they all sat within. Her anger seemed to be under control, for the time being.

"There should only be one Regent for King Harthacnut. He'd not welcome two Regents. And I caution everyone here, he'll come to England with the advent of summer, and he'll be filled with hatred for all those who didn't accord me the respect his father demanded." Leofric almost commiserated with her then as she threatened something she had no control over.

She was a woman of power, and it had been taken from her, just as her children had been taken from her. First the children of her marriage to Æthelred, then her daughter with Cnut sent to be raised at a foreign court far from her, and then Harthacnut, her son with him, shipped to Denmark to rule in his father's place, under the nominal guidance of his aunt, the powerful Estrid. Estrid, now she was a woman who could rule and command as any King could. Leofric was pleased they were on friendly terms. He wouldn't like to make an enemy of Cnut's sister.

Lady Emma had barely known her children. She'd married for political expediency on both occasions. If the second marriage had turned to love, she'd been poorly rewarded for adoring her husband. And now he was dead, and she wanted to protect her absent son's future. But it seemed beyond her, even with Earl Godwine as her steadfast supporter, with the power of Wessex behind him.

There was no one in the swirling fog of expelled breath that didn't swivel his or her head to gaze at the Queen Dowager as she found her voice. Leofric doubted there was anyone who saw no merit in the suggestion of splitting the kingdom.

"England shall not be divided again," she reasoned, her voice dropping to a whisper of persuasion. "My husband," she paused to swallow around the pain of her loss, "allowed England to be split early in his reign. Luckily the situation didn't last long, although only because of the unfortunate death of King Edmund, my step-son. No, England must stay united and together, for when Harthacnut returns to England. I'm afraid, Earl Siward, that your idea has nothing to recommend it."

At that, a murmur of unease swept through the hall, and Leofric shook into his cloak. This meeting would take all day; he just knew it. Around him, he could feel and hear people shivering and shifting as they tried to regain some comfort or warm a frozen body part.

"I disagree," a voice from the bishops called, and Leofric snapped his head to see who spoke, surprised when it was Ælfric, Archbishop of York. Although he held the Archbishopric of Northumbria, he'd long been an advocate and supporter of the House of Wessex. As he stood and walked to the front of the church, to stand beside Lord Harald, there was a hush in the muted conversation.

Archbishop Ælfric was both well respected and liked. His words would sway many within the confines of the holy place.

He bowed his tall body low to both Lord Harald and the Queen Dowager and then turned to meet the gaze of any who would return the intense gesture. He was a solemn man, and yet he was also known for his dynamic approach to the holy church, and for his ability to think quickly and act even more spontaneously. It was an attribute much needed in the North of the country.

"I would hasten to say that there is merit in the idea presented by Earl Siward, although I must confess that we'd not discussed it before we reached here, no matter what you may think." He smiled slightly as he spoke. It was easy to see why he offered the reassurance, or so Leofric thought. This shouldn't really descend into a North/South argument, although it did seem inevitable.

"There are many, even now, who don't acknowledge the Kings of England as the rightful rulers of Northumbria. To have someone more 'central' govern them, such as Lord Harald, would ensure a smoother transition than if it continues to be dictated to by the Southern kingdom of Wessex." Here he offered an eloquent shrug of his shoulders as if to apologise for the harshness of his assessment.

"As we all know, the ancient kingdoms cling, sometimes stubbornly, to their roots and their idiosyncrasies, and it's right that they do so. England is a 'new' country, 'alive' for only a mere century. In the Northern heartlands of Northumbria, on the fertile plains of East Anglia, and on the borderlands of Mercia, that is no time, a blink of an eye for some who hold on to their proud traditions."

"If England is at risk of attack, which, scare-mongering aside, is sadly a possibility now that our King, Cnut, is dead, we must accept that England could be best supported by two regional governments. It would still be whole, and ready for King Harthacnut's return, but in the meantime, government and rulership would be more closely bonded to the specific areas."

"The Earls perform that function," the Queen Dowager snapped her tone, far from beguiling now.

"The Earls govern the ancient kingdoms of Mercia, Wessex and Northumbria, on behalf of the King of England. They are proven, men. Earl Leofric has such links with Mercia that none could dare say he doesn't rule with the knowledge of nearly half a century behind him. Even King Cnut recognised that when he made him foster-father to Lord Harald."

"Earl Siward is a warrior and a courtier both. He, while reasonably new to his position, has made alliances with the powerful house of Bamburgh, he works closely with the Archbishopric of York, myself, and he's respected by almost everyone for his clarity, fairness and fierce application of justice. Not to mention his mounted warriors who keep the borderlands with the kingdom of the Scots safe."

"And Earl Godwine. He's a Wessex man, through and through, and Cnut's ally and friend."

As he named the three main Earls of England, he took the time to meet their eyes. Leofric was pleased to hear his words, to hear the respectful tone he used when he spoke of Ealdorman Leofwine, to be reminded of all that had been accomplished by his family. He was sure that Siward and Godwine were equally as pleased, but for all that, Archbishop Ælfric's point in listing the Earls as he did was obvious.

"These men need leadership. Earl Godwine can't know how to govern Northumbria, just as Earl Leofric can't know how to govern Wessex, or Earl Siward how to govern either Wessex or Mercia. These men are specialists. They can speak for their regional affiliations, but above them all there needs to be a unifying purpose, and sadly, with the Wessex-centric viewpoint that the Queen Dowager and Earl Godwine present with, this doesn't bode well for a country under external pressure for the first time in twenty years."

The words were so well-reasoned that Leofric thought no one could dispute them, but it was apparent the Queen Dowager would. Her face had turned pensive, her desire to refute the Archbishop's claims clear to see. But as Archbishop Ælfric once more bowed his tall head, and returned to his seat, the whispers of the audience began to hum with agreement.

The man had convinced many, as Leofric had thought he might be able to.

There were men and women of Mercia who decried their control by Wessex, men and women of Northumbria and East Anglia as well. No matter what the House of Swein Forkbeard had managed to accomplish since it had stolen the kingdom from the ancient House of Wessex, there were still those who thought their approach too keenly focused on Wessex. Perhaps, if Cnut had kept his first wife, as opposed to taking the widowed Queen Emma as his second wife, that skewed perspective could have been altered. But he had not. In fact, Leofric knew that his marriage to Lady Emma had been something strongly advocated by his father, as a way of uniting all of England behind Cnut's kingship; it had been a way of offering continuity when really none existed.

Hindsight was a cruel beast.

"Whenever England has been split, since it was united by King Athelstan, it has always only been reunited on the death of one of the two who have split it. Are you prepared to risk that?" the Queen Dowager spat, her eyes seeking out everyone in that room, and lingering on Lord Harald, the threat obvious. "We already have a dead King, we don't need another one."

Leofric opened his mouth to speak then, but Earl Siward beat him to it. He held his hands to either side of his massive frame, in a placating manner.

"England will still be England, ready for King Harthacnut to return to. But in the meantime, it will have two Regents. In the past, when England was split, it was between two Kings, this would be two Regents. It's completely different."

"That is a matter of semantics," the Queen Dowager returned acidly, but Leofric thought her tone sounded more resigned now. Perhaps there would be an agreement after all.

He shivered once more, moving his feet from side to side to force some feeling back into them. He was aware, as before, that there was a great deal of shifting within the church.

"I think we should have a small break," Leofric spoke into the rising sound. "It's too cold to sit for long," he apologised, but everyone was already standing, taking his words as an instruction. Although the Queen Dowager looked as though she disagreed, she quickly stalked to Earl Godwine, her back straight, her face curled into anger, and so Leofric strode to one of the braziers, keen to get there before everyone else.

# 4
## AD1035

THE BRAZIER HAD BEEN FILLED WITH BLAZING CHARCOAL WHEN LEOFRIC HAD first entered the church, but now servants rushed to refill it, and he welcomed the rekindled heat of the only source of warmth within the church. At this time of year, he often wondered why churches had not been built with the broad, central hearths always found within their homes, even in the lowliest of shacks. It made prayers and church services interminable throughout the long winter and bleak summer days that afflicted his country of birth.

His son and brother quickly joined him but didn't speak. They, like Leofric, were too busy trying to listen to the conversations of others, to determine what course of action was gaining in popularity.

They were quickly met by Lord Harald, a half-triumphant grin on his young face. No matter what was happening, it seemed he was enjoying the chaos of his appearance, and Earl Siward's suggestion.

"Good day Earl Leofric, Ælfgar and Lord Godwine," he greeted them. He was followed by a number of individuals, most of whom Leofric recognised. They were family members, the sons of Lady Ælfgifu's brothers, as well as other notables from Mercia. All of them shared the same furtive glances as they sought the safety of Lord Harald's proximity and others that they knew, stood with their lord and preferred Regent.

Leofric noted their movements with wry amusement. Here, for all to see was precisely the problem with England at present, and with the outcome of Cnut's two marriages. These men should have been welcomed at the Royal Court. They should have felt comfortable mingling with the nobility and holy men and women from Wessex. But it was more than evident that they felt only apprehension.

"My mother sends her regards," Lord Harald cracked, laughter on his lips.

"I trust she is well?" Leofric replied, almost by rote. The Lady Ælfgifu, as much as Cnut, had shaped much of his early life. He'd always admire the woman, for all that he wished not to have known her as well as he had. Or to be as intimately connected with her in the eyes of everyone else within England.

She'd not been back in England long and still mourned her elder son. But that hadn't stopped her from meddling in politics, and sending demand after demand to Leofric in his Oxfordshire home. Lady Godgifu had chastised him for complaining, saying he should be pleased to be so honoured. He didn't share her enjoyment of the situation.

"As well as any woman can be whose husband has just died." And just like that Leofric felt the years recede around him. He often forgot, as shrouded as it had become in politics and recrimination, just how close Lady Ælfgifu and Cnut had once been. He swallowed down his unease at his memories. Now was not the time for sympathy for the problematic Lady Ælfgifu.

"I'm sure arrangements can be made for her to visit his grave," was his only response, but Harald's face hardened at the conciliatory tone.

"She would rather see him alive, or not at all. My mother has words to share with her husband that will need to wait until they meet once more in the afterlife."

Leofric held his tongue on Lord Harald's flare of rage as it continued.

"I hope your brother, Northman, has met our dead King and spoken to him, honestly and openly. My father needed men as blunt as your father to show him the errors of his ways. Sadly, he never learnt them well enough, and many floundered because of that very fact."

"But your father always cared for you, and your brother."

A dramatic sigh escaped Lord Harald's hard face and Leofric noticed a slight tick to his eye. He hadn't meant to hit on this ancient weakness, but it seemed he had.

"My father sent gifts and promises he never kept. Now that he's dead, I expect to extract my own fulfilment of his promises. I'm grateful for his blood, and his kinship, even if I'd rather a man like your father had been my own or a man like you."

Leofric nodded, a smile on his face as his thoughts swirled to his own father. He still missed steady guidance of Ealdorman Leofwine. He assumed he always would.

"There's much support for Earl Siward's idea," Lord Harald queried, the conversation about fathers seemingly forgotten about in the face of more important concerns.

"There's a great deal to recommend it. And you, would you be content?"

"It'll give me an opening," Harald replied, somewhat enigmatically, and Leofric knew that Cnut's son had ideas that didn't necessarily rely on his younger brother ever returning to England.

"You would accept it then?" Leofric pushed, just to be sure, and Harald nodded, just enough to show he would.

"You should mingle with others," Leofric advised. He could tell many wished to speak with Lord Harald, standing close enough to their small group to make it obvious, while not listening to their words, but occasionally glancing over impatiently.

"Yes, we all should," Harald agreed, pulling his cloak tighter around his neck. "Bloody hell, it's freezing in here," he complained, his air pluming before him, obscuring his face as he turned away. Yet Leofric didn't miss the ambition in his fierce eyes or his pleasure at the way the meeting was progressing.

Loath to leave the brazier, but knowing that he must, Leofric stood for a moment longer. Ælfgar was silent at his side, and Leofric looked to Earl Godwine. He'd managed to extract himself from the side of the Queen Dowager and was surrounded by a number of his sons. The man had a horde of them, almost enough to fill a Viking ship and claim England for himself, and yet, for all Earl Godwine's ambitions, Leofric thought it would be a step too far even for the ambitious man.

"You can go and mingle with your friends," Leofric said into his son's ears, but Ælfgar looked mutinous at the idea.

"They aren't my friends, father, as I keep telling you."

"No, they're not my friends either, but sometimes it's good to stand and smile, make an inroad into their conclave."

"I think not," Ælfgar resisted, and Leofric relented. His father had often insinuated him into situations he'd rather have avoided. He was sure that Ælfgar could endure for a little longer before the matter became expedient. One day the boy would have to learn. Just not today.

"You should speak with Earl Siward," his brother cautioned him. "He looks quite inundated," at that Leofric turned. He'd not considered Earl Siward and the possible ramifications of his actions, or that a vast horde would wish to speak with him. Indeed, as Leofric considered the room, he saw great knots of people surrounding certain individuals. By necessity, the Queen Dowager was being mobbed, and so too was Earl Siward. Leofric could see where men and women wished to catch his eye. What he hadn't expected was to see Earl Godwine with only his sons for support. He'd always thought he held far more sway than that.

Yet his thoughts were cut short by his brother, Godwine Leofwinesson at his shoulder.

"You must speak with Earl Siward," he warned, "before they reconvene the Witan."

Leofric nodded at the repeated request and moved forward, his limbs solid with cold and from little use so that his brother's outstretched arm was welcome as he balanced himself. Lord Harald was still deeply engrossed in conversations, his voice, earnest and filled with guile followed Leofric as he walked to Earl Siward. Men and women parted for him, and he thanked them with small gestures, surprised, as always, to find he garnered so much respect.

Earl Siward had observed his progression, and he too broke away from his current conversation and made his way to meet Earl Leofric. As if by supernatural powers, all those stood in close proximity drifted away so that only the two men remained.

Earl Siward grunted his acceptance of what had happened, as though it didn't necessarily please him.

"Well met," the more substantial, slightly older man said to Leofric, his hand outstretched to grip his forearm. Leofric mirrored his words and the sentiment as they grasped each other's arms.

"A mess," Earl Siward began, betraying no hint of annoyance other than through his words.

"It could have been done better," Leofric agreed. "But then, we can't always decide when our Lord God will take us."

Siward merely grunted once more, and Leofric suddenly wondered whether Siward had meant Cnut's death or the beginning of the Witan. He'd taken it to mean the former, but he might have been wrong.

"Are you sure Cnut would have been content to let Lord Harald rule for his brother?" the Earl's blunt question was entirely what Leofric had been expecting from the plainly spoken Norse man.

"He wouldn't have allowed Harald to remain in England while Swein and Harthacnut were absent if he hadn't wanted the reassurance of an heir on hand," Leofric reasoned, and Siward grunted in agreement.

Leofric knew the other man as more than a passing acquaintance, but he couldn't always fathom the way his mind ran. It seemed he was doubting the veracity of his own words now.

"Damn boy, being in Denmark at a time like this, and damn Cnut for dying in the bloody winter. Much chaos could be caused before Harthacnut steps foot on English soil again. It's a mess, that's for sure. I suppose we should be grateful that we don't have an army camped on our borders or a Viking ship-fleet in anchor at Southampton." Leofric agreed with the other man on all those points and so held his tongue, waiting to see if Earl Siward did regret the option of a split regency that he'd offered.

"Northumbria is more than half Norse, it will accept either of the boys as their ruler. What it won't accept is bloody Earl Godwine and the Queen Dowager. I imagine that Mercia is similar?"

"Yes, perhaps not quite so Norse as Northumbria, but the Five Boroughs are still very proud of their Danish roots and hold dear to many of the old traditions. Lady Ælfgifu, despite her long absence in Norway, has always had a great deal of support there, ever since her father was murdered on Æthelred's instructions. Now that she's returned, many are keen to renew their allegiance to her."

"We must allow the boy to hold the regency then. There's nothing else for it, no matter what Earl Godwine and Lady Emma think. I'll continue to press the point."

"As will I. And, he truly does have the support of the ship-army on the Thames. They will support Harald and no other, Lady Ælfgifu saw to that on her return from Norway and Denmark. Lady Emma needs to understand that. She might be able to secure Wessex for herself, but only with Earl Godwine's support. She's the King's wife, not the King. As much as she might wish otherwise."

Leofric felt he spoke with regret for the woman. Cnut had left her in an unenviable position. She might once have shored up a kingdom for Cnut, but she'd be unable to do the same for her son with him.

She didn't have the advantage of having Swein Forkbeard for a father, as Lady Estrid did in Denmark. That reputation kept men and women in awe of her role in Harthacnut's regency and kingship there.

He only hoped that Lady Emma accepted what was about to happen with good grace.

Assured that Earl Siward would support the splitting of England between Lord Harald and the Queen Dowager, Leofric now fixed his gaze on Earl Godwine. He was speaking to some of his sons, and his words were furious and animated. Leofric felt his eyes narrow. They'd never been perfectly aligned in their political aspirations, everything that came so hard for his own family, seeming to fall into the lap of Earl Godwine and his. But perhaps not anymore.

Nonchalantly he walked toward the third great earl of England. Godwine, by dint of his age and long-standing, was regarded as the premier earl of England. While born of English parents, he was more Danish than many of his contemporaries, and his wife was a Danish woman. His children had a mixture of English and Danish names, and their attitudes toward the future seemed to reflect their mixed heritage. Or so Ælfgar had informed him.

They were proud young men, and Leofric worried for his own son's future with so many of them to stand against him.

But that was for the future. Today, for the first time in a long time, it seemed he might have an advantage over the often-gloating Earl, who'd done him so much harm in the past.

"My Lord," Leofric greeted him, a chill to his voice that had been missing when he'd spoken to Earl Siward. No matter the passage of years, Leofric found it hard to forgive the arrogant man his part in the murder of his elder brother. They'd been allies, once, but that time might now be well and truly over.

"Earl Leofric," the man replied, his eyes tracking his path to see where he'd come from. Leofric saw recognition swoop over his face as he spied Earl Siward.

"You've angered the Queen Dowager," Earl Godwine spoke bluntly, and Leofric thought it an odd way to begin the conversation.

"But not yourself?" he queried, somewhat surprised when Earl Godwine failed to answer the question.

"King Cnut was most adamant with her about Harthacnut's inheritance."

"He may have been," Leofric allowed, turning around so that he stood beside the other man, as opposed to in front of him. He wanted to see whatever Earl Godwine did as they conversed. "He was less adamant with myself, and I do wonder if it was perhaps the other way around. Was the Queen Dowager not most adamant with Cnut about Harthacnut?"

Leofric didn't miss the Earl's sharp inhalation at those words.

"You've always been more closely aligned with the other sons," Earl Godwine eventually ruminated, not quite an accusation, and not precisely recovered from Leofric's comments. Leofric held his amusement in check. Again, someone keen to forget that not only was Leofric in an alliance with Swein and Harald, but he was also Harald's foster-father.

"As King Cnut willed it, yes, I have been." It was good to speak his mind. It was no lie that his father, and then he, had been tasked with keeping Lady Ælfgifu content in her stronghold of Northampton. It had done them no favours with the Queen Dowager, and yet she'd still considered his loyalty all hers, perhaps more so when he'd become Harald's foster-father, and his sister had remained as her lady-in-waiting. Sometimes he was disturbed to consider what Lady Emma might have expected him to do to Harald on her behalf.

"Then you must do as your oaths, and your heart tells you," Earl Godwine commented, his voice dipping low, and Leofric knew he stared at the Queen Dowager. She would be enraged, but it appeared as though the Earl was giving him his tacit agreement for Earl Siward's suggestion.

"And you must do the same," Leofric answered, before walking back to the brazier, his son, and his brother, his sister as well. She had made her position clear by joining them, and he embraced her cold cheek.

"It is done," she shivered, and Leofric knew that she had distanced herself from the Queen Dowager.

"It's for the best," he offered, and Eadgifu nodded.

"It should have been done before. I have a husband, children and a home that need my attention." She didn't speak as though to convince herself, but rather with the assurance of one content with her decision.

Once more he shivered into his cloak, surprised that even the heat of compromise couldn't warm him, and he gratefully took the mug of warmed wine, heavily scented with the spices of winter that Lady Eadgifu had purloined for him.

He inhaled the heady aroma and sipped hungrily at the liquid. It warmed him as his cloak and gloves could not do. His brother watched him keenly, and he nodded to show all was well and then turned to seek out the Queen Dowager.

Lady Emma was holding court at the front of the church, surrounded by many men and women from Wessex, as well as churchmen and women. Leofric considered that as well.

There was a slightly weighted feel to the religious houses of England. Wessex was rich in them, the Northern kingdoms less so, although the Archbishopric of York was large and commanded great respect, the ancient Archbishop of Lichfield was more fragmented and suffered from its once vast reach. It made sense that many would seek out Lady Emma. She was a patron of the church and was known to support worthy causes. Leofric felt no concerns though. The diocese of Worcester was in Mercia as was the ancient diocese of Lichfield, once an archbishopric in its own right, and he knew support would be forthcoming from both religious establishments, as well as from Peterborough and Hereford.

The Witan, having gossiped and plotted, was quickly called back to order by Archbishop Æthelnoth, and in the smoky and breath-fogged interior of the church, it didn't take long for everyone to reclaim their original position. The day was advancing rapidly, and Leofric could feel his stomach beginning to clench with hunger.

Once more Archbishop Æthelnoth brought proceedings together, an expectant look on his face. Lord Harald quickly stepped into the breach, standing to the side of him.

"I'm happy to accept the resolution of Earl Siward. I will hold the Northern kingdoms for my brother, as his Regent. When he returns from Denmark, should he return, the rule of the land shall be given over to him." Harald spoke formally but with a lilt of triumph that elicited an angry tut from the Queen Dowager, sitting at the front of the church, but within easy listening distance of Leofric.

Quickly Leofric stood, as did Earl Siward, both keen to add their voices to the agreement.

"I concur," Leofric called, his cry echoed immediately by Earl Siward, and then Earl Godwine stood as well.

"I concur," he growled, his unhappiness at having to do so evident to hear, and yet this was the Witan. The laws and writs passed before the men and women gathered here would be legally binding.

It was then the turn of the lesser earls, and Hrani and Eilifr were quick to agree to the arrangement. The men looked exhausted by the contest of wills. As good Danish men, they knew their allegiance was simply to Cnut. The details were somewhat irrelevant.

Now all eyes turned to Lady Emma. She stood slowly, drawing everyone to gaze at her, even those who didn't want to. She stood, as a river of molten gold, striding to stand beside the Archbishop, on the opposite side of Harald, and when she turned, it was as though she blazed with fury.

"I will concur," she spoke clearly. "But know this, men and women of Mercia, Northumbria and East Anglia, men of the ship-army, when your King returns to England, as he will, there will be a reckoning."

Leofric could see the shadow of the young girl she'd once been as she poured scorn on all who had defied her and the ambitions for her son she held.

"King Cnut ruled this country through conquest as well as ambition, I wouldn't wish it to come to such again, for as all here know, loyalties can be tested, and enemies found to be friends when chaos and war ravages any kingdom."

Her voice flowed, and while Leofric admired her courage, all he could really see before him was a mother standing in the place of her son, and a wife, standing alone, abandoned by not one but two husbands.

For all the Queen Dowager's defiance, Leofric was unsurprised when Earl Siward's idea received resounding agreement from all the attendees of the Witan. And yet there were still trivial matters to resolve, and they took almost longer than deemed decent.

No warmth had managed to infiltrate the church, despite the press of bodies and the heat of the brazier, and Leofric was amazed by the stamina of some to still argue rather than seek a quick resolution. Not that he was surprised by the determination of some, especially when it came to the finances of the kingdom.

The Queen Dowager, far from reconciled to the agreement reached by the men and women of the Witan, was proving difficult to quell.

"The royal coffers are safely stored at Winchester," she'd announced in response to a question from Lord Harald, "and as such, they'll be mine to control. Seeing as how they are south of the Thames." Her voice was filled with a high edge of disdain. Now that she realised she had the advantage over the man who'd upset her careful plans, she was keen to exploit it.

Her anger was a palpable creature, stalking the resolve of many, perhaps even Earl Godwine. Leofric watched events uneasily.

It would be devastating should Lord Harald start his rule in poverty.

"But it's the wealth of the kingdom," Earl Siward tried to reason, only to be faced with the cutting eyes of Lady Emma.

"It is the wealth of the kingdom, yes, and it's stored at Winchester, and so it's mine to control."

"A little reason, My Lady," Siward tried to persuade, but the Queen Dowager turned her back to his question, focusing instead on the smouldering ire of Lord Harald.

"But you'll allow for the normal expenses of running the kingdom," Lord Harald choked, his voice strangled as he considered the implications dearth might have over his ambitions. He was not, despite who his father had been, a wealthy man in his own right. His mother was a wealthy and well-endowed woman, thanks to her own father's wealth, but even she wouldn't have been able to fund the running of a kingdom from her estates.

"I'll allow for those things I find necessary, but Earl Godwine and my husband's house-carls will protect it until it's needed."

"So I will rule the North, and you'll rule the purse strings?" Lord Harald queried, just to clarify, fury turning his voice to ice. Leofric winced at the display before him; already the two Regents were at each other's throats, and the resolution was only known within the church. It seemed Lady Emma would do all she could to inflict the most amount of pain on the child she'd never acknowledged as her husband's.

He considered her once more. How could she look on Lord Harald and not see her husband or even her own sons? How could she be so callous and cruel?

A small smile turned the Queen Dowager's lips upwards as she nodded.

"The treasure, I'm afraid, lies in the lands which will be mine to control."

Before Lord Harald could vent his full anger, Leofric stood and bowed to his new Regents.

"The North, I'm sure will be keen to honour Cnut's son with a newly minted coinage in his image. I'm sure," and here he turned to face the audience to ensure he didn't speak out of turn, "that no one will begrudge Regent Harald the honour?" At his words, he hoped for some sort of rousing cheer from the other assembled noblemen and women and wasn't disappointed. Those who saw Harald as Cnut's natural successor quickly shouted their assent, and Leofric turned back to find himself under appraisal from both regents.

The Queen Dowager, it seemed, had already denounced him as a traitor as her eyes smouldered, whereas Lord Harald regarded him as though he were some kind of saviour. No one in that church didn't understand the implication of reminting the coinage and the wealth that would be created.

Leofric endured Lady Emma's scrutiny while inclining his head to Harald. No matter what, King Cnut wouldn't have wanted his death to plunge England into a civil war. Leofric appreciated that it would be almost impossible to avoid that, with Lady Emma as angry and belligerent as she appeared to be.

She looked passed Leofric, into the audience and half opened her mouth to speak, only to close it again. Leofric imagined he knew precisely what her argument might have been, but she'd badly misjudged the situation. Even if the men and women of the Northern kingdoms had to pay for the privilege of having Harald as their Regent, instead of herself, they'd gladly do so. She was making no allies with the rough stance she'd adopted.

If they had to bring their coinage to the royal mints, and have those coins with Cnut's image on melted down and recast, at a reduced silver content, to show the image of Lord Harald, then they'd do so. The cost to them would be a small tax, nothing more, to have a man rule them who they thought should have been given more power by his father anyway. The fact it meant the virtual obliteration of Cnut's twisted legacy, wasn't lost on Leofric.

The more difficult the Queen Dowager became, the easier it would be for them to ignore Harthacnut's right to rule if he should ever return from Denmark. Leofric knew that there were a great many in that room who would look for any excuse to cast aside King Harthacnut.

Harthacnut was not known by the men and women of the Northern kingdoms, and while his deeds in Denmark may occasionally filter back, there were few keen to embrace the warrior king he was attempting to make himself.

Cnut may have begun his rule in war, but he'd ended it in peace, and no one within that church didn't wish that peace to continue.

The Queen Dowager, with her querulous nature, was making the rule of Harthacnut seem an even more distant possibility than it had been when the Witan had convened. Leofric had always known she was a difficult woman, keen to exert her power and influence as the Queen, but in doing so, she'd won herself more enemies than allies. As Leofric considered his final conversation with the King before his death, he wondered, not for the first time, if her dominating ways had worn away at the affection of the King's marriage. Had the King fallen out of love with his second wife, even before he'd lost his life?

His eyes once more fell on the Queen Dowager. She was still a beautiful woman, none would ever deny that, but the sharp edges of her ambitions had worn away at any softness she might once have had.

Had Cnut found any warmth in his marriage bed as he'd neared his death or only the ambition of a woman keen not to be thwarted? He rather thought the second option might have been the case.

# 5
## AD1035

The Witan lasted all of that cold winter's day. By the time Leofric was finally able to leave, he could barely move his frigid legs to walk to his horse. He was pleased he'd decided against walking the short distance to the Church from his home. He doubted he'd have been able to move his legs enough to return there.

He found himself dreaming of being fully immersed in steaming hot water until he could feel each and every part of his cold and aching body once more. But he knew he'd have to content himself with some exercise to warm up. He doubted anyone else within Oxford would think of stripping off his or her layers of clothes in order to warm up once more.

Agreements had been made, eventually, and two Regents, Lord Harald and the Queen Dowager, Emma, now officially ruled England with the support of Earl Godwine and Cnut's household troop. Yet Leofric couldn't rest easy. Much had been accomplished but not yet enough.

He knew Queen Dowager Emma too well, and for too long to think that she'd be content with the current arrangements. And yet, what could she do?

She stood with the support of Earl Godwine, who governed a vast swathe of Wessex on behalf of his King, but his King was dead, and the new one had yet to prove himself to his English supporters.

Leofric thought of all he knew about Harthacnut. He was young, just as his own son was, and he was desperate to make a name for himself. Yet, he'd been let down by his older half-brother, who'd not only lost the tenuous hold on Norway that Cnut had gained, but had allowed King Magnus and his Regents to amass so much support that the heartland of the House of Gorm, Denmark, was now threatened as well.

It was highly likely, should King Harthacnut ever come to England to rule, that he'd tax the English heavily, as his father had once done, and also that he'd bring a great swathe of Danish men with him to impose his order and command over a country that had proved unruly and unwilling to accept him.

Cnut had done the same. Some of those Danish men had proven loyal to the House of Gorm, and some had not. All had been rewarded with lands and riches in England, but few of them had been successful in their endeavour to hold them.

No, only Earl Godwine, with his English birth, Danish wife who was almost a member of Cnut's royal family, and his half-English, half-Danish children, had managed to retain his position in England. Leofric thought that he'd once hoped for more prestige in Denmark, but had quickly realised the future lay in England. It was a pity that the other Danish men didn't recognise the same about England.

He walked, on stiff knees, to where his son held his tempestuous horse for him. The air of men and women, locked up for much of the day in political debates, steamed around everyone making the dark sky appear filled with low clouds, and Leofric shivered once more. Despite his attempts to ward off the cold, there had come a point when it had simply been too much effort to try and stay warm. The cold had seeped into his bones, and now he was weary from its effects.

He was only grateful that it wasn't snowing again.

His son offered him what he apparently thought was a smile, but looked more like the rigours of a day old corpse, as he mounted his grumpy horse, and turned the beast to go back to his house in Oxford. He was hoping to avoid any further discussion with anyone until he was warm and able to move freely once more, and as such, he purposefully ignored any who called his name. All that was apart from Lord Harald.

"Come, My Lord," he managed through clenched teeth and a shut mouth. "Follow me, we'll talk in more comfort in the heat and with good food and drink. I can't stand this anymore." Leofric hoped that Lord Harald agreed with him, but he'd already turned away, allowing his horse as much speed as it could manage over the snow-crusted road. Each movement jarred his body, and he cried out in surprised pain, before resolving himself to even greater discomfort.

All he could think about was warmth, and the heat of a summer's day, politics and those who thrived on them was as far from his mind as it was possible to be.

As he staggered from his horse on arrival, he turned, surprised to see that Lord Harald was not alone. Instead, there was a small host of men following his lead, and he growled and stumbled into the house, along the pathway that his servants had finally managed to clear through the snow. The smell of smoke made his limbs crave the heat he knew would be inside, and the final few steps were an agony of expectation.

As soon as he slunk inside, he noticed the roaring fire at the centre of the hall, huge logs crackling and flaring any colour from blue to yellow depending on their proximity to its burning heart. Beside the hearth, more logs waited to be thrown on the fire. There was no way his servants were going to allow the fire to smoulder from lack of fuel.

He flung his cloak from him with the first wave of heat and tried to bend to remove his boots, only to realise he couldn't currently reach because his back was too stiff with cold. Instead, he was offered warmed wine by one of the servants as he hurried to the fire.

He could already feel slow tendrils of heat working their way over his chapped face, and the first swallow of his wine brought an almost physical pain to his innards. He sighed and then tried to focus his muddled thoughts, as he sat and a servant bent down to remove his boots.

"We have guests," he called roughly, hoping there were food and drink aplenty. It wasn't that he hadn't envisaged this gathering today. Instead, he'd thought it would be sooner, much sooner, and he hoped the meat he'd brought from his other home in Oxfordshire wasn't spoiled beyond use.

Men and women hurried about their business of welcoming the guests as he allowed his eyes to close, leaning back in the wooden backed chair placed as close to the fire as it was possible to be, without actually being in it.

He heard the shuffle of men and women entering his home, the cries of delight at heat and the size of the fire, and when he opened his eyes once more, he was happy to feel some colour to his cheeks. He imagined some would suffer from today's meeting – it was the time of year for illnesses and the chill they'd just endured wouldn't help anyone.

Quickly, he looked to those who stood within his hall. His brother and his son were there, laughing with his sister, as they drank their own warmed wine, joined by Orkning, his brother-by-marriage and commander of his household troop. It was those who visited who arrested his attention.

Regent Harald, he'd been aware of, and he was pleased he'd not minded the snatched words of invitation as they'd left the church. He was more surprised to see Archbishop Ælfric, Bishop Lyfing of Worcester and even Earl Siward amongst the number.

He also saw Brihtric, one of the more prominent kings-thegns, and Ufegat, Harald's Uncle. Leofric had never had sympathy for the man's sightlessness, and likewise, Ufegat had never asked to be consoled. Neither was he surprised to see him amongst those supporting Regent Harald. The older man had simply been waiting and biding his time, aware that one day his nephew might well be an important man.

Lord Ufegat had been one of those to support Swein's regency of Norway and had been keen for his sister to travel with her son. While Leofric had acted as Harald's foster-father in their absence, Ufegat had always been supportive and keen to visit with his nephew. He'd thought nothing of Leofric becoming Harald's foster-father instead of him, and Leofric wondered if his ambitions would surface now, or whether he was content to bask in his nephew's success.

A hound escorted Lord Ufegat, and Leofric held his slight amusement in check. His father, Leofwine, had been famed for his use of a hound to help him 'see.' It seemed he'd not been the only one to make use of the animals.

Now Leofric watched with some apprehension as his own animal, Hund, made the acquaintance of the stranger in his home, before quickly deciding there was no threat, as the two knew each other of old, and slinking back to the fire, nose high and tail wagging.

Leofric enjoyed the company of the animals, he always had. He found their ability to make snap decisions about other people, as well as other animals, was often the way forward.

Hastily, more and more chairs were pulled from the recesses of the hall. There were benches as well, for those who'd accompanied their lords, and Leofric was pleased that his servants thought quickly enough to provide them with seats close to the fire, but far enough away from the more important attendees so that the conversation couldn't be overheard. He wouldn't want anyone to leave his hall citing his stingy ways and lack of forethought in providing warmth and food for men and women who were cold almost beyond endurance.

He called greetings to those within his home, welcomes as well, but was content to allow everyone to just rest easy for some time. No one had been immune to the iciness. Hot food was soon shared; wooden bowls almost overflowing with a warm broth filled with huge chunks of meat. He was pleased to see the meat that had been prepared as a roast hadn't been wasted during his prolonged absence.

He ate hungrily, savouring the juicy meat and fat pulses, taking the time to catch the eye of Thuri, the custodian of his Oxford house, and thanking him for the excellent meal by raising his bowl as a salute. Thuri grinned in reply, unflustered by the unexpected arrival of such a vast number of people on the coldest day of the winter.

Eventually, everyone was warmer and less hungry, and Leofric turned once more to look at faces that had lost the deep white of newly fallen snow.

"Good evening ladies and gentlemen," he greeted, "welcome to my home on this less than pleasant day. Please, make any demands for food or warmth, wine, ale or mead. Our bodies must recover from the shocks of today." As he spoke, he smiled and nodded at his accomplices and then indicated that Lord Harald should begin proceedings. He, after all, was their regent now.

Lord Harald stayed seated, but he'd cast aside his cloak, and Leofric could now appreciate the clothing he'd worn to become, what he'd hoped at the start of the day, would be a King. It was the clothes of a warrior at rest. His arm carried two arm-rings on either side, made not from finest, unblemished silver, but instead ancient silver, nicked and dented with time – the gloating reminders of trophies won in battle, probably not by Harald himself, but rather gifted to him by his father from his grandfather's time, or even older.

Around his throat he wore both a golden cross for his faith, but also a beautifully crafted silver Thor's hammer. No doubt a family heirloom, either from many centuries ago if his mother had given it to him, or far more recent if his father had. The House of Gorm, or the House of Swein Forkbeard as it was also known, had been Christian for a much shorter space of time than the English.

It might even have once belonged to Lady Ælfgifu's father, the Ealdorman Ælfhelm, murdered many, many years before by Ealdorman Eadric on King Æthelred's orders.

At his fingers, a few rings flashed in the candle and flame light, but it was the weapon's belt that spoke of who Harald was and, more importantly, what he was.

The leather was laced with the image of the House of Gorm, a representation of the massive burial mound where the great king himself had first been interred, and the short seax that rested against his hip was wickedly sharp, although it lacked decoration. It was a weapon to kill with, and Leofric wondered when it had last drunk its fill of blood.

The sight of so many family weapons, had Leofric reaching for the double-headed eagle emblem on his cuffs and at his throat. He also thought longingly of his great sword, stored safely for the winter in folds of silk and fur to keep the rust at bay. He missed the weight of the weapon around his body but knew he might never have much use for it in the future. Provided the twin regencies were a success.

"My thanks for your warm, very warm, and as such, very welcome hospitality, Earl Leofric, and for your support today. It seems that my father's second wife is a little unhappy with our new arrangements." As he spoke, a hint of a smile playing around his mouth, framed with a light blond moustache and the traces of a beard, the other men quipped or laughed softly. Leofric doubted that any wished to humiliate Cnut's second wife, but he was sure they would if she proved intractable. Even his sister smirked, and despite everything, she was fiercely loyal to Lady Emma. She carried the taint of her family's greatest attribute as openly as everyone else.

Lady Emma might well have been the means by which Cnut cemented his own hold on England, but if she weren't careful she'd be the reason King Harthacnut lost England. And. Well, Leofric knew the lady had more than the one son, but they didn't share the same father. Still, all three boys, or rather men now, had a claim to the kingdom of England, and he could only hope that the Queen Dowager spent her time more wisely than trying to unite the three men to claim a kingdom that they were all virtual strangers within.

Harald's face sobered then, and he washed his face in one of his hands, as he considered his next words.

"England is calm and at peace. We must ensure that remains so. I hear worrying reports from all our borders, and action must be taken to ensure they stay strong. And as Earl Leofric says, it's essential we make money to ensure that's the case."

Harald spoke as he thought, and Leofric admired the personal nature of it.

"It's also imperative that we marry you, to a good and fertile woman," Harald's Uncle cackled softly. His hand rested on the head of his hound that sat attentively at his side, and Leofric shared a warm smile at the image, so reminiscent of his father, so many years before. "If you should ever hope to be more than just a Regent you'll need sons to govern after you."

The words seemed to shock Harald, who glared at his sightless Uncle, but Leofric could see both the advantages and disadvantages to such a suggestion.

"Respectfully Uncle, I should sooner have a kingdom to govern first, than a woman round with child. And anyway, I don't have the best experience of life with a man who's a King and the wife he took before he was a King." Sympathy marred Ufegat's face, and Leofric nodded again. How much different Harald's life might have been had Cnut married Lady Ælfgifu once he was King, as opposed to when he fought to become a King.

Leofric noted how calmly all of the men accepted Harald's future ambitions. He took it as a good sign. Should, and Leofric hoped he would, Harald prove to be a good Regent, it seemed there were many keen to allow him to become King. He dismissed his seeping worries about the self-interests of those involved. Politics was a dirty business.

"There's also the matter of the churches," Archbishop Ælfric commented when the conversation had turned away from women and children. Harald eyed him with interest, apparently unsure what the man was about to say.

"There's great wealth and land tied to every church and monastic house. Should the need arise, I'm sure that some of that can be diverted to help the Regency, with some assurances, of course.."

Only then did Leofric become aware of the close scrutiny of one of the men on the other side of the fire. In fact, Leofric realised, he'd been slowly edging closer and closer ever since the meeting had convened.

"Good," the other man burst, finally giving up his pretensions of not listening, and walking to join the rest of the men. Harald watched him with no expression on his face, and Leofric assessed the man.

He was tall, an almost typical Dane, and yet he had something of an Englishman about the way he dressed, discarding the more warrior-like tells that gave away a man of war. His face was creased, even in the depths of winter, with darker lines across his face and his hands appeared rough and well-used. Leofric knew him then as the leader of Cnut's ship-army. No doubt, like the vast majority of the ship-army, he owed his descent to Danish parents but was English to the core.

He settled himself on a stool he'd brought with him to the fire and looked to Harald. Harald nodded his head to him.

"This is Bovi, the commander of the king's ship-army, and supporter of my regency. He brought my mother safely home to me. Be welcome," Harald further expanded as recognition and understanding flooded the face of the rest of the assembled council.

"The men are in London, keeping watch on any ships that limp into port, but there are few, and none had left since before the King died. Harthacnut doesn't yet know about his father's death, and the weather is terrible this year. It'll be a long time before word can be sent to him."

The man spoke with satisfaction as he folded himself onto the small stool. Here was a man keen not to have Harthacnut as his king.

"My thanks," Harald commented, although it was clear he knew all this already. "The ship-army will keep vigilant?" he asked, just to be sure, and Bovi nodded briskly.

"Aye, they will. There are always four ships watching the approach to the Thames. On clear days they'll venture further out, but until the worst of the storms have passed, that's all the men can do. Other than train, drink and whore." He spoke with a fierceness to his voice, as though the men would apply the same dedication to all of those three tasks.

A small smile played around Lord Ufegat's mouth, and Leofric considered that he must dream of such freedom.

"I must, with all haste, have an account drawn up so that I can press the Queen Dowager for the initial funds needed for the kingdom," at this Harald looked to the Archbishop. It was the scribes of the king's household who would know most about money, and they were almost always monks, trained in the skill of reading and writing from an early age.

"I'll see what can be done," Archbishop Ælfric commented, a slight grimace on his face. "It may be difficult to extract anyone from the King's scriptorium in Winchester. They're always closely bound together by their secrets and insights into how the kingdom is run, just as my own men are in York. But if I were to find someone, where should they be directed? Where will you govern from?"

"I plan on making London my home, the place my grandfather declared his kingship from. All should seek me there. It's the best site, close enough to Wessex to know what is happening, and far enough away to keep a good distance from my father's wife." He too spoke with a frown, and Leofric felt the weight of the future settle on his shoulders. Nothing in this would be easy, and Harald would need to learn to dodge and weave his way through whatever might happen in the coming years. Leofric only hoped they had the time they needed for Lord Harald to prove his worth as both Regent and a possible future king.

That Lord Harald didn't mention the presence of the ship-army in London spoke of an underlying fear. Harald wanted to know that should an attack come, either from King Magnus or from King Harthacnut, there would be someone to protect him.

Leofric found relish in the challenge of the future now his body was warm and he could think clearly. In the church, it had all felt overwhelming. Now, while still being aware of the disadvantages to the scheme, he could also see many, many advantages. Not least of all was upsetting Earl Godwine and his careful plans. It was especially crucial for Leofric to restrict Earl Godwine's reach.

The man had too many children, and all of them, should their father remain in his current position, would soon be demanding their own small areas to govern. It would start with small sheriffdoms, but, if the children were anything like the father, the ambition would quickly expand.

The only solution was to chip away at his current position, as opposed to allowing it to expand. Leofric had deduced, from his last meeting with King Cnut, that even he had come to appreciate earl Godwine had grown too powerful within England. Leofric had decided it was his duty, not only to assist Lord Harald but also to stop Godwine encroaching further. He knew there was something that Earl Godwine held over Lady Emma or perhaps King Cnut, just as once before, and until he deciphered that, little action could be taken, but it was always good to plan.

"Why not Northampton?" Lord Ufegat asked sharply, and a faint hint of irritation marred Lord Harald's face, shown so openly, no doubt because the blind man could not see it.

"Northampton is too closely associated with mother, and with you," Harald countered, his attempts to keep the irritation from his voice, failing.

"She did birth you, you ungrateful git," Ufegat growled, but Harald merely rolled his eyes and looked around at his supporters, as though asking for forgiveness for the petty family argument taking place.

"And I'm forever grateful to her, but I must stand as my father's son, not my mother's son, no matter the fact my father all but abandoned me. I claim my right to be Regent through my father's line, not my mother's."

Lord Ufegat subsided with a grumble, and Harald squeezed his eyes shut, in an effort to focus his thoughts. Leofric watched the exchange with raised eyebrows. Unity was important. He might need to speak to Ufegat about his behaviour. Or perhaps to Lady Ælfgifu. She held sway with Ufegat.

"London is where the ship-army are stationed. If I need to face an armed invasion few will welcome attacking London, even my father failed, and my grandfather, on many occasions. London is a stronghold. Far more than bloody Winchester. All Winchester has is a lot of churches, and the bodies of long dead kings." At that point, Leofric hoped Lord Harald would cease his ranting, but he continued.

"And a very stubborn woman claims it as her own. Winchester is not mine, and never will be. London can be mine, Northampton gives its allegiance to my mother. I need somewhere that's mine."

Bovi spoke then, his voice thinly laced with a threat toward the older man.

"London is where the ship-army will stay. The ship-army will support whoever holds London." He spoke as though pronouncing a death sentence, and Leofric noticed Lord Harald's furious glare at the man.

Regent for not yet a day, and already strains were showing.

It fell then to Bishop Athelstan to speak, and try and distract from the arguments about London.

"I would recommend sending a small force to the borderlands with the Welsh. There are rumours of an uprising, and a name I keep hearing is gaining in popularity. It behoves you to protect the borderlands."

"And what of the border with the Scots?" Lord Harald asked, nodding to Bishop Athelstan to show he understood and agreed, before looking to Earl Siward. The other earl was ensconced in a comfortable wooden-backed chair, his feet and face angled toward the fire, which he studied, rather than meeting Lord Harald's eye.

"I have it on good authority that the kingdom is peaceful – the new king is untried – and they still smart from Cnut's attack on them a few years ago. I don't foresee any problems, but I'm being careful. Donnchad Mac Crinain is much under the influence of Mac Bethad mac Findlaích. I've yet to decide the best steps to take."

Archbishop Ælfric was nodding along with Earl Siward, as though the two had discussed the matter.

"I agree, I believe the land of the Scots is more concerned with events within its borders. Just like the English are." There was a slight note of censor to the words, and Leofric agreed. England was weak when it was divided, and men and women squabbled over the spoils.

Lord Harald needed to act decisively to ensure that the unfortunate death of his father didn't allow England to stand weak and defenceless under her two Regents.

"Gruffudd ap Llewelyn is the threat to England north of the Thames," Godwine Leofwinesson said, joining the conversation and Harald nodded once more as Leofric's brother continued to speak.

"Come the better weather, we must have small forces patrolling the area, and I'll consider whether to make overtures of friendship with him. Perhaps it would be better to avert a battle, although possibly not," he countered, fingering his sharp seax as he spoke. Leofric felt a wave of unease engulf him. Now was not the time for war, not if the threat from King Magnus or King Harthacnut manifested itself.

"And what of my brother?" Lord Harald said, meeting and holding the eyes of those who counted themselves as his closest advisor.

All looked to Harald now, and Leofric wondered just what he had planned.

"It's of course to the benefit of everyone here that King Harthacnut remain in Denmark for as long as possible. I don't believe that he'd look too favourably on what has happened in England in his absence, no matter the justification, on that I fear the Queen Dowager spoke the truth."

A faint menace hung in the air at the pronouncement and Leofric held his tongue. Cnut had not sworn him to an oath that prevented Harthacnut from becoming king, he had merely demanded that Harald be given a chance. Yet, the danger of recriminations from Harthacnut was a real one.

"Surely he'll be busy holding onto Denmark?" Archbishop Ælfric offered, unease on his face. "I hear the men behind King Magnus' kingship are powerful warlords, with the backing of the previous king's wife, who is not the child's mother, but overlooks that, and that she is the sister of King Anund Jakob of Sweden."

"Yes, I'd hope the same. Still, it would be good to have some sort of reassurance of that," Lord Harald continued, and Leofric felt a faint worry. Just what was Lord Harald asking them to do?

"England has been allied with Norway before," he continued, a dangerous glint in his eyes and Leofric thought back to his childhood, when his father had been an acknowledged ally of Olaf Tryggvason, who'd claimed Norway as his birthright. Then, the alliance had been drawn up to protect England from future attack from Norway. The same situation didn't currently apply, but he didn't want to be the one to caution the new Regent.

Yet, it seemed no one else wanted to either as an uneasy silence fell amongst the assembled nobility and senior churchmen. He watched the faces of men he knew and respected. Some gazed at the fire, others returned his gaze as though reminding him that he was Harald's foster-father, and he could speak as he saw fit. Others wouldn't have the same lee-way with the new Regent.

"Norway has no claim to England. The King's mother, I understand, was an English slave," Leofric eventually stated. "We can be assured that no King of Norway could possibly claim England, except through conquest, and that is unlikely while it battles Denmark, and unlikely because we're aware of the danger, now." Before anyone, including Lord Harald, could interject, Leofric continued. "Harthacnut is King of Denmark, and still our ally, despite everything that has happened today."

This earned Leofric a furious glare from Lord Harald, but he ignored it, instead seeing something that looked suspiciously like relief on the faces of the other men, all apart from Bovi.

"Our sons and daughters have been raised in a wave of peace not known since the reign of Edgar the Peaceable, sixty years ago. There's no need to go looking for an enemy."

A heavy silence hung in the air, broken only by the creaking and crackling of the wood on the massive hearth, and Leofric felt a small bead of sweat start to drip down his back.

"Well said," Earl Siward eventually answered, only for others to also nod their heads and mutter soft agreement once they knew the two great Earls spoke with one mind.

"If we seek an enemy it should be on our island, not across the seas," Earl Siward continued. "There are always many, many men who could threaten England, women as well," he admitted with a wry shrug. Leofric didn't know if he meant Lady Emma, and so he held his tongue.

Leofric finally hazarded a glance at Lord Harald, and what he found on the younger man's face was resignation. He was pleased. Leofric knew the rage that pulsed through Harald. No doubt he'd have happily done anything to make King Harthacnut's current position in Denmark even more unstable by supporting the Norwegians, but Leofric was adamant that England wouldn't be used as a battleground for a family feud. Not again. And even if it seemed inevitable.

"So we'll focus on Wales," Harald interjected, his voice a little flat. "And on building a relationship with the Queen Dowager, and providing the continuity my father would have wanted." It didn't sound exhilarating, but it was what England needed, and Leofric was pleased Lord Harald understood that.

"Agreed," Earl Siward said, with Archbishop Ælfric chiming in at the same time, while others nodded. If Lord Ufegat looked a little rebellious, Leofric ignored it. There was no need for war. Men and women could be known for dispensing justice and good government as opposed to killing enemies.

"Secure the funds, appease the Queen Dowager, keep Earl Godwine neutered, and prove my abilities," Lord Harald spoke with an upturned lip, a quip in his eyes. "Easy," he breathed, shaking his head as he did so. But triumph still shone through him, and Leofric knew that if he could just be prevented from pissing his half-brother off in Denmark, he'd get the chance his father had wanted him to have. More importantly, Leofric would be freed from his oath.

# THE ANGLO SAXON CHRONICLE ENTRY FOR 1035

This year died king Canute (Cnut) at Shaftesbury, and he is buried at Winchester in the Old-minster : and he was king over all England very nigh twenty years. And soon after his decease there was a meeting of all the witan at Oxford; and Leofric the earl, and almost all the thanes north of the Thames, and the 'lithsmen' at London, chose Harold for chief of all England, him and his brother Hiirde-canute (Harthacnut) who was in Denmark. And Godwin the earl and all the chief men of Wessex withstood it as long as they could ; but they were unable to effect any thing in opposition to it. And then it was decreed that Elfgive, (Lady Emma) Hardecanute's mother, should dwell at Winchester with the king's, her son's, household, and hold all Wessex in his power ; and Godwin the earl was their man. Some men said of Harold that he was son of king Canute and of Elfgive daughter of Elfelm the ealdorman, but it seemed quite incredible to many men; and he was nevertheless full king over all England.

# 6

## LONDON, AD1036
### LONDON

Leofric watched the panting shape of Lord Harald, a faint line of worry furrowing his brow. Harald was the angriest he'd ever seen him. Even though they were friends and allies, family even, Harald's hand hovered unconsciously over the seax on his weapon's belt, and Leofric doubted it would take much to have him draw it and use it on whoever spoke to him next.

Not that he didn't understand. Or at least he thought he understood.

"My Lord, please," he cautioned, his hand outstretched as he tried to placate the furious man. He needed a rational conversation with Harald, and at the moment Leofric thought that might be impossible.

Leofric looked around him. He'd just arrived in London, at Lord Harald's new hall, but it seemed that others had been on the sharp end of Harald's rage for much longer. Even Lord Ufegat, a man always sure of himself despite his blindness, sat quietly by the hearth, stroking his hound, more for his own comfort than for the dog's, a faint tremor running through his body. Hund, who'd escorted Leofric to London, couldn't tempt the creature from her

Lord's side and had instead returned to Leofric, with a whiff of haughtiness about her.

What had happened?

Or rather, what else had happened?

"My Lord Harald, I would understand all of this," he said, moving his head to indicate the subdued nature of Harald's home in London, where the servants and slaves were too terrified to carry out their normal duties, but waited for Harald to look away so that they could escape into the bitter winter's day unnoticed.

"That bitch," Harald hissed, and Leofric knew exactly of who he spoke. The next words he was more unsure about. "That bastard," Harald said, his words erupting in a fountain of spit and spite.

Did Harald speak of Earl Godwine, King Harthacnut, or Æthelnoth, Archbishop of Canterbury? None of those three had been any help to Harald in his Regency to date, and Leofric knew they all deserved to be strung up for their actions, but what new event had occurred as he rode to meet his Regent's summons?

At that moment, he was surprised by the arrival of someone he'd not been expecting to see. As he was handed a mug of ale by the only sheepish looking servant left in the hall, a belated welcome for coming to calm down their lord, Lady Ælfgifu entered the main room of the hall.

She was surrounded by a handful of women, all richly dressed, and the majority much younger than she was. Leofric almost choked in surprise and met Lady Ælfgifu's eyes only to see amusement there. No matter Lord Harald's rage, Lady Ælfgifu had enjoyed her moment of shocking the Earl who'd been her ally for so many years.

"Earl Leofric," she called, coming to stand before him without even a glance for her angry son. No doubt she was aware of what angered her child.

"Lady Ælfgifu, I hadn't expected to see you here. If I'd known, I would have invited Lady Godgifu. She'd have been pleased to meet up." A warm smile touched Lady Ælfgifu's lips at those words.

"I didn't know I would be here either," she announced, her voice light and airy as though it was of no concern, but there was evident apprehension, in her stance, if not her words. After her failed role in King Swein's governance of Norway, Lady Ælfgifu had vowed to stay away from the day-to-day running of Harald's Regency. Her presence here, at the centre of his administrative hub, was not a good sign.

As she spoke, her eyes flickered to Harald, and a steely countenance settled on her welcoming face.

"Come, we must talk, in more privacy," she chastised her son, as she led them toward the hearth, others scattering at their approach. Harald followed as though against his will, and Leofric quickly released the double-headed eagle clasp on his cloak and handed it to the waiting servant. There had been a bite to the wind outside, and he was now almost too warm to be comfortable near the hearth, but he accepted the inevitability of sitting beside it. Lady Ælfgifu wore fine court clothes, not designed for warmth, but rather for show. She'd always been a woman who understood the importance of 'show', no matter the weather. In that, she shared similarities with the Queen Dowager that he'd never, ever, voice.

He admired her resolve.

As soon as they were settled, Harald opened his mouth to speak, only for a grimace to mar his face. He'd aged in his short time as Regent. It had brought a worry line to his forehead that Leofric was appalled to see in a man only just into his twentieth year, and it looked as though he hadn't shaved for days, his beard and moustache resembling a bird's nest and not the carefully trimmed appearance Leofric had come to associate with Harald.

Harald was acting well in his limited capacity as Regent, but he found obstacles continually prevented him from achieving what he wanted.

"The Queen Dowager has refused my request for funds and sends word that the 'King of England' Harthacnut, as she insists on referring to him, will be arriving in England within months. And bloody Earl Godwine has allowed the slaughter of two members of my own personal household guard sent to collect the payment requested from Winchester. If I can't pay the fleet, they'll abandon me," Harald grumbled, his fury ending on a plaintive tone that belied his utter despair.

"But the coinage has been recalled, and reissued, the tax levied as agreed at the Witan, surely funds are coming from that source?" Leofric queried, trying to make sense of Harald's utter dejection. A fiery gaze met his query, and he leaned back on the chair in shock.

"The reminting continues apace, of course, but it takes time, and my men need paying, and I need to bloody eat." Hopelessness filled Harald's voice, and Leofric looked to where his own son was deep in conversation with one of his own ally's. There was little to divide the two concerning age, no more than five years, and yet Leofric looked to Ælfgar as a child, while he expected Harald to govern the kingdom of England.

"It was agreed that funds would be shared?" he continued, just to be sure, only for Lady Ælfgar to shake her head slightly from side to side, as though warning him off.

When Harald didn't respond, Leofric tried a different tact.

"The Queen Dowager still stands alone, with only Earl Godwine and the Archbishop as her allies?"

Immediately, he felt the interested gaze of Harald.

"And?" Lord Harald asked, as though annoyed with Leofric for stating the obvious, but curious all the same.

"How many men did you send to Winchester?"

"Just the ten were allowed into Winchester itself, to accompany my clerics. The Queen Dowager was insistent on that."

"Have you questioned the men about Winchester?"

"What about it?" Harald asked with exasperation.

Leofric leaned forward on his elbows, thinking carefully before he spoke.

"How many men are there in attendance upon the Queen Dowager? Is Earl Godwine always in Winchester there? Or his sons? Do the housecarls still support the Queen Dowager? Does the royal treasury remain filled with Cnut's resources?"

"Why would I ask those questions?" Lord Harald asked, his anger temporarily forgotten as annoyance tinged his voice, but Leofric was thinking carefully once more. Some actions were easily reversed, but some were not, and he knew making the wrong suggestion to Lord Harald would cause dreadful consequences.

"An agreement was reached between the Witan of England and her two Regents, yourself and the Queen Dowager. That agreement stipulated that the Northern Kingdom, under your rule, could call upon the royal treasury for funds for the acceptable costs of running it. Yes?"

He pressed the point, hoping that Harald would seize the initiative.

"Yes, Earl Leofric, you know all this." Aggravation still consumed Harald, but Leofric hadn't finished yet.

"I do yes, and I know it was witnessed by all and ratified by them."

"Yes, it was. But I can't do anything if the Queen Dowager and sodding Earl Godwine break their pact."

"Yes, but you can. You have a legal claim to those funds – an agreement from all, from the Witan, that governs England. You have the right to the funds, and if she denies you, then, unfortunately for her, you have a legal recourse to demand that which is yours, by force if necessary."

Lord Harald's mouth had dropped in shock, whereas Lady Ælfgifu had allowed a small smile of pleasure to touch her tight cheeks. Leofric looked at the woman. Traces of her beauty remained in her sharper features. Some women grew fat as they aged. Lady Ælfgifu had grown thinner, and more pointed. The loss of her eldest son had wounded her deeply, as had her fraught journey home to England, pursued by the Norwegians even when Swein was dead and buried. She'd been rescued by the English ship-army who now supported her son, and as such, she was doubly in their debt.

Returning only to then lose her husband had taken much of the joy from Lady Ælfgifu, what little had been left to her, anyway.

Leofric knew she'd spent a lifetime plotting her revenge on Cnut for his abandonment of her. To have all that come to nothing had disappointed her. Now she hoped only for Lord Harald's victory as a means of winning her vengeance against the Queen Dowager.

"You're within your legal rights to take more than the specified ten men, and take your share of the kingdom's treasure to ensure it can meet its financial obligations. There's nothing that either the Queen Dowager or Earl Godwine can do. It's your lawful right. Although, you must only take what you're owed." He added the last comment as a warning because he could already see Harald formulating a much larger raid on Winchester, a way of seeking recompense for his humiliation at the hands of Earl Godwine.

"So we would need to know the strength of Winchester to overwhelm it," Lady Ælfgifu added, her voice firm as she considered the possible outcomes, as her son did.

Leofric knew the time for caution was now. "It would be best if there were no bloodshed, but again, the Queen Dowager has been the first to draw blood. You must demand the wergeld for the men murdered. If the Northern Regency appears weak against the Southern, they'll do worse in the future. We must counter their actions, but with no violence."

Leofric was already formulating his own plans as he spoke, considering who could be trusted to carry out the raid-like attack on the King's treasury. He was thinking of the strong room, and how it might be guarded, and for once, he let his gaze slip away from Lord Harald and his mother.

"A fine idea," Lord Harald said into the silence. "I'll lead the party myself, and take a hundred men with me, some of the ship-army I think. They'll revel in the idea of going to get their pay."

Leofric swallowed his unease at the idea but quickly reconciled himself to it. It would be best for Harald to lead. He was, after all, the Regent, and must appear strong-minded.

"You have copies of the amount owed to yourself, drawn up by the Northern Chancellery?" Leofric questioned, just to be sure, and Lord Harald nodded.

"Your son, he'll accompany me?" Harald asked, almost a demand, turning to glance at Ælfgar and Leofric nodded. He thought that might be Harald's next move.

"Yes, it'll be good for him to spend time with the men of the ship-army. He enjoyed his time with my own ship. I'll ask his Uncle Godwine to accompany you as well. Godwine is keen, as ever to meet any injustice."

"Your brother should have been born during a different time," Harald laughed. It was well known that Lord Godwine was a man of his sword and his rage, Lord Eadwine, a man of letters and justice. Any injustice could be dealt with swiftly, in Godwine's eyes, needing only a sharp-edged blade, Eadwine was more prone to relish the challenge of using words and bringing about a compromise.

"And as to King Harthacnut. I've no word that he's yet beaten the Norwegians. And even if he had, I doubt he'd be prepared to leave Denmark when it's so recently been under attack. I've sent my own ship to Denmark for more recent news. The seas are still rough, and all crossings fraught with peril, but the men enjoy the challenge."

"So the Queen Dowager lies about that as well?" Harald growled, and Leofric nodded.

"She reports her hopes, not the actual events. She's lost much of her ability to think and act calmly in the wake of Cnut's death. He wouldn't be pleased by the implacable stance she's adopted."

Harald nodded, his face twisting as he thought of the Queen Dowager.

"I never liked the bitch," he growled, before standing and striding away. Leofric watched him go with only a twinge of apprehension. The lad needed more guidance than Leofric had thought, but then, he'd never been raised to rule. It was his father's fault, but Leofric understood he'd have to guide Harald more than was comfortable in the first years of his regency.

"Harald is a good ruler," Lady Ælfgifu spoke into the hush. "What he lacks is the conviction in his abilities. I blame Cnut. He should have accorded his sons' far more prestige than he ever did. No doubt because that witch of a woman wouldn't allow him to. That is why Swein failed in Norway, you know." She spoke as though conferring a great secret and Leofric was surprised. Lady Ælfgifu had offered no explanation to him before of what had occurred in Norway.

"Swein is a great miss," Leofric said softly.

"He is yes. He would have risen to the challenge that Cnut's death has caused. He would have known how to rule better than poor Harald."

Leofric stilled at the deliberate slight, as a small smirk of triumph touched Lady Ælfgifu's lips.

"What happened in Norway?" Leofric asked, curious, despite himself and wondering if now was the time to finally learn the truth. Unshed tears glittered in Lady Ælfgifu's eyes, and her hand trembled a little as she held her goblet, but she spoke.

"Earl Hakon had already made allies. He and his family, they were well known to the Norwegians, from the time they ruled Skane for Swein Forkbeard and then for Cnut. Cnut should have been pleased he died before more damage was done." She spoke with an edge, excuses pouring from her that Leofric dismissed with a pinch of salt.

"It didn't help that Olaf Haraldsson, the new King's father, had only recently been killed, and not by Cnut or Earl Hakon, but rather by his own people. They rose against his leadership and killed him at the Battle of Seiklestad. I hear his half-brother, Harald Hardrada, stood with him, but he ran off, to the lands of the Rus after the battle."

"But it was too much for King Swein. The people of Norway are not keen to be ruled now that they understand they can have whoever they want as King, and they didn't want King Swein precisely because he was Cnut's son. They want a Norwegian to rule them. They are strongly nationalist, just like the English." She spoke with a tilt to her chin.

"But King Magnus was no more than a child, or rather, is a child."

"Yes, he is. I met him, you know. I thought him sweet. I should have known better. The two men who stand as his regents, who chased Swein and I from Norway, Einar and Kalf, were nothing but trouble while we were there. Swein could make no decision that they wouldn't argue against. They didn't want Swein. They roused public support for King Magnus, even managing to convince Olaf Haraldsson's widow that she should throw her weight behind the little bastard."

"I understand," Leofric commented, keen to cut off her snide remarks.

"King Swein needed his father to stand behind him, the strength of the House of Swein Forkbeard. Instead, he sent Swein and me into a pit of vipers, with few clear allies and an impossible task. I'll not forgive Cnut for his ridiculous expectations of us both, and I'll ensure poor Harald doesn't meet the same fate."

"He's performing admirably," Leofric hesitated. "It's a strange situation for him, to be in limbo, unsure when, or even if, his half-brother will return."

"It's to be hoped the bastards who killed Harthacnut's half-brother are killed by Harthacnut. I'll take it as an insult if he fails to avenge his brother's death."

Lady Ælfgifu spoke harshly, her eyes still glittering with unshed tears, and Leofric felt pity stir within him. He doubted it would be easy to heal from the death of a son. He still mourned his brother.

"Yet if he kills them, he'll return to England," Earl Leofric commented, and Lady Ælfgifu choked down laughter.

"I know, Earl Leofric. Fate is a strange beast." At that, she ceased speaking, lapsing into her own memories and Leofric found himself doing the same.

His brother was never far from his thoughts. Not that he thought exclusively about him, but instead, since Cnut's death, it had become more comfortable to think about him. For too many years he'd had to hold his anger and grief in check, unable to fully vent when his King was the man responsible for Northman's death. Now that Cnut was dead as well Leofric knew he'd thought more about his brother than he had for many years.

His nephews, a similar age to Lord Harald as opposed to his own son, were a credit to their father's memory, and yet, they still bore his taint, that of a traitor. Leofric rubbed his forehead once more. Earl Godwine was the only man who yet lived who'd been involved in his brother's murder. That would, despite everything, forever taint any chance of genuine reconciliation between the pair of them, and, Leofric realised, he really was done with being allies with men who killed without thought.

"Memories take you to strange places," Lady Ælfgifu said, standing slowly and placing a consoling hand on Leofric's shoulder. "It's grief, rather than joy, that so often shapes our lives. And now, if you'll excuse me. I really must be alone."

Leofric watched the woman walk with as much composure as possible, out of her son's hall in London, and he considered the wisdom of her words. It sounded very much like something Wulfstan would have once said to him. Perhaps, he thought with a wry smile, there was an advantage to a little bit of a life well lived to add perspective to everything.

Unsettled by his thoughts, he stood and indicated to Ælfgar that he too was going to leave the hall. Ælfgar remained behind as Leofric stepped through the wooden doorway and into the brisk day outside. He was engrossed in conversation with his cousins, and Leofric was keen to be alone.

The number of buildings in this part of London did something to diminish the strength of the blustery wind, but, as Leofric fastened his cloak once more, using another catch that carried his house's emblem of the double-headed eagle, he appreciated that it would be colder near to the water, and that was where he planned on going.

Harald had built his new hall some distance from the water's edge, and all around was a hive of activity, as shop-fronts spilt into the through-fare, owners calling to those they thought had coin enough to purchase their goods. The sound of iron being hammered filled the air, the sizzle of meat being cooked, and the stench of the leather-curers all mingled, so that Leofric wrinkled his nose while smiling at the industrious nature of it all.

The walkway was busy as he stepped ever closer to the water's edge, seeming to fill with more and more people, as opposed to less, as expected. No matter the season, and provided ships could still get through, London thrived as a trading port, of both goods and gossip. Leofric appreciated its acceptance of exotic trading vessels because it brought to England goods that he didn't even know he desired; warm spices, warmer wines, sharper wines, and the much-prized furs from the far Northern Kingdoms.

There were often fish to be had, in all shapes and sizes, some from as far as Iceland, and he loved to hear the stories all seasoned shipmen could conjure as if from nowhere, that gave a life to the trading goods they brought with them. Stories of whalers and the exotic excitements from the far South were just some of those that Leofric caught snatches of as he strode.

He'd always liked the time on-board his own family's vessel, still sleek even over thirty years later, and much rebuilt and repaired, but his current responsibilities more often than not kept him land based. He was always jealous when his ship's commander was asked to travel to Jelling or Trondheim.

He almost envied Harthacnut and Swein their adventures in Norway and Denmark. His own time in Denmark and Norway had been concerned with war and defence. Just once he'd have just liked to 'see' what else there was that drove the fierce Northern men and women to travel as far as they could by ship.

The wind whipped his cloak as he walked and he pulled it tighter to his body. He wished to seek out Bovi, and he knew, without having to ask, that he'd find the commander of Harald's ship-army as close to the ships as possible, if not actually in them. The men had patrolled the Thames, as Bovi had promised back in Oxford, all winter long, but now those ships that hadn't been brought ashore for repairs in the nearby long wooden sheds during the coldest winter for many years were in need of their own repairs.

Others, those who'd spent much of the winter drinking and whoring, now rode the river and the seas further out. It was they who waited for news of King Harthacnut, or any other Viking war-leader who fancied his chances in a divided England.

Bovi saw Leofric before Leofric spied him out, and called a greeting. Leofric redirected his path so that he'd cross Bovi, a small smirk when he noticed the other man issuing terse commands about the state of one of the ship's that had been pulled up on the side of the dock.

"Bloody idiots," he was grumbling when Leofric finally stood before him. "Sometimes I wonder what they've got between their ears, 'cause none of the buggers can think about the more practical nature of their ships. Why should ship-men know about the timbers the ships are built from, they moan at me, and every time I have to remind them that their bloody lives depend on the bloody timbers and they should sodding well know!"

He finished with an aggrieved sigh, running his calloused hand through thick black hair, and then down an even fuller beard.

Leofric allowed him a moment to recover his good humour before he opened his mouth to ask his questions. Bovi forestalled him.

"No, I have no news of Lord Harthacnut or the Wessex bitch," he sneered, but Leofric shook his head.

"I didn't come for that. I know there's little news. The season has been late to turn, the seas are rough. My own ship-men tell me as much."

Large black eyebrows peered at Leofric with interest, perhaps wondering what question he had come to ask.

"I came to ask about the payments for your men and yourself. Are they up to date, as promised?"

Bovi's mouth made an 'O' of surprise, as though reminded of something he'd been told, and Leofric held his annoyance in check.

"Another month has just been paid, in good silver, with Harald's image on it," Bovi replied, far too enigmatically for Leofric's liking. He considered just how much of Harald's worries and fears might have been stoked by the ship-army who were apparently keen for greater riches than they perhaps were due, given their desultory winter spent on-land.

"Then everything is as it should be," Leofric responded, turning to walk away, only for Bovi to continue speaking.

"The ship-army chose Lord Harald. We stand by him. We'll support him without pay if we must, but men must eat."

"But not oysters," Leofric countered, "and spices from the east. Men just need to eat the basic foodstuffs that make them warriors and rowers."

"Well yes," Bovi agreed, his brow furrowed. "But the best ship-armies are those who are feted and rewarded well for their work."

"No, the best are those desperate to be fed, who know their life depends on supporting their Regent and ensuring the success of his governance. Surely it would be much more problematic for you all should King Harthacnut return and install his own ship-army in England, ousting you from your current position."

Fear crossed Bovi's face, but he had the good grace to nod in agreement.

"Perhaps we've been too harsh with Lord Harald. I'll reconsider our approach. But rest assured, Lord Leofric, we support Lord Harald and hope to one day call him King, just as his mother promised us." For a long moment, Bovi held Leofric's gaze. When he turned away, Leofric knew that he'd measured the length of the man, and was almost content with what he'd discovered. Still, he wished that it had been Lord Harald who'd sought to question his commander, and not himself.

Harald still had much to learn. Hopefully, his visit to Winchester would imbibe him with the guile he needed to rule men who were always out for their own gain.

But before he turned away, Leofric thought of another question.

"Bovi, tell me, what happened to Lady Ælfgifu in Denmark. Who killed King Swein?"

Bovi spat, as though reminded of something unpleasant at the question.

"Lady Ælfgifu sought assurances from King Harthacnut that should they make land-fall in Denmark, he would not attack them, but rather would offer aid to the remnants of the ship-army. The Regents had attacked those twenty ships that travelled to Norway with King Swein. There were many casualties."

Bovi sighed as he spoke.

"King Harthacnut offered no such assurances and did nothing when the Regents' ships caught up with King Swein and Lady Ælfgifu. The men fought on, but Swein was killed. Only the intervention of Lady Estrid saved Lady Ælfgifu. She sent one of her sons at the head of small fleet to counter the attack."

"The Danish men were good warriors, all of them. They rescued Lady Ælfgifu and those who yet lived out of the ship-army. Lady Estrid allowed them to recover in Jelling, but King Harthacnut did nothing."

"Ah," Leofric commented. "So it's no wonder she hates Harthacnut then."

"Oh, she doesn't hate him, Earl Leofric. She dreams of his death at her hands." Bovi spoke with a wink of his eye, as he turned away, but Leofric felt a shudder of premonition, he tried to swallow down.

"My thanks Bovi," Leofric called, but the ship's commander was gone back to shouting at his ship-men and issuing terse instructions to the carpenters keen to make repairs to the ships.

There was no love lost between King Harthacnut and King Swein, and there'd be even less should Harald ever be declared King of England, as opposed to just her Regent.

# 7
## AD1036

THE MESSENGER FOUND HIM WATCHING HIS HOUSEHOLD TROOP TRAINING, enjoying the feel of heat on his face, and content to just be doing 'nothing'.

"Earl Leofric," the man called, and Leofric squinted into the blazing sun to try and see the man, as opposed to the blackness of a face in shadow.

"Good day," he responded, unable to focus on the man until he stood before him, but aware that no one would have gained admission through his closed gateway unless they were welcome.

Then he gave a start. He recognised the man, and he didn't come from Lord Harald in London, as he'd expected, but rather from the Queen Dowager.

"Earl Leofric," the man greeted him again and bowed his head low. "I bring news from the Queen Dowager. She was most adamant that I seek you out as soon as possible."

Carefully he held his face blank, hoping not to show any trepidation for the next words.

"The Queen Dowager is pleased to inform you that her daughter, the Lady Gunnhilda, has been married to her betrothed, Henry, son of the Holy Roman Emperor." Surprised by the news, Leofric still squinted at the man, his response delayed by just a moment too long.

"The Queen Dowager, Lady Emma, has my best wishes for the future happiness of her daughter and her husband." It had been so many years since either Emma or Leofric, had laid eyes on her daughter with Cnut that Leofric had almost forgotten about the girl's existence, even though he'd once escorted her to Denmark on Cnut's instructions. It seemed that not only had the Queen Dowager never forgotten her daughter, she wasn't above reminding others of the reach Cnut had once laid claim to, the King of the North with his own Empire at his fingertips; an Empire to rival that of the Holy Roman Emperor.

"I'll pass on your good wishes," the messenger bowed, as Leofric signalled for food and ale for the man.

"You'll stay and eat?" he asked, but the messenger was already shaking his head.

"My thanks, Earl Leofric, but I must continue my journey North. The Queen Dowager is desirous that all the Earls hear the wonderful news as soon as possible."

"You travel to Northumbria then?" he quizzed, a slightly amused smile on his face.

"I do, My Lord. I have a beautiful horse, and we'll ride quickly."

"Then my thanks for your news. But tell me, when did the wedding occur?"

"The wedding took place at the Easter festival."

"My thanks again," Leofric nodded, thinking quickly as the messenger, having taken his fill of ale and food, promptly mounted up and moved away. It seemed the Queen Dowager was asserting her motherhood over all of her children. Gunnhilda was almost forgotten about in England, but the fact that the marriage had now taken place meant that Harthacnut, King of Denmark, was also brother-by-marriage to the man who would one day rule the lands of the Holy Roman Emperor. Henry would be a powerful man, and it seemed that Cnut's grandchildren might one-day rule there as well.

Would Lord Harald realise that he might gain from conciliatory action toward the Queen Dowager? After all, the wife of the Holy Roman Emperor was his half-sister too. That might be a powerful tonic to a man keen to rule as wisely as his father had once done.

But it was also a strong warning from the Queen Dowager. Another to add to her attempts to circumnavigate Lord Harald's ability to rule in the North, should he prove blind to the opportunities.

"Who was that?" his wife called as she joined him. She was warmly wrapped in a fur cloak, and Leofric laughed to see her so.

"It's the summer," he exclaimed to her, temporarily ignoring her question, but all he received in return was a shake of the head and warm smile.

"It might be, but I don't feel like casting off winter just yet. Anyway, the wind is cold." She spoke defensively, but with a smile to remove the edge to her voice, the wind forcing her hair to swirl across her face.

"That was a messenger from the Queen Dowager," he explained, and his wife watched him fondly. Their marriage hadn't been the source of calm and comfort that his father and mother had attained, and yet his wife had softened of late, and he was beginning to think that they might yet achieve the perfection of his father's marriage. Should time allow them.

"She'll never accept what's happened with any grace," his wife commented, and he nodded. It was no secret that his wife was a firm ally and friend of Lady Ælfgifu. It had been the cause of many ructions in their marriage, and Leofric could admit to himself that now freed from his constraints to Cnut, he found it easier to overlook his wife's obstinacy where Lady Ælfgifu was concerned. The friendship between the two women had never faltered, despite the fact it might have been politically expedient to stand aloof from Lady Ælfgifu.

Before he could say more, a further disturbance at the gate distracted him, and in a flurry of sweating horse and angry shouting, he watched his son rush through the busy work yard, scattering chickens and small children with wild abandon.

Leofric worked hard to keep his face impassive. His son was never one for impulsive actions, and he should have been with Lord Harald in Winchester, not here.

"Son," he called as Ælfgar slipped from his horse, thrusting his reins into the hand of a surprised member of the household troop. Leofric made a face of apology toward the man, and he nodded, as though assured this wasn't his usual task, and no insult was intended. He'd not suddenly been downgraded to one of the stable-hands.

"That bloody bastard," Ælfgar growled, rushing to his father's side, as a handful of other men followed him into the work yard on sweaty horses. Dust was kicked up, more chickens scattered and more children rescued from the affray by attentive adults in those few moments than had happened for many a year. Leofric watched with a wince of worry, pleased when nothing untoward befell his own people.

"What bloody bastard?" Leofric demanded, but already he had a sinking feeling in the pit of his stomach. "What happened?" Leofric asked, hoping it was Earl Godwine that his son railed against, and not Lord Harald.

His son was breathing heavily, but he mastered himself, and met his father's concerned expression with remarkable calmness, considering the haste and angry shouting only moments ago. He was dressed for riding, but the emblem of his house, the double-headed eagle flashed on his cloak buckle, and his tunic, poking out from the front of the cloak, had stitching of the eagle as well. Lady Godgifu was keen to flaunt their emblem, spending hours embroidering it on anything.

And the blacksmith never had idle hands either. All of the family hounds and servants carried the emblem in some form, and Leofric could see where it flashed at the top of Ælfgar's seax as his son sought calmness to speak clearly and explain his fury.

"Lord Harald has been to Winchester, run the Queen Dowager from the royal palace and stolen the treasure of England. All of it. Not one piece of silver or a scrap of gold did he leave behind. Nothing. He vowed he went in peace and with the lawful agreement of the Witan of the Northern Kingdoms, but he's virtually declared war on Wessex, the Queen Dowager and Earl Godwine."

"What?" Leofric gasped, while his wife laughed softly at his side. He rounded on her, fury making him forget his thoughts of earlier about reconciliation and a quieter life in the future.

"Did you expect Lord Harald to act with any restraint," she asked. "You gave him the idea to raid Winchester, and now he has. He's no intention of being a Regent when he could make himself a King. Money is a delightful way of greasing the palms of those who might not welcome his kingship any other way."

"Was anyone hurt?" Leofric asked, hoping no one had been while trying to ignore his wife's laughter. No doubt she and Lady Ælfgifu would retell the story for years to come.

Hund circled the family, as they stood and spoke, and Leofric knew the animal warned others not to interfere.

"A few cuts and bruises. Most stood aside," Ælfgar confirmed, watching his mother laugh with anger writ on his face once more, his hand opening and closing as though he wished to grab his seax.

"Mother," he admonished, but Leofric shook his head.

"Don't waste your breath boy," he confirmed. "Your mother is no doubt proud of Lord Harald and unaware of the problems for the future."

"I'm neither of those things. But I'm not surprised," she crowed, stalking from their presence although her amusement filtered back to her simmering husband and son across the busy work yard.

"Did you know?" his son asked him angrily, and Leofric was reminded of the times he'd confronted his own father when he thought he'd been told half a story and made to look a fool.

"No, I cautioned Lord Harald to take only what was necessary. There was no need to incite further difficulties, not when the seas are clear, and King Harthacnut could come at any time."

"Ah, well that might explain it then," Ælfgar offered, pacing in front of his father. If he was aware that every man, woman and child watched him, he gave no indication of knowing it. "When we arrived at Winchester, Regent Harald met with the Queen Dowager and Earl Godwine, at the palace, and the Queen Dowager was forced to admit that King Harthacnut had sent word he'd not return to England this year. The war with Magnus of Norway and his regents goes poorly."

Leofric had suspected Harthacnut would dally in Denmark, but he'd not expected such a fierce rebuttal of his duties.

"So Lord Harald chose to act knowing he faced no possible recriminations from his half-brother."

"I assume so. I didn't know, or even suspected; otherwise I'd have sent for you. He toyed with the Queen Dowager and Earl Godwine for two days, gaining admission to the King's treasury on the third day, when he had Earl Godwine surrounded by armed men of the ship-army. Earl Godwine was powerless to act, as he was when Harald then went to the palace of Winchester. He sits there even now, counting the coin and planning how he'll spend it."

"So he's become a tyrant already?" Leofric mused, wondering how the situation could affect him. Perhaps it was best that England had only one Regent.

"You left Winchester with or without his permission?" he asked, dread consuming him.

"Oh, with his permission. Lord Harald demands your attendance in Winchester. He says you must travel there with all haste, and I'm to see it done."

"Ah," was all Leofric could think to say. He doubted that the Queen Dowager would take this well. He suspected that Cnut's close allies within Wessex and Mercia would not welcome it either. A complicated arrangement had just become far more complicated. He could only hope that Harthacnut genuinely had no plans to return to

England anytime soon. If he did, he could only foresee a war such as Cnut had once fought with King Æthelred and King Edmund; a war that had seen men lose their lives.

Leofric sighed. He had intended to avert war on English soil. It seemed that those hopes were as feathers on the wind. Gone with no trace of ever having existed.

He moaned heavily and reached out to grasp his son's arm.

"You did well," he reassured the lad, and then he turned to watch his household troop once more. It might just be that he would have need of Olaf and Orkning, and their skills with weapon and blade, once more.

"I was a witness, nothing more," his son tried to reassure him, and Leofric nodded, his thoughts elsewhere.

"They'll interpret it as they want, they always do," he tried to explain, but his son looked rebellious.

"I touched nothing," he asserted, his face colouring with anger.

"I understand," Leofric said again, trying to reassure, but failing miserably, and shook his head before trying once more. "I understand. Never doubt that. I always understand, but you must learn as well. You'll be used when it suits them. It's rare that we ever have more than a modicum of control to our lives."

He held his hand up then, sadness swamping him, so far removed from his earlier joy.

"I felt the same when I was your age when my brother was taken from me. Your grandfather endured all that he could, but that was too much for even him to reconcile with his perception of kingship, nobility and power."

Still, Ælfgar's eyes looked filled with rage at what had been done to him.

"Lord Harald will have given you no thought. It's always those who stand to gain from our helplessness who give it the most thought. I know you'll worry. I know it goes against your honour, and I'm sorry about that."

"Lord Harald acted irresponsibly."

"He did, but he's a Regent, perhaps nearer a King. Time will give its answer to that. But it means he can act with a disregard denied to yourself. His actions will be tried by history, yours by those who would gain from your immediate or imminent disgrace."

"What will happen next?" his son pressed, worry furrowing his forehead.

"We'll go to Winchester and find out," Leofric sighed, turning once more to face his son. "There are always new possibilities," he concluded. "We just need to determine what they are." At that, his son perked up, and Leofric noted it with relief. He'd never thought himself a father on a level with his own, but there was still time to grow into the man his father had been. There was still time for him to earn his son's, and his wife's, respect.

INSIDE HIS HALL, HIS WIFE WAS BUSY REGALING ALL WHO WOULD LISTEN about Lord Harald's achievements. Leofric winced as she laughed, time and time again, but he left her to what enjoyment she could find in the situation. Instead, he issued instructions for his journey the next day, and sent for his brother, Eadwine, and also his sister's husband, Olaf who just happened to be visiting with him. Godwine had remained in Winchester with Lord Harald. He thought it only right to consult the other members of his family.

His father's home had been taken over by his sister and her husband, too far for him to get immediate word to her but Eadwine was less than half a day's ride, and so he sent for him to meet him in Oxford. Eadwine would caution him against violence. He doubted any of the others would.

What he didn't expect was the arrival of Lord Hrani. The Danish Earl rode calmly to Leofric's gate, calling for admittance and was swiftly granted it by Orkning, standing his watch for his lord. Leofric held his reticence in place. Hrani, unlike many of Cnut's other Danish Earls, had made his home in England for much of Cnut's reign, although age had dimmed his interest in politics, as had the disdain of his English subjects. His countenance now showed that might no longer be the case.

"Good evening," Leofric greeted the man, holding his horse's reins so that he could clamber from the animal's back. Hrani had always been a warrior, and never really a politician, content, in the end, to allow Leofric to govern much of Mercia, no matter what Cnut's intentions might once have been.

"Don't 'good evening' me," the older man quibbled. "How can it be a good evening when Lord Harald has acted so irresponsibly?"

"You've heard?" Leofric asked, but Earl Hrani grunted his answer, and made his way into Leofric's hall, griping all the time.

Leofric followed behind him, peering into the far distance first, in the hope that his brother might be close to arriving. He'd welcome his support with the grumpy older man.

"Come on Leofric," Earl Hrani grumbled. "We have much to talk about. Stop dawdling." With nothing for it, he settled beside Hrani, calling his son over to listen, but not speak. The lad came willingly enough, and Leofric suppressed his reservations about including him. His father would have done the same. The lad was too old to be shielded from the realities of politics, and, as a witness to Lord Harald's actions, he had every right to be included.

"Does the fool intend to proclaim himself King over all, or just Regent? What of King Harthacnut? What of bloody Earl Godwine and that shrew of a wife of Cnut's." Hrani had never had a kind word to say about the Queen Dowager. He'd been much happier with Lady Ælfgifu as wife to the king but had tried to reconcile himself to the fact that King Harthacnut would rule after his father, one day.

"I don't know the answers to your questions, Hrani. I advised Lord Harald to take only what he was owed, and nothing more. I even spoke with Commander Bovi and received assurance that the need to pay the ship-army was not as imperative as Harald thought. The reissuing of the coinage is running smoothly. There should have been money in Lord Harald's royal coffers."

"Hum," the Dane grunted, settling himself before the hearth and looking around for ale to wet his mouth. "What you think of as 'enough' money, might not be the same as the young hot-head, and his mother. No doubt he dreams of money he could only ever have imagined once when he was all but abandoned by his father. Bloody fool." Hrani shook his head, and then reached for the welcome mug of ale and drank deeply. His eyes closed as he savoured the flavour and Leofric took the opportunity to study the man.

He'd been one of Cnut's most loyal followers when he'd first come to England. He'd fought at his side, been rewarded with land in and around Hereford, close to the borderlands with the Welsh kingdoms. Then he'd fallen from favour, and his influence on Cnut had waned with Cnut's more imperial ambitions, and his constant absences from England. Earl Hrani had not always leapt to follow his king. His rewards in England, of land and wealth, had been enough for him to settle into a life of mundane routine.

Perhaps he welcomed Harald's Regency. It was impossible to know. By rights, Leofric thought he should have favoured Harthacnut, but that special bond was missing. Harthacnut had been in Denmark for seven years. He'd grown to manhood, or nearly to manhood, without Hrani even seeing him. Perhaps Hrani was also fearful of King Harthacnut's eventual return.

Leofric thought back over the older man's words, suddenly puzzling over who he called a 'bloody fool'.

"The Queen Dowager will be pissed," Hrani muttered, a gleam in his eyes that Leofric thought might be delight at such an event.

"The others will come," Hrani stated, looking to have his mug refilled, and Leofric almost choked on his own tongue.

"What Earl Eilifr will come, here?" he sought to clarify.

"Yes, and that other hot head, Thorkell's son, I forget his bloody name."

"Harold," Leofric answered, his voice a little distant as he hoped his brother would hurry up and arrive. He didn't much fancy being outmanoeuvred in his own home.

"I didn't know that Earl Eilifr remained in England. I saw him at the Witan but have heard nothing since. I assumed he'd returned to Denmark?"

Leofric thought frantically. It was Eilifr's sister who was married to Earl Godwine. Not only did Leofric not like knowing he was back in Mercia, he was even more pensive about the thought of Earl Eilifr meddling in the current morass of English politics.

The news that Earl Thorkell's son was also coming to this impromptu gathering was even more bewildering. Thorkell and Cnut had long had a strange relationship; allies one moment and enemies the next. Yes, they'd also reconciled before Thorkell's death, and yes, Cnut had gone to Thorkell's aid when the stronghold of the Jomsvikings was attacked, but Leofric had little idea about how the man would face the current difficulties.

He thought then of Gunnhildr, Earl Thorkell's son's wife. When Earl Hakon, her first husband, had died at sea, Leofric had thought that would be the end of her meddling in the land close to Hertford. He'd been wrong to think so. No sooner had news of Earl Hakon's death arrived than she'd remarried, with almost indecent haste, another close member of Cnut's old warrior cohort.

When all the men gathered, and he wouldn't be surprised if Gunnhildr put in an appearance as well, there might well be a civil war within his own home, let alone throughout England.

"Excuse me," he muttered, standing and striding toward his wife. She'd been watching events closely, and Leofric assumed she'd determined what was happening.

"Husband," she greeted, chill to her tone, but Leofric ignored it. The time for their lack of unity was past.

"We will have guests tonight," he informed her. "All the old guard are coming here, my brother as well, can you make arrangements should our conversation continue long into the night." A spark of interest ignited in her bright eyes, but she nodded demurely.

"Of course husband," she said, a faint note of mockery in her voice. "Is the Lady Gunnhildr coming?" she queried, and Leofric shrugged his shoulders.

"Her husband is, so no doubt she will. She never lets the poor bastard make any decisions on his own."

As she turned to command her servants, Leofric heard her mutter 'as it should be' under her breath and he sighed. His day was becoming more and more difficult by the breath.

Turning back to face Hrani, he saw his son had taken the initiative and was speaking with the older man. Hrani was not really much older than Leofric, and yet he looked sunken and far from the warrior he'd once been. The years in England had allowed him to grow soft and ill-prepared for battle. But, his mind was sharp and always had been. He'd find a way of meddling if possible, and at the least, he'd find a way of ensuring his own interests weren't harmed by what was about to happen.

Leofric admired the man while finding him testing. Earl Hrani had usurped much of his father's command in Mercia and never uttered a word of apology for it. Betrayal like that was hard to ignore, even as the years passed and Leofwine died. Once more, Leofric was reminded of how few powerful Mercian families there were within his earldom. Most had fallen from grace when Cnut had raised up so many of his own, Danish, men.

He considered the possibility that if Lord Harald did become King, those Mercian families might re-emerge but quickly stifled the hope. Lady Ælfgifu might term herself English, but Lord Harald was overly fond of his Danish half-blood, even if it had not, until now, been quite as fortuitous as he might have hoped.

It was his younger brother who entered the hall next. Lord Eadwine came with little fanfare, the household troops on watch duty at the gate, used to the comings and goings of Leofric's own family. He and his brothers might not spend a great deal of time together, too busy with their own duties, but they governed Mercia with one mind, the lessons instilled in them by their father too ingrained to ignore.

He brought with him the smell of horses and the dampness of the rain that had begun falling not long after Hrani's arrival. Leofric was pleased to see his wife attend to his needs so that they could quickly settle by the hearth, Olaf, his sister's husband, joining the gathering as well, for all that he still dressed as the warrior he'd always been.

Leofric blinked, and for the briefest of moments, he saw not his son and Olaf, but instead his father and Horic, Olaf's father. The two would have settled the matter of Lord Harald's actions quickly and decisively. Leofric doubted he'd be able to do the same.

Hrani eyed Leofric's two brothers with some interest, a slight frown to his face as he took in Lord Eadwine. The two men should be allies, their lands abutting each other, but it seemed to have the opposite effect, and often the only land disputes Leofric was called to settle were between the two men. It was both tedious and amusing in equal measure.

Leofric greeted his brother fondly. As did his son. The resemblance between them all was easy to see. No one could ever say they weren't members of the House of Leofwine, and no one, having met only one of them, ever failed to recognise the others when they met them as well. It was useful to have them all look so alike, added to which they too all carried the emblem of the House of Leofwine. Lady Godgifu wasn't the only one to enjoy her embroidery.

Leofric could tell that his brother had already heard the news of Lord Harald's attack on Winchester, and he knew what he'd say, even without having to ask. Eadwine would caution peace and reconciliation between Lord Harald and the Queen Dowager. It had always been the same.

"What do you make of it all?" Hrani growled to the new arrivals, a slight sneer to his face when Lord Eadwine spoke first.

"A foolish action," Eadwine said. "But one that can be resolved should Lord Harald take conciliatory action now. Before it's too late."

"Hah," Earl Hrani barked. "It's already too late. He's shed blood. The Queen Dowager will ensure all know."

"Yes, she will, but she shed blood first," Leofric interjected, only for Hrani to ignore his words.

"It's never too late," Eadwine almost intoned, but Olaf was shaking his head as well.

"Lord Harald has stepped outside the boundaries of an agreement endorsed at the Witan. The Queen Dowager would be just as much within her rights to claim all England for herself, as Harald would have been had he acted with more restraint."

"Why did he go to Winchester?" Earl Hrani demanded, and Leofric knew he was being held accountable for Harald's actions.

"I suggested it," he announced. "I told him he had a legal recourse to take what was agreed and to claim the wergeld for his dead men, nothing else."

Hrani grumbled, and Leofric knew he wouldn't be the first.

"Did you caution him?"

"Yes, I did, and my son and brother went with him as well. Ælfgar witnessed what happened, and then he returned to me. Lord Harald demands my presence in Winchester, and Godwine Leofwinesson remains there even now." Leofric indicated his son when he spoke, and Earl Hrani licked his lips and glared at the younger man.

"Hah, he seeks to have you there to give some semblance of a majority to his theft. He'll use you as a bolster between him and Earl Godwine. You'll have to go."

"I know that," Leofric replied, irritation in his voice and his son cautioned him with his eyes. It had been only earlier that he'd tried to teach his son this lesson, and still, it infuriated him to understand his own position. He might well be Earl of Mercia, but he was still subject to the whims of others: both of those above him, and sometimes those below him in the hierarchy of his society.

"I will go. I know I will have to."

Before the conversation could continue, there was another commotion at the door, and a man and woman walked into his hall. Leofric suppressed his groan of annoyance and instead stood to welcome Lady Gunnhildr, and her husband, Lord Harold.

Yet Lady Gunnhildr had no time for him, instead sweeping past him to hold her arms out to Lady Godgifu. Leofric didn't take it as a dismissal. The women might pretend not to be interested in the discussion, but come decision time, there was little chance of Lady Gunnhildr allowing anything to happen that didn't please her.

"Well met Lord Harold," Leofric said when the women were settled, and the other man smirked and then clasped Leofric's forearm.

"Well met, Earl Leofric. I would have wished for a better night to travel through."

"Wouldn't we all," he agreed, and settling himself, the conversation resumed.

Earl Hrani and Lord Harold, Gunnhildr's husband, were not precisely allies, but neither were they, enemies. Instead, they bonded over a shared heritage, and Leofric envied them their ease, each to the other.

"Is it true? Is Lord Harald about to claim the kingship?" Amusement filled Harold's voice, and Leofric sighed on his annoyance that the Danes loved war and conflict so much more than peace.

"He's taken command of Winchester and the treasury," Leofric confirmed, nodding at Ælfgar as he spoke. "My son witnessed it."

"So Lord Harald is King then?" Harold grunted, but Ælfgar shook his head.

"He's yet to make such a statement, but the Queen Dowager has fled, and Earl Godwine threatens him with the might of the fyrd."

"What does he plan now?"

Ælfgar shrugged.

"He plans for my father to meet him in Winchester, and then he intends to formulate his next moves."

"Why does he need another to advise him? Can he not act on his own wishes?"

Again Ælfgar shrugged. "I don't know. I was simply sent for by my father."

"Then Lord Harald may be claiming the kingship even as we sit here twiddling our thumbs and trying to second guess him."

Leofric's face grew still at that assertion. He'd not considered that possibility, but it made sense.

"So Lord Harald sends my son away, intends to claim the kingship and then have me arrive as though I knew all along, while my brother witnesses it all first hand?"

Earl Hrani chuckled at that.

"He'll use you to legitimise his claim. Your family will suffer the same fate as under King's Swein and Æthelred."

Leofric felt his face flaming with anger. It was one thing to understand his family's position himself, quite another to have it flung in his face by others.

"Was a messenger sent to Earl Siward?" Leofric asked his son, but his son shook his head.

"Not before I was sent to fetch you. It may be that the Earl has been summoned since."

"The Regent places my family in a precarious position," Leofric rumbled, trying to keep his rage in check.

"He honours you," Earl Hrani laughed once more, enjoying Leofric's discomfort far too much and Leofric worked hard to ignore him.

"You will accompany me?" he asked, looking directly at Earl Hrani.

"Why would I do that? Hrani demanded, and Leofric smirked.

"If Lord Harald is to proclaim himself King, then we should all be there to see it done."

"No, we shouldn't" Earl Eilifr commented, his arrival inside the hall passing almost unnoticed in the intensity of Leofric and Hrani's discussion.

The Danish warlord, like Hrani and Cnut before him, wore his age more heavily than other men. He'd fought for Cnut, fought against Cnut, been accused of treason with his dead brother, and spent much time in Denmark, no doubt under the influence of Harthacnut, and his nephews.

"The Danish men need do nothing for the Regent. He should be ruling in King Harthacnut's name. Not his own. If he tries to take the kingship, none of the Danish men can be seen to have supported Lord Harald. We'll lose our influence in England and in Denmark should we do so. King Harthacnut is not someone who forgives treachery easily."

As he spoke, Eilifr looked at Leofric, and Leofric nodded. He was unsurprised to hear such words on Eilifr's lips. It made sense to him. The older Dane, a warrior and a statesman, had only been reconciled with Cnut just before his death. Yet it seemed the King hadn't trusted him with his ambitions for Harald, any more than he had Earl Godwine.

"You support King Harthacnut over Harald then?" Leofric asked, and the man nodded, stray raindrops falling from his sodden hair.

"I've long been an ally of the House of Gorm or the House of Swein Forkbeard. I've had my moments, but then, who hasn't," he croaked a laugh at his own folly in the past, and especially at that of his dead brother's. "But now I owe my return to England to King Cnut and my positions in Denmark to King Harthacnut and my nephews. I'll not risk either to support the son Cnut abandoned in Mercia. If Cnut had wanted Lord Harald to be king after him, he'd have named him as such."

Leofric opened his mouth to speak and then closed it again, reconsidering his words. It seemed now wasn't the time to share Cnut's words with anyone.

"Never forget that Lord Harald is Cnut's son, despite what all might say," Leofric said instead.

"Hah," Eilifr barked. "Cnut had ample time and opportunity to settle his son in his place. He chose not to. I think that speaks for his intentions." Eilifr seemed to taunt Leofric with his words and his stance, and yet Leofric felt that logically, his words made far more sense than Cnut's sly attempts to bring about his son's command of England.

"Do you understand that King Harthacnut has any interest in England?" Leofric probed, keen to hear Earl Eilifr's opinions, despite everything, as someone who'd seen Harthacnut far more recently than anyone else he'd yet spoken to.

"He'll come, he's made no secret of that, and when he does, those who were disloyal to his father's demands will be destroyed."

"And when will that be?" Leofric taunted. He could feel the walls in the hall closing around him, trapping him, depriving him of an easy route out, or even a more difficult alternative route. Or he could until Earl Eilifr spoke again.

"When Denmark is secure, not before. And if Denmark is never secure, then Harthacnut will never come."

Leofric kept his face straight as Eilifr spoke, but the words offered enough comfort to settle his worries.

"King Harthacnut says it will not be this year. The Queen Dowager has heard from him."

"Then Lord Harald, or King Harald, should he so chose to style himself, can enjoy his triumph for now, but mark my words, war will come next year, or the year after." Earl Eilifr spoke with finality.

Leofric bowed his head low so that none could see his expression, but no one else spoke to counter Eilifr's words.

Too much could happen in a year, and certainly in two. By then Lord Harald might well be secure in his kingship, and King Harthacnut could express his intentions toward England all he wanted, but not being the warrior his father had been would hamper his endeavours. None of Cnut's sons had inherited his martial abilities, and without them, Leofric doubted that King Harthacnut would succeed in claiming England by force. If he'd been as battle hungry as his father, Denmark would be secure, and Norway returned to his command already.

But he didn't say that out loud. He'd not be punished for speaking so openly, or for criticising Harthacnut.

"It's done then," Leofric announced instead, meeting the eyes of those within the room, including his wife and Lady Gunnhildr. "Lord Harald will be able to claim the kingship, and none will be able to stop him, not even Earl Godwine. I'd suggest you all do what you must to ease your consciences. England will soon have a new King, and no matter your personal opinions, to keep your earldoms, you'll all need to bow the knee to Harald."

His words fell heavily into the silence, but none spoke to object, not even Lady Gunnhildr, related as she was to Cnut and Harthacnut.

"You will be the foster-father to a king," Earl Hrani finally taunted into the strained quiet, and Leofric glared at the older man. This was it. Many would think his involvement in Lord Harald's attack would be more significant than it ever had been. The fact he'd suggested it meant he'd be damned, should it all backfire. He only wished he'd never taken his eyes from Lord Harald and his mother on that fateful day in London, and that he, and not his son and brother, had gone with Lord Harald to Winchester. He'd have stopped him. If at all possible.

The future, never secure, was complicated and once more, his family were at the heart of the turbulence.

# 8

## AD1036

Leofric strode into the King's Palace at Winchester with murder on his mind, and as calm a countenance as possible.

Ælfgar escorted him, as was so often the case, and he followed his father without speaking. For once they were of one mind and had no need to discuss their current predicament, for that was what it was.

The journey to Winchester had been swift, almost too quick for Leofric's liking, but he knew it was better to get some things over and done with as soon as possible.

The Palace was a forbidding place. Leofric knew that in the past many kings had made Winchester their home, but it was fast falling from favour, and Leofric wasn't surprised. Cnut had preferred Oxford to Winchester, and while Lord Harald might be enjoying his brief seizure of Winchester, Leofric was sure he'd soon return to London.

Mercia was Lord Harald's home. He might need Wessex to be King of all England, but he was a Mercian.

The buildings, although kept in immaculate repair, exhibited a design that was fast changing. Yes, the great hall had never changed, but the tangled web of outbuildings, built at odd angles, and when the thought took their instigator, was a mess that few lords and kings would tolerate.

Even Deerhurst, his sister's home, was undergoing substantial redesign, and Leofric knew his sister would take great pride in her new passion. He wished her well, although he would miss the comforting familiarity of his childhood.

The day was warm, the air filled with the hum of insects and a gentle breeze that teased the budding crops. Leofric, while pleased to see the growth on his journey to Winchester, was irritated by the buzzing now. It seemed to him to be the combined uproar that he would face from those unhappy with Harald's audacious attack on Winchester.

Two men guarded the door to the great hall, and Leofric nodded to them in thanks as they pushed open the door onto a quiet hall. Inside few moved, and those who did, simply raised goblets to lips, or sat and played their games, in almost silence.

Leofric squinted into the gloom and haze caused by the great hearth, trying to determine where Lord Harald sat so that he could direct his steps that way. He saw a shadowy figure, on the small raised dais, and proceeded forward.

Each of his steps on the wooden boards seemed to fill the hall with the crash of thunder, and he almost winced as every eye turned his way. He was used to being the centre of attention, but it didn't mean he ever liked the intense scrutiny.

"Earl Leofric," his name was called from the dais, and he raised his hand in welcome, catching the warning look from his brother, where he sat amongst Lord Harald's warriors. A pained expression and a nod of welcome for Ælfgar were the only clues his brother gave, but they were enough.

Lord Harald was pleased with himself. That much was obvious, as he sat at the front of his father's hall, a small pile of newly minted coins running through his fingers, the clink of silver audible in the near-silence.

"Lord Harald," he greeted him, his hands to either side of his body, as though to indicate their new surroundings.

More he didn't say, waiting for his foster-son to offer an explanation. Lord Harald offered a sardonic grin, before reaching for his goblet of wine. Leofric didn't miss that his hand shook slightly. Ah, he thought to himself, a man who suddenly regrets his actions.

"My thanks for coming with all haste," Harald continued, his voice quiet, perhaps even quivering a little. Leofric was surprised. He'd expected to find him belligerent and stamping his authority all over Wessex.

"I come when I'm summoned," Leofric half-bowed. He tried not to mock, but it was an effort.

"Come, we will talk outside. I've something to show you." So decided, Lord Harald stood and stepped from the dais. "Ælfgar, your Uncle can fill you in on recent events." The dismissal was poorly done, and Leofric winced for his son's feelings, but Ælfgar, a smile on his face, seemed pleased to be excused from the awkward conversation that was about to take place.

Stepping once more into the brightness of the day, Leofric took a moment to orientate himself as he followed Harald's steps. Harald was dressed very much as he had been on the day of the Witan, all apart from the white cloak which had been tossed aside due to the warmer weather. Leofric caught a glimpse of the iron armrings that circled his forearms and suppressed a grimace.

Had Harald decided to be a warrior king after all?

They didn't speak as they walked, Leofric content to see how others reacted to Lord Harald walking amongst them. None ran from him, and most of the servants and slaves instead offered a smile or a respectful bow as he passed. There was nothing like the arrival of young blood at the King's Palace to renew respect for the ruling family. Leofric watched it with relief. He wouldn't have wanted to think that Harald had acted anymore the tyrant than he already had.

They strode through the myriad collection of halls, workshops, sleeping halls and stables, before, on the outskirts of the palatial complex they came across the smoking fire of the blacksmith. Leofric sniffed the air, appreciating the tang of iron and fire, and the fact that it seemed to have driven all the buzzing insects away.

It was here that Lord Harald came up short, and Leofric squinted into the gloom of the blacksmith's workshop with understanding dawning on his face. The blacksmith, as was so often the case, was a large man, muscles bulging in his forearms as he worked away.

"Coins," Harald offered, and Leofric nodded. He'd thought as much.

"This," and he indicated a huge pile of seemingly discarded coins scattered and overflowing from a large wooden chest, closely guarded by four armed warriors, "was my father's treasure. And now it is mine." He spoke with a smile, clearly enjoying his triumph, and turned to thump Leofric on the back.

Leofric was surprised by the show of affection and allowed some amusement to show on his own face. Harald was worried and exhilarated in equal measure. Leofric understood his emotions far too well.

"Look at it all," Harald crowed. "And the bitch didn't want to share any of it. What did she need all this for?" as he spoke, Harald bent down to run his hands through the dulled coins of the chest. "Look at it all," he picked a coin at random and held it out for Leofric to examine. "He didn't even have his own coinage recast to reflect the newer design. Bastard avoided even his own sodding taxes."

Leofric took the coin, its surface fresh and glimmering. The currency had apparently been struck and then placed in Cnut's treasury, and then never moved for nearly a decade. The design, as Harald said, was the second of Cnut's reign, showing his pointed helmet, as opposed to the cross that had been adopted in more recent years.

Leofric ran his fingers over the firmly struck coin, noticing as he did so that the blacksmith watched him with disinterest.

"A good moneyer made these," Leofric commented, hoping he complimented the brutish looking man.

"Aye, with a good dye, a fresh one. Look, it's in the chest with the coin!" As he spoke, Harald held up the curved barrel of the king's coin and examined it. It too looked freshly made.

"Arrogant bastard," Harald said again, as though daring Leofric to deny his words.

"There is an irony," Leofric agreed, thinking of Cnut's motivation for his actions. "Perhaps he needed the coins with a higher silver content for some reason we don't know about."

"Hah," Harald laughed. "Of course he didn't. He just wanted his personal coinage to outweigh that which anyone else had. Sneaky bastard."

Leofric couldn't help but agree.

England's coinage system was elaborate and effective both. Cnut, as far as Leofric could remember, had reminted his coinage three times during his reign. Each and every time, just as Lord Harald had been forced to do in the Northern kingdom, the restruck coins were issued at a slightly lower weight. And it really could be just a fraction lower, no more. With the massive amount of coins in circulation, even just a scraping from each coin restruck could afford the king a considerable tax.

Neither was there any choice. Other than the king himself, no one would have allowed their coinage to retain the incorrect image, for the coinage wouldn't always be accepted as legal tender. To use their coins, everyone in England had to have their coins restruck when the king issued new dyes.

Not that they had to come to Winchester, or even Wessex to have their coins restruck. No, the king would issue new dyes to all of his moneyers, be they in Mercia or Northumbria, and those moneyers, of course, paying for the privilege as well, were then able to melt down others coinage and recast it in the correct image and into the proper weight.

"Look, I'm having my father's coinage melted down, and restruck in my own image. Ceolnoth here has had to make a dye, for I didn't bring one with me, but it's excellent. The image is clear, and it's easy to see my image. He will make more dyes as well, and I'll distribute them throughout Wessex."

Harald bent to pick up one of the coins from a much smaller pile, undoubtedly the recast coins. Holding the two, one in each hand, Leofric could virtually feel no difference in weight between the two. Neither, if someone had come upon them without understanding what was happening, would the uninitiated be able to tell which coin was the newer.

"So you plan on staying with Wessex then?" Leofric questioned. He didn't speak loudly, the hammering of Ceolnoth obscuring the conversation.

"No, of course not. I'll return to London as soon as I can. But I can't go anywhere until I know what to do about bloody Earl Godwine."

Harald didn't mention the Queen Dowager, and Leofric realised that was because Harald had already dismissed her as a threat. Leofric didn't necessarily agree with that assumption, but he didn't press his foster-son about it.

"And that's why you sought my advice?" Leofric pressed, as Harald nodded. He was still fingering the coins in his image, a lopsided grin on his face.

Leofric had worried that Harald had become a tyrant, but as he watched his foster-son fondly, it was really more that Harald was a child deprived of his favourite toy, but now able to claim it for himself. He was pleased with himself. There was no other way to describe it.

"A new design?" Leofric asked, suddenly realising the coin of Harald's he held in his hand was different to the ones he already carried.

"A new design yes, for Wessex," Harald grinned, turning with delight to Leofric. "But what of Earl Godwine?"

"Where is the Earl now?" Leofric asked, turning as though he expected him to step from behind one of the many buildings.

"Gone home to sulk," Harald chuckled.

"You should banish him," Leofric offered hopefully, but Harald was already shaking his head.

"Wessex is Earl Godwine, and Earl Godwine is Wessex. I can't banish him. My father never could. I doubt I'll have any greater success."

"But he supports your brother for the kingship."

"Yes, he does. A problem. And one that Earl Godwine will have to work hard to overcome."

Harald began to move away, a new pile of coins in his hands for him to join to the others he already had, indicating that they should continue their conversation where it couldn't be overheard.

"What do the men and women of Mercia say?" Harald spoke with a wide grin. Clearly, he expected Leofric to regale him with tales of rejoicing.

"Mainly favourable, as you'd expect," Leofric tried to downplay his conversation between Earl Hrani and Earl Eilifr, but Harald squinted at him.

"Mainly favourable? Who did you speak to? Bloody hell. I was expecting something a little more ... positive!"

"I only spoke with a few people before reaching Winchester. Obviously, people just crave peace and continuity."

Harald's face clouded at the words, and Leofric wished he could offer more than that.

"Who did you speak to?" Harald pressed, an amused outrage threading his words, but Leofric didn't want to speak inappropriately of what, had, to all intents and purposed been a private conversation.

"What of Earl Godwine. You cut me off back there. What do you plan to do?"

"Now that I don't know." Harald pondered, apparently not wanting to change the conversation, but alert enough to realise Leofric would offer no more.

"He's gone from Wessex. I may have had him apprehended while my men emptied the king's coffers, but he wasn't injured in any way, and I allowed him to walk free afterwards, just as I let the Queen Dowager."

There was a hint of justifying his actions when Harald spoke, but Leofric ignored the slightly injured tone.

"How did Earl Godwine respond to that?"

"Oh, he went off, huffing and puffing, and threatening me with a reckoning when King Harthacnut arrives in England. Honestly, it's as though those are the only words Earl Godwine and the Queen Dowager know. 'When Harthacnut gets here this will happen,' 'When Harthacnut gets here that will happen,'. Don't they tire of their hopes and lies?"

Harald mimicked both the lighter voice of Lady Emma, and the deeper of Earl Godwine as he spoke, and Leofric laughed out loud at the mimicry. He could see how young Harald would chafe at the words of the older man and woman. He only hoped that his foster-son didn't impersonate him, but was too fearful to ask.

"And do you fear Earl Godwine?"

"No, I bloody don't. But I need to bring him to heal, ensure he understands that threatening me with my brother is no real threat at all."

"Earl Godwine is powerful within Wessex. He has a great deal of support. You have two options, you either undermine his support and claim it for yourself, a hard task to accomplish, or you show your support for him, and then he'll throw his weight behind your bid for the kingship as well. I prefer the first option, but I know you won't."

"I just want it done as quickly as possible. The second option is the quicker option, and then I can become King, as I always should have been."

Leofric nodded as they walked.

"Then you'll have to treat with Earl Godwine. It would, perhaps, have been good to hold him here, against his will, but actually, in allowing him his freedom you've shown yourself to be reasonable."

"High praise, indeed," Harald chuckled, at Leofric's grudgingly given praise. "You will speak to Earl Godwine on my behalf?" a statement not a question, but Leofric was already shaking his head.

"No, My Lord. I am not the man to broker any sort of arrangement with Earl Godwine. He would take it as an insult, and I wouldn't be able to help myself from exasperating the bastard. You will need to send another. Earl Siward would be a good option, but of course, he's far away, and if you want this done with haste, you'll need others to speak for you."

"What if I ordered you?" Harald taunted, his disappointment evident on his dropped face, all traces of humour gone.

"I would have to disobey you, and then you'd have two unruly earls to contend with."

"Damn," Harald muttered, but he didn't press Leofric, and he was pleased.

'Earl Hrani?" Harald suggested, but again Leofric shook his head.

"Your best option would be Earl Eilifr, Earl Godwine's brother-by-marriage, but I'd not trust the pair of them together. They'd have Harthacnut crowned before you could blink. No, someone else. Maybe the Archbishop?"

"Maybe your son?" Harald announced. "He has the right heritage to negotiate for me. He's my foster-brother, and your son, and the mind of a skilled negotiator."

"Well, I appreciate the compliment, as I'm sure he would. But do you not think it too much for him?"

"No, no, of course not. It's perfect. Ælfgar can take Earl Godwine my demands, and they will be demands. No matter that I need him, I can make it awkward for the traitorous bastard. Not that Ælfgar will go alone. No, we shall send others. Ha, ha," Harald grinned once more.

"But you don't berate me for the attack on the king's treasury."

"It hardly seems worthwhile to do so after the attack, but Harald, tread carefully. It was almost an act of war and should things go badly with Earl Godwine, who will be at his family home licking his wounds and plotting his revenge, he just might say it was a declaration of war. I know you want Wessex, but Earl Godwine is an ..." Leofric strove to find the correct word. "An unsettling foe, believe me."

Harald laughed once more and slapped his foster-father on the back.

"He might well be, but I have the entire contents of my father's treasury at my beck and call, and the support of the kingdom apart from Earl Godwine and Wessex. Only a fool would fail to see his options are limited."

"Yes, I agree, but equally, only a fool would think the matter settled before it actually is."

Harald growled at the warning but nodded all the same.

"Fine, I shall put the plans for my coronation on hold, and wait for bloody Earl Godwine to realise he's surrounded and out of options. Would that please you foster-father?"

"Yes, foster-son, it would," Leofric agreed, his face serious but inside he rejoiced for Harald. This was what Cnut should have done, all those years ago, brought Earl Godwine to heel before giving him any power.

Leofric reached out and gripped Harald's forearm.

"I don't approve of what you did, but what's done is done, and now we wait and see what Earl Godwine's next move will be."

"Agreed," Harald said, all humour gone from his serious young face. "But, warn your wife. I know she'll need time to stitch some fancy clothing for you," Harald indicated Leofric's rich tunic as he spoke, where gold thread shone in the dappled light beneath the trees they walked amongst. Leofric batted his hand away, a smirk on his face. Yes, Lady Godgifu had much to do now that her closest friend's son was about to be declared king.

# 9
## SUMMER AD1036

The night was dark, and so too Leofric's anger as he rode without thought for his horse's safety or his own life.

Around him, he knew his son and younger brothers rushed to keep up with him, but it was Orkning who did the best. Orkning urged his horse on, riding with a brand to the side of him, flaring in the wind. Sparks drifted lazily to the ground, but Leofric was too fast to notice them, hoping only that they settled and died without causing any considerable damage to the parched countryside. Wildfires had caused problems a few years ago, gorging on the harvest and only careful food management had ensured everyone survived the following winter. He didn't want to be the cause of any other fires, but his need was urgent.

Speed was essential, but in his heart, he already knew, just as on that day years ago when he'd escorted his father to London to save Northman from the allegations of treason, that he'd be too late.

News of events in the south had come to him only slowly. He already imagined that much might have happened that could never be undone.

He wished he could blame only one person, but he knew better.

The Queen Dowager might have set this chain of events in play, but Lord Harald had forced her hand, and now Earl Godwine's had been compelled by both of them.

He had news from Denmark, direct news from Orkning and Olaf's family, informing that the war with Magnus of Norway progressed both slowly and badly. While it was accorded the status of war, much of it was an impasse. Neither side sought reconciliation, and until that happened, the message was clear, King Harthacnut was a long way from coming to England. In fact, if King Magnus and his Regents prevailed in the war of attrition, he might never come. Leofric had long thought that might be the ultimate outcome, but still, it unsettled him.

For now, trade between Denmark, Norway and Iceland was severely disrupted. Any who clambered into their ships to head out did so with the constant worry that they'd be seen as a traitor by the kings of another country and lose their lives. The situation was complicated and likely to continue that way for much longer. Leofric thought that King Anund Jakob of Sweden must be thoroughly enjoying himself while his neighbours leaked money and trading opportunities that were his to profit from.

The Queen Dowager, in an audacious move that shocked even Leofric, and he thought he'd imagined all she could do since Lord Harald's raid on Winchester, had informed her other sons that England was theirs for the taking.

The knowledge that Edward and Alfred, the sons of Æthelred, were in England for the first time since their banishment over twenty years ago, had floored Leofric. He hadn't known what to do or even if he should do anything.

He'd never dismissed the two men. After all, they had a valid claim to the English kingdom, but he'd never thought the Queen Dowager would just try and install them in England. He'd expected years of negotiations before either Edward or Alfred actually came to England.

It had been Ælfgar who'd ridden in with the news, as always. It seemed his son was always in a place he shouldn't be, overseeing events that could prove catastrophic to England and to his own family.

That news had Leofric ordering his men to ride from Oxford. There was no time to lose if a life was to be saved. Yet he feared he'd be too late.

He wondered how the Queen Dowager could have forgotten about Earl Godwine in her plans. Or rather, he wished he could wonder. In all honesty, he knew she thought of no one but herself.

Lord Harald was barely a step away from being declared King of England. He had control of all the royal mints, including those within Wessex, and his image was replacing that of Harthacnut's on all the coinage in Wessex. He had the support of everyone, and the stamp of authority from all of the Earls north of the Thames, even Earl Eilifr, and against his wishes.

There had been little that the Queen Dowager could do to stem the tide that was turning away without her, little that she could do to save England for her absent son in Denmark. Or so Leofric had thought. Now he knew differently.

Luckily, he'd been in Oxford when Ælfgar had found him, and now he rode to Winchester, through the short summer night, hoping that when he got there, Lord Alfred was unharmed and safe with his mother. From there, it would be relatively easy to keep him free from harm until he could be escorted from England's shores and returned to Normandy or the Vexin, wherever he'd originated from.

Yet he doubted it, for Ælfgar had not come from Winchester, where the Queen Dowager still sheltered, despite her humiliation at the hands of Lord Harald, no, Ælfgar had come from a visit to Earl Godwine's home. He'd been using guile to reconcile the Earl with Lord Harald; to act as a go-between for the tedious negotiations that were all hampering Harald's imminent proclamation as king.

There was an inevitability about the way the kingdom would be run, and Harald had sent Ælfgar and other family members of his trusted followers, to speak openly with Earl Godwine about the advantages to be gained from changing his allegiance. Lord Harald wanted all of Wessex to accept him and had decided that Earl Godwine was the way to get it, not the hated Queen Dowager.

Leofric doubted the validity of the plan. He'd have thought it better to exile the House of Godwine, and have others rule in Wessex. Lord Harald and he had not agreed on the matter, and now he feared Earl Godwine's intentions toward King Æthelred's children.

Ælfgar, alone in Wessex, had been unable to gather others to do his bidding and stop Earl Godwine when he'd ridden out, furious at the news that Alfred had landed on English soil. Instead, Ælfgar had sought out his father, and his uncles, and while Leofric almost wished he hadn't if his son had stood idly by, he'd never have forgiven him.

The rumour that had so incensed Earl Godwine was that Alfred was marching across Wessex land to reach Winchester, to visit with his mother. He was surrounded by a contingent of warriors supplied by his sister, her new husband keen to prove his worth to his influential wife and powerful nephew, the Count of Vexin, and Earl Godwine had no idea how large the group was.

And this coming so soon after the fyrd of Hampshire had been forced to counter an invasion fleet led by Edward, the elder of Emma's sons with Æthelred II.

Leofric had been aghast at that news but pleased when he'd been informed that Edward had seen sense and left England's coastline without making landfall. He'd not considered, even for a moment, that Lord Alfred would also have been summoned.

Why Alfred had come via a different route, Leofric couldn't fathom.

Surely both brothers should have travelled together to visit their mother, or claim their patronage? Alone they were vulnerable, and now Alfred was in dangerous peril.

And so Leofric rode. He hoped to make it to Winchester before the first streaks of pink lit the summer sky, but that meant riding through the short, but very dark, night, with no moon to light the landscape. It was fortuitous that he knew the way so well, he almost felt as though he could have ridden with his eyes closed, and at times, felt as though he did. The darkness was absolute, just the tiny point of light, Orkning's brand, providing any illumination.

Around him his son and brothers kept pace with him, all of them silent as the wind whipped their hair with the speed of the chase. Out front, Orkning swept in and out of view, but he led a strong horse, the animal as tried and tested in the route as any of them. He could only wish it had been the same season when he'd ridden to protect Northman, instead of the middle of winter, with snow thick on the ground.

Thoughts of his brother ran rampant through his mind, as they skittered and skidded through the landscape. Never more than now did he appreciate that he was a creature of capricious lords and that none of them cared about others' welfare, provided they retained their position, wealth and the support of men who would allow them to keep their position.

He understood ambition, of course, he did, but not at the cost of others. His stomach churned queasily, and he leant to the side, holding his head far to the side of the horse, and heaved the contents of his stomach into the passing night.

Coughing his mouth clear, he settled back in position, aware that his son's eyes had not left him. They carried pity and sympathy and Leofric cursed events that had made his own son feel such benevolence toward him.

Winchester lay ever ahead, always out of his reach, and Leofric tried to fill his mind with anything but the images he recalled of his brother's death. He'd long blanked his father's wounded face, the incomprehension as King Cnut had spoken to him, the terrible journey home to tell Mildryth and his mother of what had happened.

He choked again but swallowed his bile.

Then his anger returned. Why was this even his problem? Could he not trust others to act responsibly, to do the 'right' thing? He only had such vague memories of Lord Alfred, why was this his challenge to contain?

But he knew the answer. He knew it had to be him because none of the others ever exercised any restraint. They believed so vehemently in their own rights that all thoughts of others pain were so fleeting as to be inconsequential to them.

It had been his father's role in life, and now it was his, to somehow soothe the clash of personalities that occurred whenever people worked against each other, as opposed to toward a mutually agreeable goal.

As he hoped, the faint hint of pink lit the grey landscape as he saw the tower of Winchester's Minster come into focus before him. Still, he spurred his horse onwards, the terrain more accessible now that he could see dips and shadows as opposed to just the brand, which still burnt before him. He couldn't determine how Orkning had managed to keep the flame burning so long but was grateful it had.

With his horse heaving with exertion, he raced to the closed gateway of the royal palace, demanding admission from the astonished gate wardens.

"Earl Leofric," the first of the men to regain his wits called. "Why are you here?"

"Allow me to enter, I must speak with the Queen Dowager. It's urgent. I've ridden all night to be here for the dawn."

"The Queen Dowager isn't within," the guard offered quickly. "She rode from here last night, with, with," the man suddenly faltered, not wishing to inform Earl Leofric of the woman's intentions, but Leofric pre-empted him.

"With Lord Alfred?"

"No, with a man who represented Lord Alfred. He said he was on his way to London. The Queen Dowager went to meet him." The man seemed relieved that Leofric already knew the truth of it all.

Angrily, Leofric battered his forehead, where sweat dripped from his hairline, despite the chill of the new day dawning.

"I need fresh horses," he demanded. "For myself and my men. Are there some within?"

"Of course, Earl Leofric, of course." The man, sensing the urgency of the situation, even if he didn't understand it, hastily ordered the gates opened, and Leofric and his son and brothers, who had caught him after his wild ride through the streets of Winchester, clattered inside. Only Ælfgar had overheard the exchange between his father and the gate guard, and Leofric listened to him inform the others of what had happened. If they'd hoped for food and respite from their wild chase, they were going to be disappointed.

Hastily, he steered his horse to the royal stables, and leapt from his side, taking the time to thank him, and ensure his long legs remained without injury. His horse's sides heaved with the effort of the previous night, and Leofric was grateful to have such a fit and strong horse at his command, even if he could be bloody-minded. Around him, stable hands roused from sleep worked to saddle horses that belonged either to the Queen Dowager, the king or even perhaps, to the men of the household troop.

Leofric rewarded their quickness with a hastily tossed bag of coins to share amongst them all, and a promise that he'd return for his own horses, and then they were gone again.

He was unsure which way the Queen Dowager would have gone, but he doubted she would have travelled all night, no matter the urgency. As such he took the road to London with an eye for a travelling cavalcade that included the Queen Dowager, and perhaps, also her son, provided they'd managed to meet up.

He hoped he found the Queen Dowager before the son, and he hoped to find them both before Earl Godwine, and if not, then he yearned to discover the Queen Dowager with Earl Godwine.

As the sun climbed ever higher in the bright summer's day, exhaustion overwhelmed him, and a terrible thirst, but still he pushed the horse he'd borrowed from the King's stables.

The animal was fast and fleet of hoof, its black mane merging into the black of its neck and body. He'd barely glanced at the creature in the stables, but now, as the sun rose higher and higher, he recognised the animal as Cnut's favourite, the animal they'd watched together the last day they'd spoken, and he cursed himself for not noticing earlier that he rode Blue. He doubted the animal had been exercised much since Cnut's death, and he also knew that Lady Emma would be furious with him for risking the animal's health on this wild dash.

As the sun reached its zenith, he saw a party before him. They didn't race as his own group did, but neither did they take their time enjoying the warmth of the sun. No, they rode with purpose, and Leofric was unsurprised when Orkning called from the front that it was the Queen Dowager.

He breathed deeply through his nose, the stench of horse sweat filling his nostrils, but calming him as well.

If the Queen Dowager were without her son, he'd have to race on without her, with barely the time to explain what was happening.

Orkning encountered the first of the Queen Dowager's guards, but the men, stony-faced, refused to let him pass, and Leofric pushed his way forward, the guards standing more smartly to attention.

"Bring the Queen Dowager to me, or let me through, immediately," he ordered, his voice filled with command. The two men glanced one to the other, and then let Leofric ride through. They didn't ask him if he carried weapons, or threatened the Queen Dowager. No doubt they'd realise later and blame each other for the oversight.

"My Lady," he called, once through the first of the horse troop. "Lady Emma," he called again, his voice carrying easily, although no one seemed to be listening to him. On and on he pushed, through perhaps twenty mounted men, before he found the Queen Dowager.

She was riding with her back straight, and her eyes on the road ahead.

"My Lady," he called, much closer now, and she finally turned at the sound of his voice and rage burned in those eyes, as she tried to speed her horse up and avoid him.

"My Lady, please," he gasped. "I've ridden all night to

Winchester, and then all day to overtake you. Is your son with you? Is he here?"

She laughed, a high brittle sound, and Leofric noticed the rouge of her cheeks, as she tried to avert her eyes.

"As you know, my son is in Denmark, defeating the Norwegians."

"I meant Lord Alfred, my lady. Is he here?" Her gasp of surprise annoyed him, as did her general attitude toward him. He didn't ride one horse half to death for his own amusement.

"It's imperative that I know his whereabouts, is he here, is he close?"

"He rides to London, to claim Wessex for himself, in the name of his father, and his half-brother. He'll hold Wessex against the pretensions of bloody Lord Harald."

"He'll ride to his death." Leofric countered, with an angry shake of his head. "Earl Godwine is tracking him. I don't know what he means to do when he finds him, but I can imagine."

"Why would Earl Godwine want my son?" Emma trilled, but Leofric saw the fear in her eyes. She knew only too well that she was being caught out in lies and subterfuges.

"Where is Lord Alfred?" he asked once more, trying to persuade rather than frighten. "Tell me quickly, I must get to him first?"

"Why, so you can take him to Lord Harald?"

"No, My Lady, so I can protect him from both Lord Harald and Earl Godwine. He must leave England. There's no place for him here, as there's no place for his brother." He tried to beguile, keep the fear from his voice.

"What?" the Queen Dowager questioned, but Leofric had listened enough and made to ride on. And then fury lit Emma's eyes.

"How dare you take Cnut's horse from the royal stables. He's not yours to ride." Her voice was filled with outrage.

"I've ridden all night to Winchester from Mercia. My horse is exhausted. I claimed the best the stables could offer, but I meant no insult. I didn't recognise the beast in the early morning light. But enough. I must get to your son. Does the fact I ride Cnut's horse worry you more than the fate of your son?"

"Lord Alfred will be fine, he has a force of two hundred men, provided by his sister, Countess Godgifu. He's safe." But her voice was tinged with worry, and Leofric knew the truth of it then.

"Quickly," he demanded, and she pointed onwards.

"We were to meet at Guildford. And then travel to London together."

"Guildford?" Leofric peered into the distance, judging how much further he must go.

"You must return to Winchester. I'll bring Lord Alfred to you if I can, and send word if I can't. You mustn't be seen with him. Now go."

"I will not," she stubbornly responded, but Leofric had heard enough. He could see his men to either side of the Queen Dowager's force, as they worked to overtake the slower moving horses, and he shouted to Orkning.

"He's not here. They were to meet in Guildford," and as one the small force rushed to the front of Emma's followers and continued their journey.

Leofric didn't even say goodbye to the Queen Dowager. His journey had just become even more urgent, now that he understood that not only was Lord Alfred riding to London, he had with him a small army. Earl Godwine would claim it an invasion force. He would let his men savage Lord Alfred and his small, mobile force.

On they rode. The road was soft underfoot, summer rain had fallen a few days ago, and dried sporadically, leaving soft dints in the roadway. He gasped as he rode. The day was advancing too quickly, and there was too far to go.

He was tired, exhausted, thirsty and fearful, and his horse, once belonging to a king and having been untried for many months, was faltering beneath him.

Within sight of Guildford, Orkning called a sudden warning, and the horses slackened their forward canter eagerly.

"What do you see?" Leofric called, but Orkning was silent. A bad sign.

"Only a handful should go on," Orkning cautioned, his voice ominous, as his eyes met Leofric's. They held fury, and the haunted memories of past battles they'd both fought within. They knew what to expect.

"Come, show me," Leofric demanded, and Orkning nodded. Behind them, Ælfgar had arrived, and Leofric knew better than to banish him from escorting them.

Cautiously Leofric and five of his men went forward to where even he could see black crows had congregated. The stench of spilt blood carried on the gentle breeze, and Leofric already knew what would be found. He was too late.

Hastily he looked behind him, fearful that the Queen Dowager would be close behind, but only his own men milled around unhappily, his brother's eyes angry, his son close to retching. They knew they were too late as well. From a distance, Eadwine caught his eye, sorrow etched there, as Leofric dismounted and went to walk amongst the sea of bodies.

The Queen Dowager was right. Her son had come with two hundred warriors, and many of them lay on the trampled ground before him. Already men and women from the local villages and farms had been alerted to the unclaimed treasures on the dead bodies,. They scurried through them, calling one to another, and flapping their arms to drive crows from faces, and other exposed wounds.

Leofric swallowed heavily. He was thirsty and sick to his stomach, but he needed to discover the fate of Lord Alfred.

"Search the bodies," he instructed, beckoning the rest of his men to join him. As he did so his brother, Eadwine, caught his gaze.

"Send me back to the Queen Dowager. She shouldn't come across this unprepared."

"Are you sure? She'll be wrathful."

"I don't fear the woman," Lord Eadwine replied. "I'll try and halt her progress. Do what you can, and do it quickly."

With that, his brother turned back along the road they'd just travelled, and Leofric bent to the task. He had no idea what Lord Alfred would look like as an adult but assumed he would carry a resemblance to his father, and perhaps his older brothers, men Leofric had once looked up to and respected; the older brothers, not the father.

Picking a path to walk, he strode forward. Men stared without seeing in various positions on the floor. For each of them, he bent and turned a face, either one way or another, if the man lay on his back, he lifted him by the shoulders until he could see enough of the face to dismiss it. He recognised none of them, but winced at the wounds, as he heard others in his party heaving at the atrocities committed on the men.

Dull eyes met his own. They would never see the sunset again, and sorrow swamped him. To die in battle was one thing, but this had been a massacre.

The warriors provided by Alfred's sister had been well provisioned – they had thick byrnies and well-forged blades, well those who still had them did. The attackers or the foragers must have claimed many. They all wore thick cloaks, for night riding, and their boots were well-heeled and without holes. They'd been wealthy warriors, no doubt hand-picked by Lord Alfred's sister to support her brother's claim to the English kingdom; a kingdom they had thought would welcome them, as their mother had urged.

It wouldn't have been possible for Lord Alfred to have heard of the failure of his brother's invasion fleet. It had been too recent.

Still, he found no trace of Lord Alfred, and neither did his son or brother Godwine, Orkning or Olaf.

Reaching the far side of the battle site, he crouched down low to the final body, shocked and horrified when air gurgled through the dead man's open mouth.

"The ætheling," the man spat bloody phlegm. "He was taken. The Earl."

Leofric closed his eyes in distress at the news, as before him the last survivor whimpered his last as his chest stilled.

Leofric paused a beat, his eyes remaining closed as he whispered a prayer over the fallen man, and then he stood.

"Lord Alfred's been taken. Bring the horses. We must ride on."

"Taken by who?" Ælfgar called, at the same time that Orkning asked the question.

"By bloody Earl Godwine, who else. He'll have taken him to London."

"What of the bodies," his son asked, and Leofric shrugged.

"Ask the men of the local village to bury the dead. They'll be paid. Arrange it for me, and speak with the Queen Dowager, should your Uncle Eadwine fail to stop her. I'll go on. Try and intercept them, but I fear this happened at daybreak or even during the night. How else would so many armed men have been caught unprepared?"

"But father," his son questioned and Leofric shook his head.

"You've ridden further and longer than I have. You'll drop from your saddle and die on the road. I can't risk it. Anyway. I want to keep your involvement from Earl Godwine for as long as possible."

His son seemed to accept the explanation, but before he turned to retrieve his horse, he grabbed his father's arm.

"What should I tell the Queen Dowager?"

"Tell her I'll do my best for her son, but I fear it'll be too late. Tell her to return to Winchester, secure her own house there. Lord Harald will not take kindly to this."

"Yes father," Ælfgar bowed his head and then he spoke again.

"Ride safely."

Leofric was touched by the words, and as he rode away from the stench of death, he considered his son. He could never have put him in the sort of danger that the Queen Dowager had inflicted on her own children. Even if he'd not laid eyes on him for twenty years, he'd never have ordered an attack on a country he had no support within. How could she have done so?

At the next settlement, he paused briefly for food and water, provided by fast hands when he showed his coins bearing Lord Harald's image and allowed the horses to walk for a good portion of the afternoon.

London was little more than half a day's journey. No matter how slowly, or how much he dawdled, he knew he'd be forced to face Lord Harald and Earl Godwine too soon for his own liking. And when he came upon them, what would he do?

He could see nothing but self-interest in Earl Godwine's actions but what about Lord Harald? He grimaced at the thought. Lord Alfred was Harald's father's wife's child, yet they shared no blood. That would probably go against Alfred, but would Harald risk inciting King Harthacnut's rage even more by killing his half-brother? Harthacnut and Alfred shared a mother, if not a father. It might prove too much for Harthacnut to ignore, should he come to England.

And what should he say to his foster-son? He thought the time they'd spent together would have prepared Lord Harald better than this. He felt his teachings would have made the folly of this act clear for him to understand.

His men remained quiet, apart from the occasional grunt as a horse tripped or one of them slipped in their saddle. He knew they were all exhausted, but still, he pushed them ever onwards as the day continued.

He cursed when he saw the sun begin to slide in the sky. He'd been in this saddle since daybreak and would be in it long after dusk fell, but on he went. He must still try to save Lord Alfred from whatever Lord Harald and Earl Godwine had planned for him. He must still try and reason with them.

Eventually, Orkning shouted back along the roadway. He'd lit brands some time ago and still rode at pace, although with more care than the previous night. No one there doubted that the outcome of their mad dash through the countryside would be to find the apprehended, or dead body of Lord Alfred. The one option was recoverable from, for Lord Harald, Earl Godwine and the Queen Dowager. The other wasn't for any of them.

Earl Leofric rode to him, and Orkning turned to him.

"There are fires ahead, a camp of some sort. Not very big, but big enough."

Leofric squinted, cursing his poorer eyesight for he could see nothing.

"Can't you smell it?" Orkning queried, and now Leofric could detect damp, burning wood on the night air.

"We go carefully from here," he cautioned, turning to ensure the other men had heard him, pleased he'd cautioned Ælfgar to remain in Guildford. He wouldn't want to risk his only heir on such a fraught battle. "They'll be jumpy and quick to act and ask questions later. I'll go first," he decided, but Olaf called him back.

"I should go first, Lord Leofric. I'd rather not answer to your sister and wife if it's all the same to you."

Leofric grunted his agreement but only under duress. He'd happily argue with his sister and his wife, but Olaf preferred a quieter life, in that he was much like his father, Horic, who could always be cowed by his wife, Agata.

"Be my guest," Leofric agreed but tailed Olaf's every move carefully. He heard Olaf's sigh of annoyance but ignored it. They'd ridden into too many stressful situations in their time, for him to allow Olaf to go alone, and vice versa.

Soon he heard the voices of men floating on the breeze and then he heard the call of men challenging his approach, as he finally saw the impromptu campsite in all its glory.

"I'm Earl Leofric of Mercia," he answered, unsure whether this was Earl Godwine's camp, or perhaps Lord Harald's, but prepared to speak out to gain speedy admittance. He needed to find Lord Alfred.

He didn't have to wait long to find out whether he faced Earl Godwine or Lord Harald.

A stunned silence greeted his words, as though men conferred, and then Earl Godwine himself appeared. He wore the clothes of a warrior, a deep byrnie protecting his chest and his weapon's belt gleaming with the high sheen of iron and silver. His hands were on his hips, his cloak hooked behind them so that weapons flashed in the firelight. There was no mistaking the malice that poured from Earl Godwine, even before he opened his mouth.

"What do you want?" Earl Godwine demanded, from behind his helm, and Leofric felt his rage flare.

"The ætheling Alfred, and quickly. His mother is waiting for him."

"Who?" Earl Godwine said, but Leofric's patience was at an end, and Earl Godwine's voice had lost its edge, no doubt surprised that Leofric knew as much as he did.

"Where is he?" Leofric demanded, dismounting from his blowing mount so that he could stride forward and look Earl Godwine squarely in the face. He was so close he could smell the stale ale on Godwine's breath, and clearly see each hair on his two-day-old facial growth. Only his teeth flashed pale in the gloom.

Behind him, Blue nosed the ground, and Earl Godwine's eyes narrowed. He recognised the animal and knew it must have come from Winchester, from the Queen Dowager.

"It's no business of yours." Earl Godwine countered angrily. "Why are you even here?"

"I'm here to stop what you plan. If I can. Now, tell me, before my men attack yours, where's Lord Alfred."

"You'd threaten me?" the other man laughed as though it were the funniest thing in the world. "You have what, twenty men, if that. I have close to eighty. I think it would be easy for my own force to overcome yours." As he spoke, Earl Godwine raised his arm and indicated the camp behind him. Leofric didn't move his eyes from Godwine's face, although he was aware of the scrutiny of those eighty men as he spoke angrily to their lord and commander.

"And yet your men still sit, sleep and eat, whereas mine are ready to attack your men, string them up if need be, and march them back to Winchester, to face the Queen Dowager."

"The Queen Dowager has even fewer men than you. Even between the pair of you, you'd be no threat to my household troop."

"You'd be surprised, Earl Godwine, trust me. You might have the greater numbers, but my men have the greater skill. But enough. Tell me of Lord Alfred, or I'll raise this campsite to the ground." Leofric growled. The time for conversation was well passed.

"Do what you will, Lord Alfred is gone," Earl Godwine spat derisively, a great gob of saliva landing just inches from Leofric's boots.

"What do you mean gone? Where could he have gone when all his men are dead, no doubt at the hands of your warriors? Have you lost him?" Leofric joked, looking around as though Lord Alfred might appear from beneath the undergrowth, ignoring the spittle on the ground.

"He's gone on to London," Earl Godwine countered, as though he spoke of a gentle ride on a late summer's night.

Cold fear started to shake Leofric, his faint spark of humour tasting like bile.

"Who's taken him to London?" he growled, convinced he already knew. But his question was met with laughter, a dark chortling sound that emanated from somewhere deep inside Earl Godwine's cavernous chest.

"Go see for yourself, Earl Leofric. Go and then see how self-righteous you are when you have the answers you seek."

It was too much for Leofric, his fist clenched, and he would have punched Earl Godwine, if not for Olaf's speedy intervention.

"Come, My Lord," Olaf cautioned, his hand on Leofric's forearm. "Our journey isn't yet done. We must travel on."

"Yes," Leofric responded, his mind returning to the task at hand.

"How many men escorted Lord Alfred?"

"Enough," was the unhelpful response, and Leofric stepped forward again, but once more Olaf restrained him, and as he met the triumphant eyes of Earl Godwine, he was glad not to have hit him. A petty revenge would never erase the injustices of this moment. No, he'd have to think long and hard about how best to belittle the other Earl, at another time. It would have to be enough to punish him for Northman's death, as well as Lord Alfred's.

"Tell me," Leofric thought to demand then. "Why did Cnut not banish you, when you threatened the Queen Dowager. What is it that you have over him? What is it that made him fear you?"

Earl Godwine stilled at the angry words, a fleeting look crossing his eyes, as though he wished no one to overhear the questions.

"I don't know what you mean." Earl Godwine refuted, but Leofric shook his fist angrily, the one not held by Olaf.

"I know, you fucking idiot. I know what you did to Lady Emma. Now tell me why, even after that, King Cnut kept you by his side. He was to banish you, deprive you of your land and your power. Why didn't he?"

"Cnut was my friend as well as my King," Earl Godwine opposed, while Leofric stood his ground, determined to finally have the answers he'd been seeking for nearly five years.

"Cnut did not count you as his friend, and you made his final months a misery. Now tell me?" he refuted, pleased to see the shock on Earl Godwine's face, and perhaps a dawning realisation that explained more than it should. But still, no answer was forthcoming from the word struck Earl.

Purposefully Leofric turned his back on Earl Godwine, heading back toward Blue and another night in the saddle. Weariness dragged at his resolve, but the laughter of Earl Godwine's men drove him ever onwards only the knowledge that he'd just debased Godwine of his friendship with the King made the weight he carried a little lighter.

There'd been little hope to begin with as he'd started his quest. He knew there was even less now.

# 10

## OUTSIDE LONDON, AD1036

Another night of riding brought Leofric, and those of his men who'd managed to both stay in their saddle and keep up with him, to within sight of London. Orkning still rode ahead, but even he was starting to loll in his saddle, and Leofric felt sick with exhaustion and hunger both.

He was in no state to seek out Lord Harald, and yet he'd been left with no choice.

As the sky once more flooded with the pink of a new day, Orkning shouted for his attention. He'd been nodding off in his saddle, Cnut's horse walking at a slow trot, but suddenly he was wide-awake.

"What do you see?" he called as Orkning peered into the gloom of dawn.

"Some small campfires, a score or more of men."

"It must be Lord Alfred," Leofric stated, the faint stirring of hope forcing him ever onward. He'd felt nothing but grief all night, but if he could just make it to Lord Alfred's side, he knew how to convince Lord Harald of the futility of his intentions.

As he trotted his horse forward, another five of his men caught up, and so it was seven who rode into the small camp of no more than twenty men.

There was clearly someone on guard, but they'd long since fallen asleep, leaning against a nearby rock, and Leofric heard nothing but the snores of tired men.

They had horses, just about one for each of them, but the animals drifted in their own sleep, and Leofric ordered his men to search for the missing Lord Alfred. They worked none too carefully or quietly, but not one of the men awoke, and Leofric was unsurprised. The smell of strong ale hung in the air. They'd clearly drunk themselves into a stupor.

"He's not here," Leofric quickly concluded, and Orkning agreed unhappily.

"He might have been though. This cask didn't get here on its own," and he turned to kick a wooden barrel that rolled slowly and sloshed emptily, down the slight rise the men had made their camp upon.

"That looks like a product from London. It even has a stamp on it from one of the winemakers."

"Rouse one of them, ask them where they've been and what they did to earn such payment."

Orkning obeyed Leofric's instructions, a rueful smile on his face as he tipped a skinful of water over his chosen target, the man who'd been on guard duty and had slumped to sleep.

A sharp slap of flesh on flesh filled the air, and Leofric grimaced.

"Tell me where your captive is?" Orkning barked, grabbing the man by the scruff of his cloak. The man squawked in outrage and shock at his abrupt awakening.

"Tell me now, and I may not harm you." There was menace to Orkning's voice, and Leofric sympathised with the captive man. One moment he'd been sleeping, the next a bear-like man, who wore the departing night as a cloak, threatened him.

"I..I," the man gulped, his hand settling over Orkning's as he tried to catch more breathe, but Orkning merely shook him all the more, Olaf at his side to double the menace. The captive looked from one to the other, panic on his face at the sight of two such skilled warriors. The scars that littered Orkning's face only adding to his fears.

Realising there was nothing for it the man spoke.

"Someone came," the captive coughed, "from London. They were taking the bound man to a ship. I don't know who it was." Orkning released his grip slowly as the man spoke, and convinced that he'd be released without harm, the captive began to gabble. "I don't even know who the captive was, but we were told to bring him here by Earl Godwine. Earl Godwine didn't give his name, but I recognised him all the same. I didn't know the captive, not at all, but he'd been badly beaten, he had black eyes, bleeding lips and couldn't stand without support."

Their captive was dressed as a warrior, but one a little down on his luck, and Leofric suddenly thought he could be a ship-man, perhaps one who'd been away from England for some time. Maybe a man who'd once served Earl Godwine and King Cnut in Denmark, or someone who'd escaped from the attack on Lady Ælfgifu and King Swein and had slunk back to England in ignominy.

"I heard men calling him lord, but I don't know his name, they never used it. They were respectful but only just about. They nudged each other a lot as though they knew something that we didn't. It angered our commander."

"Was he young or old, what was the colour of his hair," Orkning might have released his grip, but he fiercely growled to bring the prattling man back to the here and now.

"Your age," the man gasped, "but there was something about him. He didn't take the man himself, others did it for him. He, he had a hound," the man shouted with delight, as though pleased to remember the fact. "The animal never left his side. It was a hunting hound, but I don't think it was used for hunting."

At the news, Leofric turned toward where he knew London, and the great River Thames meandered through the landscape, almost scything England into North and South, Wessex and Mercia, as it went. He was pensive and upset.

He knew one thing for sure. Whatever he might have hoped to accomplish, he was too late. Lord Alfred was gone, and he doubted he'd be found in London.

No, Lord Alfred was long gone, somewhere into Lord Harald's stronghold around Northampton, where Lady Ælfgifu would keep him hidden. There was no way Lord Harald would have allowed him to enter London, even as a captive. London could be hot-headed and easily swayed. There was no way that Lord Harald would have let Lord Alfred enter. None at all.

"Let the man go," Leofric said to Orkning. "He's told me all I need to know."

Their captive hit the floor with a bang and scooted backwards until he felt he was far enough away to stand and turn his back on the massing horsemen, riding in one at a time as they caught up with Leofric, Orkning and Olaf.

"Do not fear," Leofric called to him, but the man was beyond listening. Stepping over his comrades, who he stamped on or stumbled over, rousing them as he went, he dashed for one of the horses and was gone into the grey light of dawn, leaving behind him the waking shapes of disgruntled men who'd drunk too much the night before, and had the headaches to regret it. Leofric watched the formerly captive man in frustration.

Leofric sighed, weariness and vexation warring within him. He could simply have mounted Cnut's horse and ridden for one of his own homes on the Mercian border, the closest would be Oxford. But there was still work to do. His obligations tore at him, and he turned to Orkning and Olaf, where he saw his own tiredness reflected.

"We must sleep," Leofric quietly said, and Orkning seemed to shrink with relief as he spoke.

"Where Lord Leofric? I don't even know where the last house we passed was. We must be close to Southwark, perhaps we can find a hall there to sleep within."

"Here is as good as anywhere, and they have a fire that's well lit already." The fire was stacked high, and Leofric longed for its heat and comfort.

Orkning and his brother were too tired to argue, and Leofric was pleased. More of his men were catching them now they'd stopped, and he quickly informed them of his orders, and what they'd discovered. Sure the men could determine who would stand a-watch, and who wouldn't, Leofric retrieved a bundle from his saddle, inside a spare cloak awaited him. Swirling the fur cloak he wore around his shoulders so that his body was well covered, he settled to the rough ground, within warming distance of the flickering fire, and used the other cloak to cushion his head. He closed his eyes, fearing he might never sleep again, so conflicted was he by the events of the last few days, but knew nothing more.

He woke to the soft laughter of men, and a pattering of rain on his face. The sky was grey, the sun unseen behind the clouds, and he had no idea of the time of day.

Groaning, he sat and looked around, rubbing his lower back as he did so. Some of his men still slept, others sat around eating hare, and there was no sign of any of the original party of men that they'd happened upon that morning, their horses either. As Leofric had slept all of the men had rushed away. Leofric couldn't blame them.

The fire had been restocked and burned wildly with damp and dry kindling intermingled, while Orkning, Olaf, Godwine Leofwinesson and Ælfgar laughed as they tried to cook the hare on stakes over the fire. It was clear that the Danish men were far more self-sufficient than the English, who had to keep leaning into the fire to reclaim fallen pieces of sizzling meat. It all seemed very normal and calm, and then Leofric remembered why he'd spent the day curled in his cloak on the hard ground, and why he felt as though every bone in his body had been broken and poorly healed.

'Ah, you're awake," Orkning called his good cheer enough to set

Leofric's teeth on edge. "Come eat. We have news, and then you can decide on our next area of search."

Leofric struggled to his feet, all the time taking in the state of the make-shift camp. Some of his men still slept, but most were up and about, ensuring their horses were fed and that they were as well. There was a silence to the camp that unsettled Leofric, and he wondered just what it was that the others knew.

"Your brother arrived earlier, with Ælfgar, here. He's sent the Queen Dowager back to Winchester, with the promise of updates, and he's gone into London to get food and information."

Leofric nodded at that. His brother, Lord Eadwine, never seemed to need sleep, it infuriated Leofric.

"What of Lord Alfred?"

"No sign of him here. I went down to the banks of the river, and there's evidence of a ship being moored there, but the ship's long gone. The tide was swift last night. They're either already in London, or gone out to sea. Poor Lord Alfred could be almost anywhere by now." It was his brother who spoke, and Leofric hoped he looked less drained than Godwine Leofwinesson.

Leofric agreed with the sentiment as he wolfed down some part-cooked hare his son offered him, uncaring of its heat although he burnt his mouth. Quickly he reached for a water bag and upended it into his mouth, but not before he'd burnt his tongue.

"Damn," he complained but continued to pick meat from the skewer. He was ravenous.

"At least you can't taste it that way," Orkning consoled, and Leofric nodded. It had been many years since he'd relied on the cooking skills of his household warriors. In that time he'd forgotten both how bad, and how good, half-cooked meat could taste to the ravenous.

"Where's your cousin?" he asked Ælfgar and his son pointed with his chin toward the river.

"He went with Uncle Eadwine. Probably looking for some mischief or a woman, more than likely." Ælfgar smirked as he spoke and Leofric let it lie. His son and his cousins were always teasing each other. If not about women, then about horses, or hounds, or past fights. The three of them never tired, even when their parents did.

Leofric sank to his knees as soon as the first hunger pangs faded.

"What to do?" he muttered. Now that he'd slept, his anger at Earl Godwine felt fresh in his mind, as did his disbelief at the Queen Dowager's actions. And poor Lord Alfred. He couldn't stop thinking about the terrible situation he might now be in, especially when he considered his captor.

"We can't track a ship?" his son offered. He and his Uncles had apparently been discussing the problem.

"No, we can't," Leofric agreed.

"We can't ask Lord Harald outright?"

"No, we can't," he agreed once more.

"We could ask Earl Godwine again."

"He won't say anything, the arrogant bastard," Leofric growled, gazing into the heart of the fire.

What could he do? He was loath to admit defeat. There had to be a way of undoing Lord Alfred's capture, provided he was still alive.

"Where do you think he'll have been taken?" he asked Orkning and Olaf. Orkning lapsed into silence as he considered his response. Leofric waited patiently, alongside Olaf who ate with the determination of one who'd not eaten for nearly two full days.

"If Lord Harald has him, he'll have taken him to somewhere he feels safe and secure," it was Olaf who eventually spoke.

"Northampton then? Do you think Lady Ælfgifu knew of this?" Leofric couldn't keep the disbelief from his voice at the thought. She'd always been a conniving woman, but having just lost a son, he couldn't envisage her doing the same to another woman. Although. Well, she did hate the Queen Dowager. He reconsidered, in the wake of that knowledge but still held with his original thought.

"I believe Lady Ælfgifu is capable of anything," Orkning retorted, a trace of annoyance in his voice. He didn't much like Lady Ælfgifu and her waspish ways.

"But surely everyone in Northampton would know that she held the Queen Dowager's son?"

"Yes, but they're her loyal followers, all of them. They wouldn't speak against her. They never have."

Leofric considered again. "So we should return to Mercia and then to Northampton."

"Would that be wise, father?" his son asked. "Lord Harald wouldn't like the thought of you questioning his actions."

"No, he wouldn't, but all men who want to be kings must have someone to put checks on them. Otherwise, they run wild." He spoke despondently. It hardly seemed a fair outcome if Earl Godwine ended this matter higher in Lord Harald's estimations than he was. Why was he even concerning himself with the problem of Lord Alfred's disappearance?

"Come on, we should go to London as well. I'm sure Lord Harald is there. I'll seek an audience with him."

"No need, brother," a voice called, and Leofric turned to see Lord Eadwine riding back toward them. A trail of packhorses followed behind with supplies for their horses and for themselves. It looked as though Eadwine had purchased everything that London's market had to offer.

"Lord Harald isn't there. He disappeared abruptly in the night, according to the gate wardens." He jumped from his horse as he spoke, handing freshly baked bread to Leofric as he did so.

"Where did he go?" Leofric asked, handing the loaf to his son, who hastily broke it into four pieces, offering one back to his father and one to each of his uncles.

"They didn't say, but toward Mercia, on horseback."

"So not toward the river then, on a ship?"

"No, not at all, but the gate warden also confirmed that his Uncle Ufegat has been in London and that he hasn't been seen this morning, although he didn't know if he'd left during the night or was just lounging in his bed."

"I think we know where Lord Ufegat is," Leofric offered sourly. "How do we find them then?" he asked no one in particular, unsurprised when he received no response. His unease at the situation he found himself in was growing. He did risk a great deal by going against Lord Harald, but equally, he didn't want to be subject to a King who was ruled wholly by his whims and desire for revenge. Æthelred had been a capricious king. He's almost ruined his father's life, and Leofric had no intention of allowing another man to wield such power over his family again if it could be avoided.

As he considered the possible outcomes of his actions, he was pulled from his ruminations by the arrival of another horseman.

"Earl Leofric," the man called, searching amongst the assembled men while astride his horse, and only sliding from the animal's lathered back when he spotted Leofric.

"My Lord," he said, bowing his head just enough to show respect. Leofric recognised him as the man who'd ridden to tell him of Lady Gunnhilda's marriage at Easter. "The Queen Dowager is asking for an update on the whereabouts of her son." At that Leofric sighed. This was the problem. Lord Eadwine had spoken directly to Lady Emma only late yesterday, and here she was today demanding answers that Leofric simply didn't have.

"There's no sign of him," Leofric answered truthfully, inviting the rider to sit and eat.

"But the Queen Dowager?"

"Should never have invited him to England," Leofric rumbled, cutting the messenger off mid-flow. "Tell me, good man, what does Lady Emma expect you to do?"

Here the rider swallowed nervously, his Adam's apple prominent in his throat. Leofric thought him a strange choice of outrider for the Queen Dowager, but then, if Earl Godwine had abandoned her, it was probable that she had to rely on men who were merely riders to act as her warriors.

"I've promised the Queen Dowager that I'll return with her son, alive."

"Then you're a fool," Godwine Leofwinesson jutted into the conversation. His voice was rich with contempt for the man before them all.

"Despite all we did, Lord Alfred has been exchanged between Earl Godwine and a representative of Lord Harald, no doubt so Earl Godwine can show his loyalty to the Regent. I doubt that Lord Alfred yet lives, and if he does, I don't envy him his captivity."

"My Lord Leofric?" the messenger gasped. "Lady Emma will be distressed and angry beyond words."

"Then the Queen Dowager should be careful with the commands that she issues. Did she truly expect Lord Alfred to take the rule of the kingdom from Lord Harald, without even informing her, until now, staunchest ally, Earl Godwine?"

"I don't know what the Queen Dowager thought, only what has happened."

"A worthwhile response," Leofric sighed, rubbing his hand over his tired face and grimacing as his hand touched the days old bristle on his chin. He needed to shave, and bathe, and sleep and eat some more.

"I suggest you don't return to the Queen Dowager with this news. She'll be most discontent and may even punish you in her desperation."

"I will find him," the man reasserted, and instead of laughing, Leofric looked at the man. His face was serious, his resolve hard to doubt.

"Whatever she's promised you, won't be reward enough. But tell me, where would you begin your search?"

"London," the messenger answered straight away. "It's close to here. Men and women must have seen something or heard something. There are always those keen to trade secrets for coin."

While the man spoke the truth, Leofric knew that there was nothing to be gained from such an approach.

"And what if someone overhears your questions, someone who would rather you didn't ask them? What will you do then?"

"I'm a warrior, I can defend myself." Leofric tried not to laugh at the pronouncement.

"Maybe, but the Queen Dowager's name will bring you no protection in Mercia and certainly not in Lord Harald's London."

"I'll do what must be done," the man answered stiffly, rising as he did so. "I'll go on, and find Lord Alfred for the Queen Dowager. You, Earl Leofric, can sit here and think of obstacles all you want. I'm a man of action and will therefore act."

With that, the Queen Dowager's man bowed his head once more and turned away. Before he was out of earshot, and the outrage had faded from his brother's face, Leofric called after the man.

"Should you find yourself in trouble in Mercia, say my name, or seek me out. I'll do all I can to save you from your doomed quest."

The man's steps faltered as he heard those words, and he turned back, a confused expression on his face.

"The rumours about you are right, Earl Leofric. It's not often that's the case, but my thanks for your cautions and your offer. I hope not to use it, but will, should the need arise."

As the messenger rode off toward London, Leofric watched him go with a perplexed expression. He wished the man luck but knew he was more than likely walking into a trap that would bring about his own death. The thought was disturbing.

Lord Eadwine turned to his brother.

"What do you think will happen now?" he asked.

"Lord Harald will have himself declared as King, he'll rule England. The Queen Dowager will be punished in some way, either with imprisonment or banishment, and Earl Godwine will float to the top of the pile, as all good turds do. But still, my concern is with Lord Alfred."

"What would you have us do? Knock on each door, and ask if they have an imprisoned son of the Queen Dowager locked up somewhere?"

"No, I wouldn't do that. I'll go to Lord Harald, support his move to claim the kingship, and we'll listen, all of us. We'll ride from one end of Mercia to another, and we'll listen until we overhear something that tells us whether Lord Alfred lives or dies, and where he is, should he live."

"And if he's alive?"

"I'll return him to his mother, and damn the King to hell."

"What if Lord Alfred is no longer in England? What if he's been sent to King Magnus of Norway, a gift from Lord Harald to ensure that he continues the war with King Harthacnut?"

"Then we'll be even more ineffective. We can't reach out across raging seas. Why, do you believe that Lord Harald is deliberately prolonging King Harthacnut's war with King Magnus?" He asked his brother, surprised that he wasn't the only one to have the thought.

"Why else would the bastard have needed all the treasure he took from Winchester?" his brother grumbled, uncaring when Ælfgar sucked in a shocked breath at hearing his Uncle defame the would-be-king.

"Quite," Leofric agreed. "Quite. Come now, we'll return to Mercia. I need to bathe and shave."

# 11
## AD1036

Leofric touched his face to the wooden floorboards of the Church. He'd not visited Deerhurst for too long. He sought the oblivion of peace that the family church always gave to him.

The summer had been long and terrible, and still, there was no sign of Lord Alfred. He'd sent all of his men the length and breadth of Mercia, even as far as Earl Siward to the North, seeking news of Lord Alfred. But he'd disappeared, just as Lord Ufegat seemed to have done.

Leofric felt sick with worry and fear whenever he thought about his midnight travels to prevent the capture of Lord Alfred. If only. There were always so many if-onlys.

He'd been grumpy, grouchy, even his son too fearful to speak to him, his wife stalking off to Northampton to be with Lady Ælfgifu. He'd begged her to intercede on Lord Alfred's behalf, but she refused. She was too concerned with finding Ælfgar a wife and had no idea why her husband worried himself as he did about Lord Alfred.

So now he sought the sanctuary of wiser men who'd died before him. He only wished that his father, brother, and Wulfstan could materialise before him and offer him the answer that he needed.

He was deprived of sleep, riven with new possibilities, his mind working overtime to try and determine just what Lord Ufegat might have planned for his captive.

He ignored summonses from Lord Harald and sent his son and brothers to do his duties for him, while he raced from one end of Mercia to another, and still nothing.

Closing his eyes, his hand resting on Hund's neck so that he'd be able to stand when his praying was done, he sought the calmness so long deprived him.

Yet, even here, he was not left alone, and although he tried to ignore the noises filtering through from outside, eventually he lifted his head, surprised beyond words to meet the haunted eyes of the Queen Dowager.

Stumbling to his feet, Hund helping him, he turned to greet her.

He was horrified by the grief that veiled her and knew what she'd say even before her mouth opened.

"Lord Leofric," she began, and he nodded.

"I fear we may have done this before," he interrupted her, and she inclined her head in agreement.

"My apologies," she said, "for interfering with your prayers."

"It is no matter. I can come whenever I want to." He spoke without rancour. Here, in Deerhurst, it was as though the misunderstandings of the past were forgotten about. It was here that they could talk to each other as openly as they needed to, without fear of the other ever using those words against the other.

"It has been years," she apologised, a small posy of bright flowers in her hand, and Leofric nodded.

"Come, we shall go outside, by the grave markers," he escorted her with a flourish, and a last lingering glance at his family's cross, glittering in candlelight on the altar. But she turned away and strode to the magnificent object.

"This has always been the way I think of your family," Lady Emma said simply, and Leofric was aware of his sister behind them both. Lady Eadgifu had returned to Deerhurst after the kingdom had been split between the two Regents, and it was probably her intervention that had brought this meeting to fruition. She offered a shoulder-lift of apology, but Leofric knew he would never be angry with his sister.

She was as much a peace-weaver as his father had been. Her strength and courage never failed to surprise him.

"It was my grandfather's. My father was devastated when he lost it."

"And overjoyed when it was returned to him on the instructions of King Olaf."

"A long time ago now," Leofric countered, as they made their way outside.

"You come to beg me for news of Lord Alfred," he asked quietly, the shock of his words still making Lady Emma wince.

"I do, yes. It's been a long time. Lord Harald will not even allow my messengers to speak with him, and my letters are returned unopened."

"You must know that I've never ceased my search for him. If he remains in Mercia, I am at a loss to know where he is. His survival is a mystery to me."

"Ah, I thought you would have forgotten about him," Lady Emma said with some rancour. A hot rage flooded Leofric's face at the carelessly tossed words, and for the first time ever he spoke angrily to Lady Emma.

"Forgotten! I think not. I risk my marriage, and my earldom to trace your son. I don't sleep, I don't eat, I ride, from one side of Mercia to another, and so do my men. I've barely seen my son since Lord Alfred was taken. Sometimes I catch his scent, or miss him by a morning, as we search, without cease, for your son."

Lady Emma bent to place the colourful flowers on his mother's grave and when she stood there was stubbornness on her face and no hint of apology.

"Then he should have been found," she stated, brokering no argument.

"I can't find something so well hidden," he interjected hotly, as she shook her head, elegant tears flowing down her cheeks.

"My son is missing, in the clutches of Lord Harald. He must be found."

"I agree, My Lady, but it's impossible."

"Nothing is impossible," she retorted, her face bleached of colour. "Nothing. I am the Queen Dowager, you are Earl Leofric, foster-father to Lord Harald. Demand he tells you where my son is, and bring him to me. I make this ultimatum to you. You would have done the same for King Cnut."

"My Lady," Leofric countered. "I already do all of those things. I do them for you, for King Cnut and even for King Æthelred's memory and that of Lord Alfred's half-brothers. I do it because it is the honourable thing to do. I," and here he faltered. Words failed him. He was being berated when the task was already his to complete.

"I will ask my foster-son. I promise. If anyone knows, it will be him. He's always been close to Lord Ufegat." At those words, the Queen Dowager wavered, and Leofric held out his arms to steady her, and still, she crumbled through his arms and landed on the soft grass.

"Lord Ufegat?" she sobbed, as Leofric knelt before her. "But he hated King Æthelred. He will have killed my son. Why didn't I know Lord Ufegat had him?"

Leofric shook his head, indicating her position on the floor, and she nodded, her eyes mutinous.

"You kept it from me, for my own good," she grumbled.

"I kept it from you for no good could come of you knowing."

"If you know who has him, why is he not found?"

"Lord Ufegat is missing as well."

Delicately, she lay a hand on the grass, patting it before her, as though she sought comfort from the incumbent beneath the grass and mud.

"Go, find my son. Bring him to me. Dead or alive."

Leofric stood, and held out a hand for her to grasp.

"Of course, My Lady. Of course." There was very little else to say.

Lord Harald sat before Leofric, a self-assured smirk on his face. There was no doubting that he was pleased with himself, and with the current state of affairs within England. At his side, Earl Godwine drank and ate, his expression dark in the sparingly lit hall. Leofric felt repulsed by the man, but also unable to act against him, not here and not now. He should have killed him when he'd the chance in Guildford.

"Earl Leofric, it's good to see you. I take it you bring good news."

"Good news of what?" he asked, furrowing his brow. He was unsure if Lord Harald knew of his exploits, although he doubted that Earl Godwine would have kept news of their meeting a secret.

"Oh, I don't know. Perhaps your ship-men bring you stories of how badly the war goes in Denmark, or that, perhaps, Harthacnut is wounded, and close to death."

There was no humour to Lord Harald's voice as he spoke of his younger half-brother, only an implacable hatred. Leofric had never hated his own brothers and found it hard to think that he ever could have, even if his father had married another woman after his mother's death. But then, a kingdom had never been at stake for him.

"Sadly no, My Lord. I hear no such news from Denmark, although I understand the war is a stalemate and no side can make any advances."

"Well, that is good news, my thanks," Lord Harald smirked, and Leofric bowed his head low. He needed to speak to Harald about Lord Alfred but was uncomfortable and unwilling to do so in front of Earl Godwine.

"I have my own news," Harald crowed, and Leofric glanced sharply at the regent.

"The Witan will convene in two weeks, and I'll be proclaimed as King of England," Harald announced, his eyes flickering to Earl Godwine's as though for an assurance that he spoke the truth.

"The Queen Dowager has lost all support for Harthacnut then?" Leofric qualified, and Harald laughed.

"Oh yes, the Queen Dowager has lost all her support, and her son Edward is back in Normandy, where he should have stayed all the time. She should not have meddled."

"And her other son?" Leofric asked quickly, determined to take advantage of Harald's good cheer.

At the question, Leofric felt the heat of Earl Godwine's glare but chose to ignore him and focus instead on Harald. Harald flushed slightly at the subject, but waved his glass goblet of wine expansively, as he replied.

"Alfred was never a real threat. Earl Godwine saw to that, and Alfred will be bothering no one in the future." There was an admission of something there, but Leofric doubted it was that Alfred had been killed on the future king's orders. No, he rather thought it meant something far more devious and painful.

"And what will happen to the Queen Dowager?"

"I've yet to decide," Lord Harald retorted, his words starting to slur as he drank more and more wine. Leofric abstained from joining his soon-to-be-declared-king but considered the possibility that his drunkenness was a mask for guilt about the treatment of his father's wife's son.

"I would rather plan my coronation than worry about the Queen Dowager."

"Well yes, it is a more enticing prospect," Leofric encouraged, pleased to keep Harald talking. Perhaps he would say something he shouldn't, and Leofric would know the truth about Lord Alfred.

"Archbishop Ælfric will carry out the ceremony," Earl Godwine interjected dryly, and Leofric finally looked at him again. What he saw there disgusted him. Earl Godwine showed no remorse for his actions, only the gleam of future possibilities was reflected on his face.

"And where will it take place? King's Standing, Oxford, Winchester?"

"I think Oxford," Lord Harald replied. "I should be made King of England in Mercia, the place of my birth, and where my alliances are strongest. It'll be a reward for the support of the Mercians when my father died. I don't believe the people of Wessex should be rewarded in such a way."

Leofric started at the words, but it was the anger that slid over Earl Godwine's face that worried him the most. The pair might be reconciled, but it seemed neither was happy about it.

"An excellent choice of venue, already closely associated with your father, and of course, close enough to Wessex that the slight won't necessarily be understood by everyone."

"As you say, Lord Leofric. I suppose," Harald mused, his eyes were glassy, his face rosier than the southern wine he drank. "But tell me, why are you here?"

Ah, the crux of the moment. Perhaps the king was less drunk than Leofric thought.

"The Queen Dowager, she's appealed to me to help her find her son. She sends a new messenger every day. Her distress is, well evident in her frantic efforts to find him. She has been abandoned by all of her allies, or so she tells me, and reaches out to me because of my father's long alliance with her."

Leofric had thought carefully about how to phrase his request but delighted in reminding Earl Godwine of his twisted loyalties. He tried not to look but saw Godwine's shoulders tighten at the reminder.

"The Queen Dowager could approach me directly," Harald answered angrily.

"She could, but she prefers not to. I understand that when you last met the meeting ended… poorly."

"You mean I stole all the treasure from Winchester, that she was supposedly safeguarding for Harthacnut. I think she plays hard and fast with the truth on that one. She hardly put up any resistance, as though she wanted me to take it."

"Yes, well the reasoning behind the Queen Dowager's actions is not for me to decipher," Leofric countered. "I seek only the answer to her question to stop her harassing my wife and family. I'd sooner sleep more easily knowing that I'll not be disturbed from my bed each and every morning, by a new messenger demanding admittance to my home."

A glint of malice had entered Lord Harald's eye as Leofric continued speaking.

"Is that all it would take then Lord Leofric? A knock at the door each morning for a week, or perhaps two, and you'd come rushing to me, your king, for answers?"

"It's been months, not weeks, and I believe that you have the answer to the question, which is why I'm here. I'd sooner know as well. There's much at stake, as always."

"So now you threaten me?"

"How, my Lord? I ask a simple question, 'where is ætheling Alfred?' I do not try and do anything else. And I'm pleased that I'll finally be able to call you 'My Lord King,' as opposed to just 'My Lord'. I've acted as your father asked me to."

At that Lord Godwine's head shot up from where it had been hanging low over the table. His expression was unfathomable, but Leofric had spoken of King Cnut's wishes deliberately. It was evident that the king, even in his final days, had never shared the content of his conversation with Leofric with anyone; and certainly not Earl Godwine or Lord Harald.

"Ætheling Alfred is detained at my pleasure. That's all you need to know."

"So he lives then?" Leofric pressured, and now Harald hung his head and turned away from Leofric's angry stare.

"He does, just about. You need to know nothing more."

"I believe I have every right to know where he is and to see him. I would put the Queen Dowager's fears to bed."

"That won't be possible," Harald countered.

"So he's dead then?" Leofric growled, desperate for a straight answer. Lord Harald shook his head.

"Not quite yet," was his callous reply, but Leofric tried to stay calm, think about his next move.

"I would visit the man, and see with my own eyes."

"You would question your king?"

"I would always question my king when the life of another is at stake."

"You would throw away your goodwill with me because of the Queen Dowager?"

"No, I'd hope you'd see that sometimes generosity after the event can heal many wounds. The Queen Dowager is broken and without support. You'll banish her, of that I'm sure. Her son is no threat to you and could be returned to her care. She has barely seen him for over twenty years."

"That, Lord Leofric, was the Queen Dowager's own choice."

At that Leofric laughed out loud, he couldn't help himself. It seemed Lord Harald knew little of the facts about his father's marriage to his second wife.

"Why do you laugh?" Harald bristled, almost jumping to his feet in rage.

"Your father banished the Queen Dowager's sons. He vowed she'd never see them again. He refused permission for them to visit her, and in turn, he refused her permission to visit them. Your father, for all I miss him and counted him as a friend, had no softness to him. He saw people as pieces to move on the tafl board, nothing more. Just as with you and your brother."

Before Harald could respond, Earl Godwine was on his feet.

"I'll not have you speak about a dead man in such a way," he roared, shocking both Leofric and Harald.

"You'd not hear the truth then?" Leofric asked the first to recover his wits. Earl Godwine was so drunk he could barely stand, swaying where he stood and shaking his fist at Leofric, although his hand wobbled from side to side.

"It's not the truth," Earl Godwine countered roughly, spittle flying from his mouth.

"It is easier to see and remember only that which makes you comfortable," Leofric growled, eyeing Earl Godwine as he spoke. "But it's the truth that really matters, not the ideals. To love someone, and respect them, despite their flaws, is far worthier than loving and respecting someone for what you 'think' they are."

"How would you know?" Earl Godwine demanded angrily.

"Your father may have been exiled by King Æthelred, but my brother was murdered at the command of Cnut, and by your very hands, and still, I respected and cared for my king. Despite everything. And so did my father. Loyalty is loyalty, no matter the cost."

"You've always been so goddamned high and mighty about your brother. He was a duplicitous shit, and Cnut did the right thing when he ordered his execution."

"My brother served his kingdom in ways you would never understand, Earl Godwine, too concerned with your own power and reach. You'd never do anything unless it benefitted you somehow – Cnut gave you back your land and power, and then he gave you more, a wife, a greater area to govern for him, your sons, your closeness to the ruling dynasty of England. But he never trusted you, and what would he think of you now? You vowed to support Harthacnut, and here you are, with Lord Harald, and the blood of an innocent on your hands."

"And what of you then? With your righteous indignation? You supported Harald, although the king wanted Harthacnut to rule."

"The king shared more of his intentions with me than he did with you. I've done nothing 'wrong' in his eyes, until now. Ætheling Alfred is an innocent in all of this, and what have you done? Slaughtered his men and handed him over to Lord Harald? And why? To get your petty revenge on a King who's been dead for over twenty years? To ensure you retain control of Wessex? To give you leverage with another man who equally seeks revenge? You should both aim for the people who've actually caused your distress as opposed to settling your scores by proxy using a man who has no knowledge of events in England, and even less interest in what happens here."

Silence greeted his words, and Leofric looked between the eyes of two guilty men who'd disappointed him beyond words.

"Kings and Earls are men, just like every other, but sometimes we must strive to rise above petty jealousies and feuds – not for ourselves but for the good of the kingdom. Kings who spend their time punishing perceived enemies, will not be ensuring the country is run fairly. Earls who spend their time preserving their own existence, will not see the whole picture."

Leofric spoke calmly, surprising himself with his lack of rage. He spoke the truth, kings were just men, and likely to make just as many mistakes.

"My Uncle has ætheling Alfred, but I don't know where, other than it'll be near to one of his strongholds. Go, find Alfred, tell my Uncle you have permission to take him. Return him to his mother and then banish the witch. I have a coronation to plan."

"My thanks, My Lord," Leofric bowed his head at finally having the answer to his question.

"But Leofric, remember this. Earls are also just men, even those who seek to work for a higher purpose and earls can always be replaced." The threat brought a sad shake of the head to Leofric.

"And you, My Lord and foster-son, while we play this game. Remember all kings of England rule by the will of the Witan or by right of conquest, and that kings too can be easily replaced. As can earls, My Lord Godwine. Don't ever think your part in this will be forgotten."

Without looking to Earl Godwine, Leofric stomped from Lord Harald's presence.

He hadn't gained precisely what he wanted, but at least he had confirmation of who had Lord Alfred. He hoped he'd finally find him. Before it was too late, although he doubted it. Too much time had passed, too much time in which Ufegat, another who sought revenge on the wrong man, could have killed Alfred, or worse, blinded him just as he had been.

# 12
## AD1036

LEOFRIC'S THOUGHTS PROVED WELL FOUNDED.

As the long summer began to give way to the colder days of early winter, he sought out Lord Ufegat at his properties but failed to find him, anywhere. In the end, he was left with no choice but to approach Lady Ælfgifu herself. He'd hoped to do so at her stronghold in Northampton, but had missed her, and now sought her out in Oxford.

He knew he'd lost the initiative in coming to Oxford, where Lord Harald sought the approval of the Witan to become King Harald, but he had little choice. The Queen Dowager's entreaties were just about frantic, and now that it was widely known that he was seeking Lord Alfred, it would be too easy for Harald's Uncle to simply kill the man and dispose of the body. None would be any the wiser then. The only flaw in that plan was, of course, Ufegat's blindness. He might be able to kill Emma's son, but he'd not be able to hide the body without someone else being involved.

Having convinced his wife that he needed her assistance, he strode to the grand hall where Lady Ælfgifu had set up her headquarters while in Oxford, trying to decide how best to gain Ælfgifu's help.

He knew he could appeal to her better nature, but he knew that wouldn't work. She hated Æthelred as much as her older brother, and no doubt would find no shame in punishing the son for the father's crimes. Instead, he'd need to coax the information from Lady Ælfgifu, and that was why his wife accompanied him. Lady Godgifu was a firm friend and ally. Leofric was tolerated by Harald's mother, on behalf of his wife, and son, who Lady Ælfgifu was also friendly toward.

"Explain to me why you even care what happened to Lord Alfred?" his wife complained at his side, once more, and he tried to stay his irritation.

"The Queen Dowager demands it from me."

"And? I make many demands on you, and still, you don't make yourself unpopular with anyone on my behalf." He suppressed a groan.

"I would know what happened to Lord Alfred, and if he lives, I'd escort him from England. He shouldn't have come, and King Harald, as he will be, shouldn't have been lulled into accepting him from Lord Godwine as some sort of token of his loyalty. Alfred is an innocent man."

"How can he be when he brought an army to England?"

"Yes, he brought a whole two hundred men and Earl Godwine slaughtered them all. They should simply have been escorted away, as happened to Lord Edward."

"But he threatened Lord Harald."

"Only because his mother ordered him to. Really, Godgifu, I ask only that you take Lady Ælfgifu to one side and ask her if she knows the whereabouts of her brother."

"I understand that, but she'll know that it's you who wants to know."

"Of course she will. Why would you be interested in where Lord Ufegat is?"

His wife sighed unhappily. "I would simply rather not be involved."

"As would I?" Leofric answered sharply. "But my honour dictates it, as does my father's honour. It is, after all, just a question."

"Fine," Godgifu complained, her face pinched with annoyance. "I'll ask Lady Ælfgifu your question."

"My thanks, wife. I will remember this."

"And so will I" his wife whined, and Leofric knew she'd indeed remind him of the need to rely on her in the future. It was rare that she let anything go, reminding him years later of all the times he'd inconvenienced her. For that was what she thought of his requests upon her; that they were an inconvenience. She rarely took the time to appreciate the demands she made upon him, as though he should live to follow her wishes. He sighed. He wished his marriage had been happier.

Inside Lady Ælfgifu's hall, he mingled with the men and women of Mercia. Almost everyone of importance from there – even Earls Hrani and Eilifr making an appearance, for all that they would rather Harthacnut were king. Leofric watched them closely, keen to see who they spoke to, but unsurprised when they kept very much to themselves, and other thegns who'd been born in Denmark.

Should Lord Harald fail in his kingship, he was sure that the Danish would quickly seek out Harthacnut. In fact, he hazarded a guess that even now, they were in contact with the Queen Dowager, despite everything they'd ever said about her, and they too made some attempts to uncover where Alfred was being held.

He pinched his nose between his fingers. Nothing had been simple since Cnut's death. He'd appreciated that it would be difficult, but he couldn't have imagined the shifting tides of politics would prove this complicated.

Leofric drank deeply of a fine wine, offered to him by one of the servants, and watched his son and brothers mingling in the crowd.

Ælfgar spoke with a group of young men just about his own age, and it took little for Leofric to determine that these were Earl Godwine's sons. He was always unsure of the correct birth order of the youths but imagined these were the older sons, the ones that Godwine had indoctrinated into the House of Godwine already.

They were well-dressed young men, similar in height and stature, all trained with blade and shield, as their arms seemed to bristle through their tunics. It appeared Earl Godwine was raising warriors in his household, not men skilled with the art of compromise.

He turned, distracted by a high laugh, and saw that his wife was deeply engrossed in conversation with Lady Ælfgifu. No doubt he was the butt of their joke, but he hardly cared.

Lord Harald wasn't due to arrive in Oxford for a day or two yet, tarrying in London so that his mother could win over the last few supporters to agree to his demands at the Witan. Leofric wanted to take advantage of that, even though he worried that Earl Godwine was with Lord Harald, damaging his reputation with the would-be-king even further.

He hoped that Lady Ælfgifu would confide in his wife and that he could support Harald at the Witan and then, finally, end his hunt for Lord Alfred. The futility of a long summer searching for the ætheling had driven Leofric to distraction. He wanted to be done with it all, good or bad. Already he understood his support of Harald was no longer unconditional, and yet there was no alternative. Not anymore. Not unless Harthacnut came to England, and that possibility was so distant that Leofric rarely even considered it anymore.

His ship, under the command of Orkning, had once more made the journey to Denmark. He was, as ever desperate for news of Harthacnut, and Orkning returned with a wry smirk.

"King Harthacnut is about as keen to come to England, as he is to freeze his dick off in the harsh northern winters. Events in Denmark are strained, but outright war has been slow to come. I spoke with a member of Lady Estrid's personal guard. They were in Ribe on some business for her. They say Harthacnut is a good king, keen to use his cousins, Estrid's sons, to rule. They speak vaguely of a war with the

Regents of Norway and King Anund Jakob of Sweden, but it's not their primary concern."

Armed with that information, Leofric felt able to face any who questioned his actions, and also to apply some pressure to Lord Harald, should it be necessary, Lady Ælfgifu as well. He expected to have his opinion sought by the other earls and was unsurprised when Earl Siward sought him out.

"Your wife is in high favour?" the earl growled when once more, everyone's eyes turned to the laughing faces of Lady Godgifu and Lady Ælfgifu.

"They were childhood friends. It seems that very fact overshadows anything I might do." Leofric spoke with a growl. He didn't want the earl to believe his position was the sole result of his wife.

"Ah, well, childhood friends will do anything they're asked, almost without question. Just look at Cnut and Earl Godwine. Well, I suppose they were not quite childhood friends. But still, I assume the same applies."

Leofric nodded, as he twirled his glass goblet between his fingers. Lady Ælfgifu's house was filled with people, jostling and talking too loudly, with too much wine and ale on hand for those foolish enough to over-indulge.

"And yet, something came between them." Siward raised his eyebrows in surprise at the words, and Leofric nodded to show the truth of the words. "I was there, I know."

"And yet Earl Godwine remained high in his estimations."

"Yes, he did. I've long wondered how, but Earl Godwine refuses to tell me, and I doubt that Lady Emma even knows."

"It worries you?" Siward pressured, and Leofric nodded. He'd not spoken of his concerns to anyone but thought he could trust Siward with his secret.

"Earl Godwine was so close to banishment one moment, and the next it was as though his lies had never been uncovered. It plagued Cnut. I know it did."

"And what, you think Earl Godwine will use what he knows?"

"I think Earl Godwine stores all the knowledge he can, determining how best to use it to his advantage, in the future."

"Ah. You think it concerns our new king?"

"No, I think it concerns Cnut, but what impact it might have, I don't know, but he wouldn't tell me when I demanded an answer from him, in the summer."

"So you believe that means it's still relevant?"

"I do yes. I think he still plans to use it, and, as I said, I believe the Queen Dowager is unaware of it."

"Then you shouldn't worry about it. Not for now. Earl Godwine might yet trip over his own feet," Siward laughed as he spoke, and Leofric tried to dismiss yet another of his worries quiet as easily but failed.

Yet he was interrupted by the return of his wife. She smiled at Earl Siward, always keen to flirt with a handsome man, and Siward was only too pleased to play along. Only when he'd gone, to plot with another, did Lady Godgifu lean over to her husband, and whisper into his ear.

"Lord Ufegat is in Peterborough. He has been for months. She knows that Lord Alfred is there. He still lives, but husband, I caution you," and here she paused. "You will make an enemy of Lady Ælfgifu should Lord Ufegat be injured further."

Irritated by the unwanted caution, he stepped away, but Godgifu quickly moved to intercept him.

"Tread carefully. Your son has expressed an interest in a girl from a family who are allied with Lady Ælfgifu. It wouldn't do to break his heart."

He grunted. He would do anything for his son, and his wife knew that.

"My thanks," he growled, and she smiled, delighted at achieving something he couldn't.

# 13
## AD1036, ÆLFGAR

**Near Peterborough**

Ælfgar's horse heaved beneath him, and he jumped from the animal and turned to wait for his cousin, a smirk on his face.

Wulfstan clattered up behind him, his own horse blowing too hard, and leapt aside as well, turning to run his hand up and down the rear leg of his beast.

"How does he gallop so bloody fast?" he whined to his younger cousin, but Ælfgar just shrugged. He was, he knew, a sensible and often, boring member of the family, or so his two older cousins never tired of telling him, but, when it came to his horse, he knew he could be reckless. Almost impossibly so.

"He's got long legs," Ælfgar joked, mirroring his cousin's actions, and running his hands expertly up and down Chester's impossibly long legs. The animal was monstrously tall, but that wasn't the only reason for his fast turn of speed. No, he and Ælfgar could move as one, and it was that which Ælfgar reasoned allowed them to outrun everyone.

Behind him, there was another clatter of hooves onto the roadway, and Leofric met the frustrated glare of Ælfwine, with no apology on his face. His other cousin was even slower than Wulfstan, and it had nothing today with any perceived slight on the pedigree of their horses. No, his father, Leofric, ensured, no matter what, that Leofric and all of his cousins had access to the same resources the family owned, and Ælfgar was pleased. An only child, he'd relied on all of his cousins when he'd been a child.

"Will you two stop bloody racing?" Ælfwine moaned, dismounting from his own horse so that both stood in front of the other two, chests heaving and a slight look of annoyance on their faces.

"It makes the journey go more quickly," Wulfstan rejoined, but Ælfwine shook his head.

"No, it draws attention to us, and before long, every bugger will know that Earl Leofric's son is going to Peterborough, and I don't really think that was what he wanted when he sent you on ahead."

Ælfgar sobered at the reprimand, but couldn't keep the humour from his voice.

"Apologies, Father Wulfstan, we didn't mean to misbehave."

Wulfstan growled at the sing-song voice Ælfgar employed, and menaced a step forward, only for Ælfwine to intervene.

"Come on you bloody idiots. We need to walk for a bit, to rest the poor horses, but I think Peterborough should be reached today."

"About bloody time," Ælfwine grumbled. "My arse is sore from all this riding. Whoever this bloody Lord Alfred is, I hope he's worth the days I've spent in my saddle this year, searching for him."

Ælfwine received no reply to his complaints. Ælfgar had long run out of patience with them, and even Wulfstan rolled his eyes at the oft-repeated phrase about Ælfwine's arse.

"I suggest you eat more, and then it wouldn't be so damn bony and uncomfortable," Wulfstan retorted, and Ælfgar laughed to see the outraged look on Ælfwine's face.

"We can't all be tubby buggers."

"Nothing wrong with a bit of a girth," Wulfstan joked, slapping his own, more than comfortable looking backside as he walked. "At least it makes riding a joy."

"What, a horse or a woman?" Ælfwine teased, but Ælfgar looked away, feeling the faint stirrings of pink on his face.

His cousins were older than him, their enjoyment of the fairer sex well known, but Ælfgar had yet to attain their level of interest. For now, he allowed his cousins to tease him, while he thought of the task his father had set before him.

Leofric understood, from Lady Ælfgifu, that Lord Alfred, kidnapped in the summer, was being held captive in Peterborough. Before his father rushed out on yet another fruitless search, he'd ordered his son, and two nephews, to visit the place and ensure that Lord Alfred was indeed in Peterborough. Only then would he come and rescue him.

Ælfgar had been pleased with the task, far more straightforward than the one where he'd been sent to negotiate with Earl Godwine on behalf of Lord Harald, his foster-brother, but it was a hot steamy day, and the stench of horse seemed to pour from him, as he wrinkled his nose in disgust.

"Come on, let's ride again, at a sedate pace," he cautioned, a smirk on his face. "I'd sooner be there than on this dusty road."

Yet by the time they arrived at Peterborough's guarded gates, the dust had long since disappeared to be replaced by a downpour of rain that had long since washed them cleaner than clean. Ælfgar was tired of his cousins' grumbling as he negotiated their entry, being careful to cover any trace of who he was. His father wanted this accomplished with stealth. Three members of the House of Leofwine arriving with flashing seaxs embellished with the family emblem, their horses saddled and bridles as well, was not exactly what his father had planned.

"Can you direct us to an inn?" Ælfgar asked the drenched gate warden, and the man uttered some almost intelligible directions, as he ran his eyes over the beautiful horses and finer cloaks the three men wore. Abruptly he changed his mind, his voice louder now, and Ælfgar smirked at the abrupt change. Sometimes it was impossible to disguise wealth.

Once through the wooden gateway, that shimmered darkly and menacingly in the glimmer of fitful brands, Ælfgar followed the instructions and quickly found the place the gate warden had mentioned, more by the raucous laughter coming from behind the barred door than the actual directions. The roadway was awash with rain, and it was almost impossible to see through the constant deluge.

Somehow, Ælfgar found the way to the stables and leapt once more from his horse shaking rain from his hood before pulling it back from his head. His cousins followed him, a foul expression on Wulfstan's face that Ælfgar grinned to see. He always felt better knowing his cousin was more miserable than him.

A surprised stable hand greeted them, and with a low whistle, admired all three horses.

"My Lords," the older man said, sucking on his remaining front teeth. "Not a night for travel," he continued, a gleam in his eye and Ælfgar tried to keep his face straight as Ælfwine rolled his eyes at the machinations of the stable hand, keen to make some extra coin from such wealthy riders.

Knowing that his father never stinted on such cultural exchanges, Ælfgar quickly pressed two of Lord Harald's coins into the man's waiting hands.

"Please care for the animals well. Two more shall be yours when we leave if I'm happy with the state of the animals."

The broad grin on the stablehand's face was all the assurance Ælfgar needed. But then he thought of something else.

"Tell me, who is Lord of this settlement?"

A sour sneer crossed the stablehand's face, and Ælfgar knew the answer without waiting for it.

"And is Lord Ufegat a good lord?" Wulfstan pressed when the man had finally answered.

"He's blind so of course not. But his cousin is a better lord, or rather lady. Lady Ealdgyth is a fair woman and often intervenes on behalf of the citizens of Peterborough."

"And where might we find her?" Ælfgar asked, keen to avoid her if possible. She was another ally of his mother's, and if she were within Peterborough's walls, it would be imperative that they shunned her to avoid detection.

"Ah, she's away, I think in Northampton. I think," the stablehand grunted, and Ælfgar nodded.

"My thanks, good man. Now tell me, how do we get inside the inn itself? I can't see a damn thing through the rain."

The noise of the rain, on the rafters above them, had, if anything intensified since finding shelter, and the stablehand winced at the sound.

"Bloody hell. The roof will develop a leak if this keeps up. But, I assure you, your horses will be nice and dry in here. Just step that way," he pointed, out across a flooding yard, and Ælfgar grumbled as he flung his cloak back over his sodden hair.

"My thanks again," he called as he and his cousins ran to gain admittance into the hall.

Water splashed around his boots, and he hammered on the door to gain entry, which was slow in coming. By the time the door creaked open, Wulfstan was moaning once more, and Ælfgar didn't blame him.

The door warden glanced at them, disgust on his face at having to allow such sodden creatures inside, but he quickly resettled his face on recognising wealth and ushered the three of them inside. Stamping the water from their boots, and removing sodden cloaks, Ælfgar glanced at the hall.

Smoke wheezed through the air, with the abrupt shutting of the door, and a damp smell hit his nostrils, but other than that, it seemed that the inn was a reasonably pleasant place. Four long boards filled the centre of the space, split two to each side by the hearth at the very centre, and Ælfgar quickly met the eye of an interested looking innkeeper.

"Good evening, My Lords," the man commented, his wise eyes also taking account of the good clothing the three cousins wore. "I take it the stablehand saw to your horses?"

"Yes, my thanks, innkeeper, he did. And now we have come to see to ourselves."

The man smiled, and Ælfgar waited patiently. No doubt the cost would have doubled because their boots were made of soft-cured leather.

"Five coins for the three of you. One night, three meals, and three more in the morning, and as much ale as you can manage. The whores and the mead are more."

Behind him, he heard his cousins' snigger at the idea of whores, but Ælfgar knew them better. Their mother was strict with them, despite their desires.

As Ælfgar counted the coins into the open hand of the innkeeper, he continued their conversation.

"I hear Lord Ufegat runs this settlement."

"Yes he does," the innkeeper responded idly, his attention arrested by the coins he'd been given.

"These new?" he asked, turning the silver first one way and then the other, so that it caught the light from the few candles. "They look different," he continued suspiciously.

"From one of the Wessex mints, I understand," Ælfgar assured, wishing he'd thought to bring some of Harald's older coins. The new dyes hadn't yet reached this far North.

"Look, the name of the moneyer is on there, and everything. I had to remint them before I began my journey North, or risk the wrath of the moneyer for delaying his work."

"Bloody leeches," the innkeeper responded, as though suddenly satisfied with his haul of new coins.

"Why you asking about Lord Ufegat? You have business with him? If you do, I wish you luck, no one's seen him for months, and whenever anyone goes to his hall, all they hear is the strangled cry of some poor bugger he's torturing half to death."

Ælfgar tried not to wince at the information. It seemed Lord Alfred had finally been found.

"Ah well, I'll try my luck with him tomorrow. Tell me, where's his hall?"

"Near the west gate. You won't miss it. It's bloody huge – bigger even than in here if you can believe it. Now, be welcome. I'll get food and ale to you and your companions."

Together the three of them made their way to a space indicated by the innkeeper. Ælfgar was content to see that the inn was only vaguely busy. A few parties mingled together, but mostly it appeared that the rain had driven many away, perhaps dissuaded from starting journeys they might otherwise have made.

Wulfstan grumbled once more as he claimed the seat closest to the hearth, whereas Ælfwine was already licking his lips, no doubt deciding on the best person to extract the information from that they wanted to hear. Ælfgar, however, felt his eyes drawn to a tight knot of warriors around the table next to him.

It seemed as though the five burly men huddled too tightly together, and only when he caught a glimpse of beautiful blond hair did he understand why. No doubt the five men, members of someone's household troop as opposed to mercenaries, were under strict instructions to keep their charge away from any undesirable, and in an inn, there were always likely to be a few.

Ælfgar allowed his cousins' complaints to pass over his head, as he considered what he'd just learnt about Lord Ufegat, while he watched the men opposite. They shifted uneasily on their seats, and Ælfgar imagined that a night in an inn had not been on their agenda for the day. The terrible deluge had interrupted them, forced them to make a stop and they weren't happy about it.

Steaming bowls of a watery pottage were soon placed before Ælfgar and his companions, and he dug in hungrily. He was surprised by how good the meat tasted and turned to compliment the innkeeper, only to be distracted as the household troop parted to allow a slight woman to escape from between them.

A tall woman, perhaps the innkeeper's wife, waited patiently for the girl and then escorted her into the far reaches of the hall. For a moment Ælfgar knew his mouth hung open in shock, only for Ælfwine to dig his fingers into his ribs to draw attention to the leering gaze of one of the household troop members.

Abruptly, Ælfgar looked away, keen to avoid the scrutiny of the man and any possible confrontation, but his mind was a whirl.

"Who was the girl, and what was she doing in a place like this?"

A bang on the table and Ælfgar looked into a glowering face that was uncomfortably close to him.

"Keep your fucking eyes to yourself," a gruff voice warned, and Ælfgar swallowed compulsively.

"A.. apologies, good man," Ælfgar eventually responded. "I hadn't expected to see such a sight on a night as this," he tried to explain, but the warrior had heard enough.

"Keep your eyes to yourself, and you might still see other 'sights' when you wake in the morning." Ælfgar nodded, struck by the emblem on the fastening the man used to draw his cloak tightly around his neck. He knew that sigil, and as he nodded at the larger man, in apology, turning his attention to his food once more, he knew who the girl had been as well.

For just a fleeting moment, he'd seen watchful green eyes, and an intelligent looking face, and in just that moment, he finally understood just what it was about women that so fascinated his cousins.

"Ohhh," Ælfwine teased, when the warrior had meandered his way back to his companions. "Did the scary big man make you wet yourself in fright?"

"No, not at all," Ælfgar tried to deflect, and it fell to Wulfstan to stop the taunting.

"Leave him the fuck alone, brother dearest. That delightful creature was none other than Lady Ælfgifu, daughter of Morcar and Lady Ealdgyth, and named after her Aunt, the Lady Ælfgifu who happens to be our soon-to-be-king's mother."

"That, that was her?" Ælfwine whistled softly. "I'd heard about her beauty, but I've never met her before."

"Well now we have, and brother dearest, it looks like young Ælfgar might just have fallen in love at first sight."

Ælfgar bowed his head even lower to avoid his cousins' inspection, but he could still hear them laughing at his discomfort, and in annoyance picked his bowl up and turned his back to them both, and ate, staring at the fire so as not to upset the warrior again.

His cousins laughed at his actions, but, all thoughts of Lord Alfred from his mind, Ælfgar was too busy determining who he should tell about Lady Ælfgifu, his mother, or his father, for one thing was certain, he did want to meet her again, speak with her, and perhaps, well just perhaps.

# 14
## LATE AD1036

It was Ælfgar who reached the gateway to Peterborough first, but he reined in and waited for his father to join him.

Leofric had sent him to ensure the information from Lady Ælfgifu had been correct before making the journey himself. Ælfgar was much less well known than he was, and the lad and his cousins had slipped in and out of Peterborough almost undetected. And yet he'd brought the news that Leofric had been hoping to receive ever since Lord Alfred's disappearance in the summer. Even so, the report had been disturbing.

It was an open secret within Peterborough itself that Lord Ufegat, brother to Lady Ælfgifu and therefore, Uncle to the regent, and soon to be proclaimed king, of England, had a prisoner who he tortured each and every night; the screams of the man echoing through the settlement.

The news had sickened Leofric, but it meant that Lord Alfred still lived. At least for now.

Leofric had opted to come with only five of his men, Orkning amongst them, to extract Alfred from Lord Ufegat. He came, not so much with Lord Harald's permission, but with his acceptance. He'd been pleasantly surprised when Lady Ælfgifu had told his wife of her brother's hideout in Peterborough.

No doubt Lady Ælfgifu knew all about the depravities inflicted on Lord Alfred but was content for Leofric to discover the truth for himself, with no forewarning. His ambivalent feeling toward Lord Harald's mother was hardening, and he'd not even managed to extract Lord Alfred yet.

His son had told him that Lord Ufegat had a magnificent home, just on the outskirts of the settlement. Wanting to waste no further time with the chill of winter in the air, Leofric had directed his son to take him straight to the hall. He was determined to approach Ufegat, resume custody of Alfred, and bring him to Winchester, should Alfred be well enough to travel.

They arrived, all seven horsemen together, with a noisy clatter of hooves, and Leofric quickly dismounted. He wasn't so much keen to conclude this matter, but rather resolved to the unpleasantness of it all.

He noted that his arrival was unnoticed, and then strode to the closed wooden door, hammering loudly on its smooth wood surface.

As his son had said, the hall was exceptionally well built, the wood warm and glowing in the late afternoon sun, but none of that mattered when echoing silence greeted Leofric's stringent knock. He could hear empty space behind his blow, and, aggrieved simply pushed it, unsurprised when the door sprang open on vacant space inside.

"Ælfgar, was it like this last time you were here?" he called over his shoulder, pointing to the deserted interior.

"No, father. It was filled with people and furniture. Bloody hell," Ælfgar growled with annoyance. "Where's the bastard gone now?" He looked behind him, as though Ufegat would appear from behind a corner.

"I've no idea," Leofric sighed, not angry with his son, but rather with the fate that kept denying him a sight of Lord Alfred. His nights were filled with dreams of the torture he was no doubt enduring, and

Leofric was fed up with the situation, and his inability to accept his inevitable death.

"Seek out the gate wardens," he called to Orkning, who was still astride his horse. "See if they have news of where Lord Ufegat has buggered off to now."

"My lord," Orkning dipped his head and turned his animal away.

"Use a bribe if necessary. I'm tired of this. I'd be done with it."

"Of course," Orkning agreed, indicating that three of the men should stay with Leofric and Ælfgar, while one of them went with him.

"I'm going to search inside. See if there's any indication that Lord Alfred was ever here."

"I would search the stables or outhouses then," his son called. "I imagine if he were anywhere, he'd have been held there."

Leofric accepted his son's words but turned back into the hall. His boots echoed hollowly on the wooden floorboards as he walked the distance from the main door, to the small raised dais and back again.

It was a reasonably new construction, the wooden beams still holding a hint of their warm brown as opposed to the black scold of fire. As he paced, he turned his mind back to the events of the summer.

Earl Godwine had taken Lord Alfred captive, no doubt at Lord Harald's insistence, but then Harald had gifted the ætheling to his own Uncle. Leofric had spent countless months trying to track the man down, even going so far as to send his son and his household warriors to knock on doors and demand answers from anyone within Mercia who he thought might be implicated in the imprisonment of Alfred.

But he'd uncovered precisely nothing until he'd spoken first to Lord Harald, and then Lady Ælfgifu. It hadn't made for pleasant listening, but it seemed that all along they'd been playing games with him. He grumbled under his breath. Not only had Earl Godwine somehow managed to escape his impending removal from the earldom of Wessex, but he was also riding high in Lord Harald's favour whereas Leofric was being given false information to make him look ineffectual and stupid.

It was clear that Lord Harald, no matter what he said, didn't want Lord Alfred discovered and returned to his mother. Perhaps, as his wife suggested, he'd pushed the issue as far as he could. Maybe it was time to forget about Alfred and his mother. After all, the Queen Dowager wouldn't keep her place in England for much longer. Not when Lord Harald was crowned as king.

"Father," his son called to him, and Leofric strode from the useless, bare hall and into the growing dusk. "I know where he was kept, but there's no sign of him now. He was in the stables, chained to the wall, I can see the marks where he's been forced to relieve himself just like the animals."

"But he's gone?"

"Yes, and there's blood on the chains and blood on the floor, but I can't see a trace of any disturbed ground where they might have buried him."

"No, I don't think they'll have killed him. I think Lord Ufegat is enjoying himself too much for that. Why else evade me as he has?"

At that moment Orkning returned, a grimace on his face.

"They rode from the eastern gate yesterday morning, taking all the furniture with him. One of the wardens said that the ætheling was with them, but that he's been blinded and is unable to fend for himself. He doesn't know where they went, other than east, and didn't name him as the ætheling either, but I know it was him, they described him."

Leofric squinted into the setting sun, considering what he might have done in the same situation.

"I believe they're aiming for the coast. I think they'll try and evade us by leaving England."

"Why would they do that? Surely Lord Ufegat can be assured of his nephew's support."

"Yes, I'm sure he can, but will Lord Harald want the beginning of his kingship marred by the news that he killed his father's wife's younger son? I doubt it. I think they'll try and dispose of him along the way. I'd rather rest and resume our search tomorrow, but I know we can't. Even if Alfred were alive yesterday, he might not be now, and he might not be tomorrow, so we must at least try."

None of his men argued the point but instead worked to ensure their riding equipment was in good order, before discussing brands and lamps to light the darkening sky. Leofric was pleased to face no opposition. He wasn't alone in being tired of the chase.

With the sun setting behind them in a stunning collection of winter reds and pinks, Leofric led his men away from the eastern gate and into the hinterlands before. He hoped they'd find a trace of the passage of Lord Ufegat and his possessions but didn't wish to expect too much. It had been a long and wearying search, and in all honesty, he could find no end in sight.

They rode through the night sky, lit magnificently by a vast shimmering moon that almost made the brands and lamps redundant. Orkning called out when he found tracks to follow, and Leofric allowed him to set the pace, riding easy in his saddle as he peered into the grey light of dawn. It wasn't so much dark as dimmed, as though the sun were obscured with heavy cloud before a rainstorm. Through it, Orkning spotted tell-tale signs of other riders so that it was no great surprise to happen upon a make-shift camp just before the sun was due to rise again.

Leofric made no secret of his arrival, and yet none called to him or demanded to know his business. No, the men slept peacefully on, some arranged on the cart that carried Ufegat's furniture and worldly goods, and others on the floor. And yet there was no trace of Lord Ufegat or his captive.

"Wake them," he eventually barked, once he was sure the men were poorly armed and no threat to his small force. "Ask them where their master has gone?" Those sleeping around the fire were warriors while those on the cart were servants or slaves. It seemed that Ufegat had abandoned them all in his haste to be gone.

It was one of the slaves who woke first, terror on his face, but also a fierce intelligence.

"Force Lord Ufegat to release me into your service, and I'll tell you where he's gone." Orkning leered at the man as he made his demands, but judging from the state of his face, Ufegat was an unkind master, and Leofric hastily agreed to his request.

"He means to take him North. To York, where he was blinded by Eadric."

"How many men does he have with him?"

"Just three, and himself, his hound and his captive. They won't be travelling at night though. We're to follow on."

"When did he leave you behind?"

"Only late yesterday, I can't imagine they'll have made it far. Ufegat is a terrible rider."

"Is it true that Lord Alfred has been blinded?"

"Just in the one eye, My Lord. Ufegat wants him to see York before he takes all of his sight."

Leofric spat bile at the thought of Ufegat's desire for revenge but quickly turned to the waking warriors.

"This man is mine now," he said. "Keep him with you, but treat him well. I'll return for him when I've found Lord Ufegat. If I find him wounded or dead, you'll pay his wergeld, in full, and it will be that of a freeman, not a slave. Heed my words."

A sullen looking man nodded his agreement, and turned to glare at the offending slave, but left off quickly enough when Orkning jumped from his horse and offered him a cuff to the face.

"Do as Lord Leofric demands," he reinforced. "He has the power of the Regent behind him. You'll be punished, just as he said."

With the matter resolved, and having eaten and drunk what little they had with them, Leofric turned his horse to take the northern trackway. Surely he would find Lord Alfred that day? And surely, he'd still have one of his eyes.

. . .

Knowing that his prey was close, Leofric enticed his horse to greater and greater speed. They'd travelled a long way the previous day and night, but the animal had excellent stamina, as did all of the horses he owned. His men were cheered as well, and so they flew through the landscape as what darkness there had been retreated beneath the advance of the sun.

In almost no time at all, Orkning called that he could see men ahead, and Leofric kneed his steed to even greater speed. He wanted to find Lord Alfred, to find him well and send him home and he was genuinely concerned that should Ufegat realise he was being followed, he'd simply kill Alfred there and then. Only the fact that Ufegat's need for revenge was so intense gave him some sort of hope.

His horse galloped faster and faster toward the men, and only when he was within earshot did any of the small party even notice him. By then it was too late.

"Lord Ufegat," Leofric growled. "I've come for Lord Alfred. I demand you hand him over to my custody."

He could feel Orkning behind him, and the rest of his men adding their menace as well.

"Who is it?" Ufegat called, his tone querulous, but Leofric didn't look at the man he'd been chasing all this time, no his gaze was drawn to the prisoner amongst the men, for there was no doubt he was Lord Alfred.

He was unrecognisable even as a man, let alone as Lord Alfred. His face was beaten and a myriad of blues, purples and vivid greens. His clothes must have been those he'd come to England in all those months ago, but they were torn and ripped, and the smell that came from him was enough to wrinkle Leofric's nose even with the wind blowing from the other direction.

He had no cloak, but shivered in the breeze, licking his lips time and time again, which were cracked and bloodied, even his tongue had lost the pinkness of health and seemed brown and drab.

But it was his eyes that most horrified Leofric, and he gasped, and then swallowed his revulsion so that the poor man would not see his pity and dismay.

Lord Alfred had been blinded in one eye, and that eye had been plucked from his head, and the wound never treated. Puss oozed down the man's nose, without cease, and Alfred couldn't wipe it away because his hands were bound behind him. He rode a horse, but awkwardly and tears streamed down his face without ceasing, although he didn't seem to be crying.

"It's Earl Leofric, Ufegat. I've come to return Lord Alfred to his mother. I have the permission of Lord Harald, and your sister, to do so."

"Hah," the older man laughed, turning to face where he thought Leofric was, his nose up in the air as though he'd become hound-like, relying on his sense of smell to track people down. "My nephew has gifted Alfred to me. He's mine, and you'll leave us to travel on our way."

Already, Leofric had silently instructed Ælfgar and Orkning to take command of the abused man, and although Ufegat was unaware, neither did his warriors make any attempt to intervene. In fact, the man who'd held the lead rope for Alfred's horse seemed relieved to relinquish his hold on the animal. It appeared that Ufegat had repulsed even his own warriors with his thirst for revenge.

Orkning and Ælfgar had their instructions as soon as they had Lord Alfred under their command, but Leofric worried that Alfred would be unable to cope with the rigours of the ride. Instead, he called Ælfgar to him, while Ufegat continued to rant.

"Take him back to Peterborough" he spoke in little more than a whisper. "Ask the monks to heal him, do it slowly. I'll follow on soon. As soon as you're away from Ufegat, take him from his horse. Help him bathe in any available river or stream and redress him. Ensure he's kept warm, feed him what you can. The poor man is skin and bones and nothing else. I fear we're too late."

Ælfgar nodded. His cousin was a member of the community at

Peterborough. He'd ensure that, despite being deep within a territory that was traditionally loyal to Lord Harald and his mother, and Uncle, that Alfred would be tended to most carefully.

"What will you do with Lord Ufegat?" his son asked, but Leofric waved him away.

"Unbind his hands. Do what you can, and be careful with him. I'll sort out Lord Ufegat and then follow on. If you're approached by anyone, then ride to avoid them, and don't make eye contact. Keep yourself, and your uncle safe."

Realising the urgency of the situation, Orkning had already taken command of Alfred and was working to release the ropes that bound his hands, and all the while murmuring to the man.

Leofric didn't think they'd ever met before, but somehow, Orkning had dredged his memory for a time they both remembered, and the tears that flowed from Alfred's eyes were unceasing, although a smile of relief touched his broken face.

"I've commands that supersede your own," Leofric began, as Orkning and Ælfgar turned to leave with Alfred, and yet somehow, despite his lack of sight, Ufegat realised what was happening.

"He's my prisoner. You can't take him," he hollered, his hand reaching for a flashing seax at his waist, as he kneed his horse to where he thought Alfred might be. Leofric moved to intercept him, a hand on the other man's reins, while his remaining warriors watched on with a combination of rage and disinterest. None looked willing to fight for Ufegat though, and Leofric trusted to that.

Ufegat tried to stab at Leofric's hand, but he manoeuvred his horse out of the way.

"You have done enough Lord Ufegat. Enough, and it's over. You should be ashamed of yourself. You have no honour in torturing a man who has no allies to his name, a virtual stranger in England."

"I had the right to avenge my father's attack, by his father."

Leofric gazed into the unseeing eyes of Ufegat. He could easily understand the rage of a man who'd had his life's ambitions severely curtailed, but the cruelty he saw there dispersed his desire to understand easily.

"You would punish a man for a crime committed before he was even born? By a man, he has no clear memory of? What sort of man does that make you? You've eroded your own indignation, any sympathy that others might have toward you? And what for? Petty revenge? I think you've killed the man. I can't see how he'll ever recover from his injuries, not now. Your brutality disgusts me, and mark my word, you'll pay restitution on his death, to his mother."

"Oh fuck off with your righteous indignation," Ufegat snarled, yanking his horse's reins to dislodge Leofric's hands. "I'll tell Lord Harald of this, and he'll punish you for supporting the Queen Dowager over your rightful king."

"You can do what you want, Lord Ufegat. You always have. But it's you that will mean your nephew's kingship starts with the taint of blood on it."

"Hah," Ufegat growled. "Cnut's reign started with blood and didn't suffer for it."

"No, Cnut's reign started with an agreement forged from blood, an agreement between two men who both accepted that the other had a valid claim to rule England. It didn't start with what will be perceived as murder. And believe me, I'll ensure Lord Harald, and Earl Godwine's part in this is well known, as well as your own."

The conversation over, he turned to the men who accompanied Lord Ufegat.

"Take him back to his possessions, return him to Northampton, and guard him well. I'd not have Lord Harald worry about the safety of his Uncle, no matter the bastard he has become. Do this, and I'll speak highly of you, and try to dispel the stigma of your torture of Lord Alfred. Do this poorly, and I'll have you tried for your parts in this travesty of justice."

"My thanks, Earl Leofric," the man who'd been holding Alfred's reins spoke. "I'm grateful for your intervention. I only wish I'd been honour-bound enough to do the same."

Leofric grunted at the words but appreciated the sentiment. It was a poor man who didn't serve his commended man as he should, but not all commended men were genuinely worthy of another's oath. It had always been a tricky problem, and one he understood all the more now.

When Leofric next laid eyes on Lord Alfred, he had at least been washed and fed, for all he still looked not far from death. There were things that clean clothes, and a cleansed face could not hide, and more, there were new wounds and injuries that were revealed.

"My thanks, My Lord," Alfred stumbled, on seeing Leofric return to the small group of men who now protected him.

"Please don't thank me. I'm merely sorry that I was unable to rescue you earlier. You've been a victim of other men's ambitions and petty acts of revenge. I must apologise to you for that."

Lord Alfred nodded when Leofric spoke, but the movement was jerky; a man who wanted to believe he was safe but was still not sure.

"I'm Earl Leofric. It was my son and my brother-by-marriage who brought you here. I rule within Mercia, and yes, I'm a follower, and I was foster-father, of Lord Harald, but your mother asked for my help in finding you, and unlike Earl Godwine, I've no intention of slaughtering you and your men and handing you to an enemy."

The milky whiteness of Alfred's other eye, the whole one, was concerning Leofric, and he turned to look at Ælfgar to see what he had made of the situation. Alfred, sitting swallowed within a substantial black fur cloak, to try and drive some warmth back into his cold body, somehow detected the movement.

"I can see but a little," he offered, tears still pouring unheeded from both of his eyes. "They took the one eye, but Lord Ufegat said he wouldn't take the next one until we made it to York. Yet, I think it's infected because of the poor healing of the other eye. The world has been slowly going dark," Lord Alfred tried to joke, but it was a poor effort, the horrors of his captivity so evident upon his skinny and bleeding body and especially upon his distorted face.

"I have other wounds as well," he offered, almost unwillingly. "It hurts to ride, anywhere." Leofric nodded and then spoke realising Alfred might not detect the movement.

"We'll take you to the Abbey, near Peterborough. I have a nephew there who'll look to your care. We'll have monks heal you, and do all they can for your eye, and only then will I return and take you to Winchester. Would you prefer to lie down for the journey? We could source a cart. It wouldn't be a problem."

"If you could bind my ribs, tightly, I might be alright to ride," Alfred offered, touching his body gingerly beneath his cloak.

"Do we have any cloth?" Leofric called to Orkning, who was settling his horse, and seeing what could be done for the poor nag Alfred had been riding. The animal was in almost as poor condition as Alfred.

"There should be," Orkning said, his attention on the injured horse. "In my saddlebags. Ælfgar," he called, "can you find it?"

Hastily Ælfgar did as he was asked, and as Alfred removed his cloak and clean tunic, Leofric hissed in anger once more. It was clear he'd been wounded in the battle at Guildford, where his men had been killed, but the wound had gone untreated. It had healed now, poorly and an angry scar laced his back, and around it, the man's ribs showed through skin blackened and yellowed with bruises.

"Are you sure you want this strapping?" Leofric asked dubiously, knowing it would be painful almost beyond words, but Alfred nodded his jerky head.

"Yes, please. It'll ease me to know I'm held together."

"Do we have any wine?" Leofric asked his son, quietly, and Ælfgar nodded and went to his own saddlebags for the strong wine stored there.

"Here," Leofric said, placing a mug carefully into Alfred's waiting hands. "Drink this. Hopefully, it will dull the pain a little."

With shaking hands, Alfred took the mug and raised it, two-handed to his mouth, wincing all the time. He gasped with surprise at the strength of the wine on his cracked lips, but then drank hungrily, and immediately a small smile touched his lips.

"That's bloody strong," Alfred gasped, and Ælfgar laughed, his young face losing his horror-filled look.

"It certainly is. I'd recommend not drinking more than a mug full. The headache is not worth it," he shook his head ruefully, as Leofric looked on.

It was good to see his son trying to ease the other man's suffering, but Leofric couldn't help thinking it was too little, and it was far too late.

Hastily, he swept the cloth around Alfred's midriff, trying to be careful but also knowing that it would be no use unless it were pulled tight enough to stop the pain from riding the horse.

As he passed under Alfred's right arm and began to tighten the cloth, he heard Alfred gasp, and Ælfgar quickly leapt to grab the man who was stumbling where he stood, the pain, despite the strong wine, too much for him to bear.

Hastily, Leofric tightened the binding and then, while Alfred was only half conscious, helped dress him with the aid of his son, and then settled the deep cloak around his shoulders once more. Still, Alfred wobbled on his feet, and Leofric looked on with worry. He wanted to ensure Alfred's safety by returning him to Wessex and his mother, but he was too deeply wounded to move far, even getting him to the supposed safety of Peterborough Abbey might prove too much for him.

"We could let him rest," Orkning suggested quietly, and Leofric considered the option, as he gazed around him, taking the terrain and judging how exposed he truly was.

"I wish we could let him rest. But there are too few of us, should Lord Ufegat or Harald have a change of heart. We need to get to Peterborough, today."

"Then we should secure him to the horse. He can't ride unaided anyway, not with his eyes the way they are. That way, if he loses consciousness, he won't fall and hurt himself any further. I fear it would be too much for him to take."

"Do it," Alfred whispered through cracked lips, his hearing seeming to compensate for his lack of sight, his body trembling as Leofric and his son held him upright. "Get me to the monks. I must rest."

"Very well, do as he says," Leofric instructed, and between them, they managed to find a cord that was strong enough to strap Alfred into the saddle of one of the horses. It wasn't the animal that Alfred had been tied to before, when under the guard of Ufegat, but rather one of Leofric's healthier animals. It rode with a smoother gait, and benefitted from a broader back, and therefore saddle as well.

"My thanks," Leofric said to Godwulf who willingly traded his animal for the pack animal. They'd redistributed all of their supplies so that Alfred's previous mount, wounded as well as his rider, could travel unencumbered the rest of the party. Leofric spared a moment of pity for it. He could never understand the mistreatment of such animals. How could a man make money if his animal was lame? He hoped that the monks would take the animal in if he provided for its upkeep until it was well again. Even then, he hoped they'd keep the animal. It deserved a more rested future.

When everyone was ready once more, Alfred rocking unsteadily in the saddle, but somehow staying upright, Leofric instructed the men to move on. He feared he wouldn't rest easy until they were at Peterborough Abbey and Alfred was inside. Once there, he knew that his nephew, a novice, and sharing his name, would be able to ensure Alfred was treated well, while Leofric knew that a large donation would ensure their finest care for the man, and also, their absolute discretion.

He didn't want Ufegat to know where Alfred was. Not until he was fully healed and able to face the man who'd mutilated him and kept him in deprived conditions for so many months.

They finally arrived when it was entirely dark. The journey hadn't been perilous for any apart from Alfred, and he'd groaned for much of the final stages of it. Leofric knew that the suppressed cries of Alfred's agony would haunt him for many years to come.

Orkning had long ago lit a brand to light the dark path when the stately building came into sight. Leofric had visited before, calling on his nephew, and as such, he and all his men knew the correct way to gain admission.

Quickly, Orkning called to the gate warden, naming Earl Leofric, and the wooden gateway eased open. The Abbot, Ælfsige, promptly appeared.

"Earl Leofric," he questioned. "I trust all is well." He was an old man, in position for many, many years, even escorting Alfred and his brother and sister to Normandy when Swein had claimed England so many years ago. That knowledge had been forgotten about by Leofric when he'd made his decision to come here, but realisation had struck on the journey, and he knew, without doubt, that Lord Alfred would be double safe within the Abbey grounds.

His keen eyes quickly took in the horses, and then settled with dismay on the broken frame of Alfred, as something like recognition swept over him. Leofric, Ælfgar and Orkning were gently dislodging Alfred from the back of the horse.

"Good Abbot," Leofric began. "Please help this man, Lord Alfred. He's been a captive of Lord Ufegat for many months. He's been blinded and beaten, and we fear for his life."

"I know you," Abbot Ælfsige stumbled, reaching out with his hand to cup Alfred's slack face. "I know you," he repeated more quietly, quickly assessing the situation, and calling for men to summon the monk most skilled in healing. With shock on his face, he personally cleared the way to a small chamber, where they were finally able to pull off Alfred's cloak and ease him to a comfortable bed.

"The Queen Dowager's son," Ælfsige breathed, when candles had been lit, and he'd seen the full extent of his injuries. "I'd heard the rumours, but thought them nothing more than that."

"Unfortunately the rumours were true. I've been searching for him for months, and all the time he was hidden in Peterborough, under the command of Lord Ufegat."

Ælfsige lapsed into silence, as Alfred met his gaze. Recognition flashed there as well, and for the first time, Leofric saw Alfred genuinely realise that he was, indeed, safe. His shoulders relaxed, and he breathed out so deeply, Leofric could almost see where his stomach touched his back.

The monk who stepped into the room, a competent looking man of middle years, quickly bent to examine Alfred's eye, and his chest, although his face gave no hint of his concern. Bending to speak to Leofric's namesake, who had been summoned as well, he listed implements and herbs he needed and the young man, a glint and a gleam to his eye, strode off quickly. Ælfgar followed his cousin, as Leofric looked at the monk.

"Earl Leofric, this man is gravely ill. I'll not be able to save the sight in his other eye, but I'll do what I can. He should have been treated much sooner."

He didn't ask who Alfred was or offer any opinion as to his probable survival, and Leofric was grateful, although Ælfsige nodded as though he'd understood much more from the brief exchange.

Alfred gasped as his wounds were prodded and poked, but seemed just as comforted by the monk's soft words as he was by Ælfsige's presence.

"I'll leave you now, to the care of Brother Eadnoth and the Abbot. And my nephew will be with you, also named Leofric, and he'll summon me should you need me. My men and I will, with the Abbot's permission, will rest here tonight."

"My thanks, Earl Leofric," Lord Alfred gasped, and Leofric, seeing Alfred's wounds exposed before him once more, swallowed thickly. He silently berated himself for not finding Alfred sooner.

"Rest easy," Leofric tried to comfort but knew his words were useless. The survival of Alfred was far from anything he could command. Not now.

# 15
## AD1036

In the week that followed, Brother Eadnoth, and Abbot Ælfsige treated Lord Alfred with great care, and every day, he ate more and seemed more and more assured of himself. And yet, Leofric grew increasingly concerned, rather than less.

"Tell me truthfully, do you think he'll survive?" he was forced to ask Brother Eadnoth after a particularly confusing conversation with Alfred. Leofric had found his speech slurred, and his sentences made little sense.

"I can't answer that," Brother Eadnoth replied, his face earnest as he considered Leofric's question. "He seems to fluctuate between days when he's well and days when he's not. I believe it's the after-effects of the conditions he's endured. He tosses and turns all night and wakes fearful and crying out for either myself or your nephew. He is, despite what he says, not yet assured of his safety."

"So you think his recovery is being undermined because he's scared?"

"He's scared and also ill. His body needs much longer to recover, his mind may take years. I can tell you that he'll not be able to travel this year. Have you sent word to his mother?"

"No, I'd hoped to take him to her. But if you advise against him travelling, then I should do so. Only, I'll have to keep where he is a secret from her. She'll not like that."

"No, she probably won't, but you're wise to keep it a secret. We're not warriors here, and would be unable to mount any defence should Lord Ufegat seek him out again."

"Yet I can't stay here much longer. Even though I assured Lord Alfred of my protection, I must return to my duties as earl. I can't even tell my wife where I am for fear others come to know. As such, I can conduct no business from here."

"I can't give you the answer you seek, Earl Leofric. Lord Alfred can't leave here, that's all I know, and Peterborough can't protect him without you and your warriors."

"But it could protect him should some of my men remain here for the foreseeable future, provided, of course, that I sent supplies as well. Would that be acceptable?"

Brother Eadnoth shrugged at Leofric's words.

"You would need to consult with Abbot Ælfsige, but with your nephew here, that would be a valid reason for you to station men here, and provide food for the winter. Perhaps one of your brothers could even come in your place."

Leofric knew he couldn't remain in Ely indefinitely. He needed to ensure that Lord Harald wasn't acting too irrationally, and also that Earl Godwine hadn't managed to in-veil himself further into Harald's affections.

"I could leave my son here, with Orkning, his Uncle-by-marriage, and travel to Worcester, and then send more warriors in my place. Or," he thought out loud as he considered the alternatives, "I could have them meet me somewhere, with their supplies and then have them brought here by Ælfgar."

"That would work," Brother Eadnoth agreed. "It would be best if there was as little to draw the eye to Peterborough as possible."

"Yes, I agree. I'll speak to Abbot Ælfsige and also to Lord Alfred. I wouldn't want anything to happen that might delay his recovery further."

A further week passed while Leofric set his plan in motion. He spoke with Alfred but found him confused and frightened, and his worries grew for the preservation of the man's life. His sight, as Brother Eadhelm had predicted, had gone even in his remaining eye, and the tremors that Leofric had initially thought had been caused by the cold, had never abated.

What saddened Leofric most was that he could see past the ruin of the man to who he might once have been. He might well have lived all of his adult life as an exile from the English Court, but he had evidently been a man of means and patronage, honoured within the country of his mother's birth, and also in the country where his sister had married the Count.

He'd made a firm ally of Leofric's nephew, and his nephew often found him to tell him stories about Lord Alfred. Leofric was pleased by the friendship as much as he was saddened by it.

In the end, he asked his nephew and his son to speak to Alfred about his plans. Alfred was always more at ease with the two younger men, rather than the older. Leofric wondered if it was embarrassment on Alfred's behalf, after all, in another life, Leofric and Alfred might have been allies. Yet Lord Alfred had never married and had no sons to call his own, and no patrimony to bequeath any he might have had.

The two young men reported back to him that while Lord Alfred had some concerns, he was content with the arrangement provided he knew he was still well guarded. Abbot Ælfsige had also sworn to protect the man he'd once known as a child.

As such, when Leofric went to make his farewells, he found Alfred a changed man to the captive he'd finally tracked down over two weeks ago.

Not that Alfred had gained much weight, or had his eyesight returned to him, but he was clean, well-dressed, and more confident, for all that he still shook and jumped at strange and unexpected noises, as rare as they were in the house of prayer he lived within.

"Good day, Lord Alfred," Leofric greeted him before he entered the room where he lived. They'd quickly adopted the strategy when the full extent of Alfred's blindness had become apparent. It ensured Alfred always knew who was close to him.

"Come in, Earl Leofric," the slightly tremulous voice responded. "Please sit, and be welcomed."

Leofric smiled sadly at the courtly tone Alfred adopted and made a point of scraping the wooden chair a little as he settled himself. It was just another way of ensuring Alfred knew who was there and that he was not alone. In all honesty, he was never left alone. Abbot Ælfsige and Leofric were too concerned for his safety to allow him to wander unaided through even the Abbey grounds. Alfred, unused to both his freedom and lack of all sight, seemed to find the presence of others comforting.

"You've come to tell me that you're leaving Peterborough?" Alfred asked. His hands trembled as he spoke, and Leofric unconsciously leaned forward and gripped those hands between his own. The shaking disturbed him, but he also sought to comfort the injured man.

"I'll leave, yes, but my nephew will of course remain, and so will my son and Orkning. In my place, I'll send more of my household warriors to protect Peterborough and yourself until you're well enough to leave or choose to leave. I'll not desert you to Lord Ufegat again."

As he spoke, he watched Alfred's face carefully. This wasn't news to him. They'd talked of it before, but Leofric hoped to see acceptance on Alfred's face as opposed to the fear he'd previously witnessed.

"I understand," Alfred said, licking his lips nervously, but also ensuring his sightless face was turned toward Leofric. Alfred needed a shave, but in all honesty, the facial hair covered some of the tortures inflicted on his face, and as he didn't demand to be clean-shaven, Brother Eadnoth had allowed his beard and moustache to grow a little ragged. It almost made him handsome, and certainly made Leofric think of the older half-brothers he'd once known.

He couldn't imagine what the honourable Athelstan would have made of Alfred's capture and treatment. It would have gone against all of his ideals of what a warrior should be.

"I'd thank you again for rescuing me. It seems no others would have made an effort. But there's something I must tell you before you leave."

Leofric stilled at the ominous tone in Alfred's voice, the other man somehow sensing his unease.

"You do well to fear. But equally, if I should lose my life here, I can't take the secret to the grave with me."

Leofric nodded, and then coughed, to show he'd heard and understood.

"When Earl Godwine, or so I understand it was him, had me captive, I overheard him talking to someone else, someone he trusted, maybe his son or some such. He must have thought me asleep, or unconscious, but he spoke of a Magnus. It meant nothing to me at the time, but having listened carefully, I think he's important to this whole mess, isn't he?"

Leofric could feel his mouth opening in shock.

"What about Magnus?" he stumbled.

"So he is important then?" Alfred quested, and Leofric nodded once more and then shook his head at his constant forgetfulness.

"He's the King of Norway. He killed Lord Harald's brother in battle, or rather his regents did, and now holds Harthacnut in Denmark with his constant attacks."

"Well, from what I heard, I believe Earl Godwine is sending support to Magnus."

"But that makes no sense," Leofric said out loud, and Alfred nodded.

"I know. I've been trying to make sense of it as well, but that was what I heard. Definitely."

"Tell me exactly what you heard."

"The other person asked them if he were still to send the shipment to Magnus, and Godwine replied that he must. That this was just another part of the plan."

"But it's impossible if he supports your half-brother, Harthacnut?" Confusion laced Leofric's voice.

"I know, Earl Leofric. I know all that. But still, I share the information with you so that you can be wary of Earl Godwine. I don't think he's to be trusted, no matter what he says or does."

"I will bear that in mind," Leofric agreed, his mind trying to dismiss Alfred's words while accepting the logic of them. Earl Godwine was never one to place all of his eggs in one basket, and he and Leofric had long been uneasy allies and far more reliable enemies, the recent altercation only the last in a long line of such.

"And my mother," Alfred continued. "She's a wasp, never forget that. As much as I know you found me for her, she too only wants me for what she stands to gain. When I'm healed, if I heal, I might decide to travel straight home, to Normandy. Would that cause you difficulties?" Alfred's voice held some fear as he spoke those words, but Leofric grunted a quick answer.

"No, I found you because I didn't want you to be used in this complicated game of kingdoms and crowns. Your mother may have pushed me to find you, but I was already determined to prevent what she'd plotted. I know what a formidable woman she can be. I would happily escort you to Normandy, rather than Winchester. She and I have been allies and enemies, and now we seem to rub along as best we can."

"Then again, you have my thanks. I know I'm far from cured, and may never be 'cured', but if I'm to find my death in England, I should rather do so here, than as a captive of Lord Ufegat. For that, you'll always have my thanks, and I'll reward you in any way I can. Would it be acceptable for me to write to my brothers?"

The phrase caught Leofric by surprise, but then, perhaps he should not have been caught off-guard to discover that while Alfred may not have set foot in England for over twenty years, he was fully aware of his younger half-brother in Denmark, and his position there as king.

"It shouldn't be a problem. However, be mindful of the weather. The winter storms might delay your messages reaching their recipients for some time."

"My thanks again," Alfred said, struggling to his feet from his place beside the bed and the small brazier that always warmed the room. Alfred was never far from a thick cloak. He was cold even on days that Leofric cast off his own cloak and shunned a fire.

"I'll send supplies to the Abbey. I'll also leave you with this," into Alfred's hand, Leofric placed a heavy coin bag, which Alfred almost dropped. He felt it unnecessary to point out that the coins held the image of his half-brother, almost responsible for his death.

"You won't be able to send messengers to me, but should you find you need something, ask the Abbot or Brother Eadnoth and use the coin to settle the cost. I'll return, as soon as I can, and without arousing suspicion, but my men are the most loyal you'll ever find. They'll do nothing to endanger you."

With that Leofric clasped Alfred's forearm, mirroring the greeting of two warriors, and strode from the room.

He'd done all he could for Alfred, and still, he feared it would never be enough.

Rage bubbled below his inner calm. Lady Emma, Earl Godwine, Lord Ufegat and Lord Harald, even Magnus and Harthacnut. They all forgot they toyed with people's lives when they plotted and planned their futures.

It was one thing that Leofric could never understand, but then, his father had been known for his honour as well as his battle-glory, and it seemed, he was tainted with his father's perceived faults.

He was really rather proud of that.

# THE ANGLO SAXON CHRONICLE ENTRY FOR 1037

"This year Alfred the innocent etheling, son of king Ethelred (Æthelred), came in hither, and would go to his mother, who sat at Winchester ; but that neither Godwin the earl, nor the other men who had much power, would allow him because the cry was then greatly in favour of Harold, though that was unjust. But Godwin him then let, and tied in bonds set ; and his companions he dispersed and some divers ways slew; one they for money sold, some cruelly slaughtered, some did they bind, some did they blind, some did they mutilate, some did they scalp: nor was a bloodier deed done in this land since the Danes came, and here accepted peace. Now is our trust in the beloved God, that they are in bliss, blithely with Christ, who were without guilt so miserably slain. The etheling still lived, every ill they him vowed, until it was decreed that he should be led to Elybury, thus bound. Soon as he came to land, in the ship he was blinded; and him thus blind they brought to the monks : and he there abode the while that he lived. After that him they buried, as well was his due full worthily, as he worthy was, at the west end, the steeple well-nigh, in the south aisle. His soul is with Christ."

# 16

## EARLY AD1037

Leofric cursed as he rode. What was it about the bloody Danish and their children that prevented them from carrying out critical political events in the heat of the summer?

It was so cold, he'd not heard the trickle of water once on his journey, and each time they'd wanted to water the horses, they'd been forced to break the ice over the small brooks and rivers they'd traversed. It was no time of year to be travelling, even if it was a coronation that Leofric had helped organise and plan, and one that he should have exulted in.

After all, he was fulfilling the oath that Cnut had extracted from him, and despite his disappointment in Lord Harald about his treatment of Alfred, he couldn't wholly blame him. No, the ultimate blame lay with the Queen Dowager, and then with Earl Godwine. If Harald and his Uncle had taken advantage of their stupidity, he could hardly fault them for falling prey to human frailties.

The news from Peterborough was poor. His son had returned for Christmas with his family, bringing reports of Alfred's continued poor health, and then Orkning had returned only a few weeks ago.

He'd taken Leofric to one side and warned him that Brother Eadnoth said it was merely a matter of time.

Alfred's blinded eye had become repeatedly infected, and nothing they tried stopped the infection from returning. And still, Alfred remained scrawny, having only a small appetite. Brother Eadnoth had concluded that the bruising to his chest and midriff actually masked a more devastating injury inside his body that made digestion difficult. Orkning had carried a letter from Alfred to his mother, which Leofric had sent on to her. Her entreaties for news of her son had quietened once she'd known he was rescued, and alive, although her rage at Leofric's continuing secrecy had not gone down well.

He found he little cared for her fits and rages now. She'd been wrong to encourage Edward and Alfred to return to England, and Alfred was going to pay the ultimate price.

As to Lord Ufegat. Rumour had reached him that the man had fallen ill shortly after Leofric had taken Alfred from his care. He'd died not long before Christmas, and Harald and his mother had mourned their Uncle. Leofric doubted that anyone else had. But, his death had come in Northampton, and Leofric couldn't be blamed for it. That pleased him greatly.

What had relieved Leofric was the fact that neither Lord Harald nor Lady Ælfgifu had demanded to know what he'd done with Alfred. It seemed they were content to know that the matter had been handled. For the time being. Leofric hoped it also meant he'd not be inadvertently punished for going against his new king's wishes.

And still, he'd spent much of his time considering Lord Alfred's words to him. How likely was it that Earl Godwine was secretly supporting Magnus of Norway? It made little sense to him, as the current situation stood, and yet earl Godwine was evidently keen to preserve his power and prestige. He'd turned his back on Lady Emma, or so it appeared with the killing of Lord Alfred's small force and the handing over of Alfred to Lord Harald, it didn't seem too much of a push to think that he might also have decided to abandon his support of Harthacnut as well.

He'd once manipulated the Queen Dowager to ensure his continued position, and for all that Cnut had tried to deprive him of that position once the truth was known, Cnut's final illness had robbed him of his abilities to fulfil his desire to get rid of Earl Godwine. Leofric also knew now that Earl Godwine had held another secret over the king, one that Cnut had died protecting.

Magnus of Norway was a young boy who had the support of two powerful regents, Einar and Kalf. Although he was not his father's wife child, being illegitimate, he also had the support of Astrid Olofsdottir, sister of the King of Sweden, Jakob Anund. Leofric, no matter how hard he tried, could fathom no reason for Godwine to support Magnus. Surely, owing so much of his wealth, and indeed his family to the Danish kingdom, he must support Harthacnut, and not a man who'd always looked to undermine Cnut and had battled him at the Holy River, almost successfully.

Leofric had considered the possibility that Earl Godwine had deliberately spoken so openly in front of the captured man. He might well have assumed that Lord Harald would question Lord Alfred, rather than hand him onto Ufegat. Perhaps he'd hoped that Alfred would blurt out the information and earn Earl Godwine even more respect from Lord Harald, as he moved to take the kingship of England.

His brother rode at his side. He'd been mostly silent on the journey to Oxford, and Leofric knew he needed to question him. It was unlike his brother to stay his tongue, and that worried Leofric more than if he'd rumbled on about his worries.

Eadwine was a powerful lord in his own right in the counties where he owned land, but Leofric suspected his reticence was concerned with problems in Shropshire. The county where Eadric Streona had once been so powerful shared a long and jagged border with the Welsh kingdoms. Whenever England faltered, the Welsh tried to take advantage, and Leofric feared that war would come.

When it did, he and his brothers, and maybe even his son, would have to stand with the fyrd of Mercia.

Leofric would caution his brother to begin mediation with the men of Gwynedd, but as the more peaceful member of the family, Leofric thought he would already have tried as much. Perhaps Eadwine feared war was inevitable. Despite his family's long-standing alliance with the kingdoms of Gwynedd and Powys, Gwynedd had grown bold of late. But one thing at a time, he had the coronation to attend, and then, he knew he would have to face King Harald, and no doubt, his king wouldn't be alone.

He was pleased to arrive at his home in Oxford, and even happier when the ceremony got underway the next day. Presided over by Archbishop Ælfric of York in the face of the Archbishop of Canterbury's continuing preference for Harthacnut, the ceremony was as cold as Leofric remembered the Witan that had made Harald, regent over the North of England.

For all the splendour of the glowing candles, shimmering outfits, clothing of gold and polished gems that glittered on King Harald and Lady Ælfgifu, none of those things dispelled the bone-numbing chill that permeated the church, even with braziers liberally littered around the vacuous building.

While Leofric appreciated that it was imperative Harald be crowned as soon as possible, he couldn't help spending much of the ceremony wishing it had been done in the summer months. But then, Harald hadn't gathered the support he needed in the summer; it had only come in recent months, with the acceptance of all that Harthacnut had no intention of coming to England.

Once Harald had been anointed, raised above all those within the church, even the Archbishop himself, and given his holy items of sceptre, ring, rod and crown, Leofric was the first to bend his knee to his new king.

He did so with an aching back, shivering knees, and a face bleached of all colour apart from the black of his eyes and the faint pink of his lips.

As he said the words of commendation, uttered before to Harald's father, Cnut, he felt a monumental shift in the way he felt. He had striven to do as Cnut had commanded him to and had almost been happy to promote Harald, his foster-son, over Harthacnut. Only the distasteful business with Lord Alfred had forced him to reconsider whether Harald was the right choice or not. But really, there was little to be done. With Harthacnut supposedly fighting for the survival of Denmark, England needed a ruler of its own. And now it had one.

He only hoped that Harald proved to be a fair ruler, as his father had been, and one he could be proud to serve.

Harald accepted his commendatory oath with a wry smile on his face. Despite the cold, and probably because he wore a cloak thick enough to shelter three or four from the wintry conditions, he seemed none the worse for the extended period of time spent within the Church, and was determined to enjoy his triumph.

Outside the Church, Leofric knew that the people of Oxford were waiting to greet their new king, just as they'd once waited to pay their respects to the old one in Winchester. He couldn't quite understand their fascination but hoped they stayed warm in the freezing conditions.

When Leofric turned away from King Harald, he felt eyes on his back and caught Lady Ælfgifu glaring at him. She might well have pointed him in the correct direction to find her brother and Lord Alfred, but it seemed she was far from happy about it. Despite their on-going alliance, their relationship was still too often prickly to be comfortable. She'd not even taken the opportunity to thank him for his care of Harald while she'd presided over Norway. It was as though she resented Leofric's involvement in her son's life.

After Leofric, it was the turn of Earl Siward to make his oath to his new king, and he did so quickly, and loudly enough for all to hear his words. His deep voice filled the church in a way akin to the churchmen themselves.

Then it was the turn of Earl Godwine, and despite himself,

Leofric was overly keen to see how his new king respected him. Leofric had been favoured with a smile, Siward with a wink, what would Earl Godwine get?

The other statesman made his way quickly to the enthroned king, Leofric strongly reminded once again of the resemblance between Harald and his father. They shared the same eyes, the same gaze, if not the quick temper and desire to appease. That desire to appease was missing from King Harald that day. He greeted Earl Godwine with the stony gaze of someone doing something distasteful and Leofric wished, for a long moment, that he could also see Godwine's face as he stared at his king, for an overly long amount of time, before taking to his knee and bowing his head.

The words he spoke, the commendatory oath, were muttered too low even for Leofric to hear, and he sat in the first row of seats, as befitted his rank. A fleeting glimmer of fury seemed to settle in King Harald's eyes at the dishonourable action before he seemed to remember himself and settled to his unruffled calm once more.

When Earl Godwine stood, an icy atmosphere had swept through the church, which, overlaid with the prevalent too cold temperature, seemed to suck much of the joy from the coronation.

As Earl Godwine returned to his seat, head bowed, and eyes focused only on where his feet were taking him, Leofric heard the angry hiss that came from Lady Ælfgifu. At that moment he knew that he had nothing to fear from his new king, nothing at all, because King Harald, despite everything, already had a powerful enemy in the form of Earl Godwine.

Once more, Leofric considered the information that Lord Alfred had given him, regarding Godwine sending support to King Magnus of Norway and his regents. Somehow, it was becoming less and less far-fetched the more time went on.

After Godwine, it was the turn of Earl Hrani and Eilifr to give their oaths, Godric as well, another from the beginning of Cnut's reign who'd recently refound favour with King Harald, and then it was the turn of the holy men and women to give their oaths to the new king. Then the thegns, kings-thegns and members of his inner circle of advisors and the men who formed and would form, the royal scriptorium all came forward. All in all, the ceremony took the best part of the late winter's day, and Leofric emerged into the late glow of wintry afternoon, unable to feel his toes or his fingers.

He worked all of his digits within his gloves and his boots but felt only a spark of pain as he did so. Cursing, he stamped his feet and shook his hands, desperate to recover the feeling before it became even more painful.

The crowd, so keen when Harald had arrived that morning, had been put off by the freezing rain that had fallen for much of the day, whipped into a frenzy by strong winds, and few still lined the pathway the King had taken. Those who remained were the ones with nowhere else to go, beggars who were desperate for any coin the King and his nobility might scatter.

Leofric took pity on the pinched faces and called his son to him.

"Take them to the palace, find them somewhere warm to settle, and ensure they're fed. It would be inauspicious to have men and women fall dead on the day of the King's coronation."

Ælfgar grimaced a little at his task, but set to it quickly, driving the few who remained, no more than twenty, like a flock of sheep in front of them. Leofric watched them go sorrowfully. He knew there would be many stories these people could tell, but right now he just needed to see that they were fed, warm and safe. Once that was accomplished he would see about finding them more permanent homes, even if they were slaves within them. Anything had to be better than having no roof over your head when the weather was so inclement.

More and more people poured from the Church, but Leofric held back. He'd long ago learned the art of being the last to leave such gatherings. It was amazing how many chose to plot as soon as one event was concluded. The relentless grind of political manoeuvrings never ceased to disturb Leofric. He already knew that the next difficulty would arise from arranging a marriage for King Harald.

Now that he was king, people needed to know who would be king after him. Many, including Leofric himself, had taken risks in supporting Harald. They needed to see that it hadn't been in vain. Already, Leofric knew there was concern about what the next news from Denmark would bring. After all, while Harald had command of his father's ship-army in England, Harthacnut had control of the Danish ship-army. Should the threat from the thirteen-year-old King of Norway abate, most assumed that Harthacnut would turn toward England. Leofric didn't share that worry. Not since Orkning had been to Denmark.

Norway and Sweden were very much out of contention for Harthacnut. They weren't so much allied against Denmark, as roughly allied between themselves. Neither country wanted to return to the subjugation of Denmark. Jakob Anund of Sweden had long lived only to thwart Cnut's ambitions. Skane was gone once more from Danish rule, returned to Jakob.

As Leofric stood and waited, he watched his brother, Eadwine, walk past him, seemingly without seeing him, so engrossed was he in conversation with another of the men who held land in Shropshire. Leofric watched him go with a slight twinge of worry. He really needed to speak to the king about events on the border. He wondered if Earl Siward shared his concerns about the borderland with the land of the Scots.

It had been some years since Malcolm had been driven back by Cnut and his army. He was long dead, and a new, very young king, had much to prove to his people and nobility. Attacking England was always the easy option for a quick outcome, especially one overawed by an over-mighty subject.

More and more people trailed past, Leofric wondering how they could bear to linger in the cold church. Although he smirked, he was standing aside doing precisely the same.

Earl Godwine tumbled from the church, surrounded by three of his older sons, their names a blur for Leofric, but he watched them carefully while pretending to examine the heavy sky above their heads. Earl Godwine looked thunderous, while one of his son's tried to speak to him, earnestness washing from the younger man who shared his father's features so intimately. One of the other sons looked merely cold and bored, while the remaining glared at all who took too much of an interest in his father and brother. Leofric only just avoided a murderous glare when he was distracted by Earl Eilifr calling his name.

Leofric beckoned the man closer, surprised by the worry evidenced in the crumbled lines on the older man's face. They'd spoken of this moment before, but it seemed that Eilifr was still concerned by the prospect of Harald as king, even though he'd sworn his oath and given his word to support him as king.

"I have news," he whispered, his bearded face close to Leofric, for all it looked as though they merely spoke of small matters. Eilifr had sworn to share all the news he could from Norway and Denmark when they'd last met, but since then, there had been very little to report.

"King Magnus grows ever stronger. He's a true warrior, as his father was before him, and the people love him for his battle craft and piety, even though he is really still a boy. The stories I hear remind me of Cnut himself as a child."

Leofric nodded. This wasn't news to him. He'd heard the same from Bovi and Orkning. Still, he was curious enough to know what else Eilifr had unearthed, to stand and listen. He could, at least, feel his toes now, if not yet his fingers.

"My nephews inform me that Harthacnut is being urged to make terms with Magnus. The people of Denmark don't want war. They want their king to settle down, produce an heir, and then go to war if need be. They say it interrupts their trading to the land of the Rus, and many have been forced to turn inland, to where Harthacnut's sister is honoured as the wife of the future Holy Roman Emperor. They don't wish to pay taxes for a war that disrupts trade they now have to seek elsewhere."

"What else do your nephews say?" Leofric asked. While Eilifr might hold little power in his own right in England now, despite his title as Earl, his nephews, and their mother, the sister of Cnut, were very powerful in Denmark itself. Leofric understood that they'd assisted Harthacnut as he'd learned to rule, and now Harthacnut rewarded them for their loyalty. Leofric assumed, should Harthacnut ever come to England, that he would leave one or other of his cousins as his regent in Denmark, his aunt as well.

Still, there was a severe enough family rift, that Eilifr had been forced to return to England when Cnut's sister had married the Duke of Normandy, a very short-lived marriage, and now he waited for a chance to return to Denmark. Leofric hoped the man got his wish. The extent of his patronage and reach had shrunk in the years he'd been gone from England, and now he seemed like a man without resources and wealth.

"They say Harthacnut will exact revenge on his half-brother when he does come to England. This coronation is not the beginning that Harald might hope it is. I fear Harthacnut will interpret it more like the first act in a war for the kingdom of England."

Leofric sighed to hear that but also understood it. Bovi, and others who'd been to Denmark, Norway and Sweden since Cnut's death, offered him the same warnings. Some were offered in far less conciliatory phrases.

Should anything befall Harald, Leofric knew that Harthacnut would punish the people of England. That was why Lord Alfred's request to contact his brother had so touched Leofric. He'd agreed to his request without thinking through any possible consequences, and now he found he little cared. If Alfred recommended any of the people of England to his brother, Leofric hoped it would off-set some of Harthacnut's anger.

"What do you plan on doing?" Leofric asked Eilifr, and the other man shrugged.

"I thought to seek out Lady Estrid. After all, she was once married to my brother."

"You would do better to go straight to your nephews," Leofric cautioned. Lady Estrid was very much her brother's sister. She'd be slow to forgive any perceived slight done her by Eilifr, and rumour had it, she still smarted from her rejection by her second husband, the Duke of Normandy, dead now.

"Appeal to the young men. Clearly, they already respect you. And Eilifr, whatever you do, go with care. Family feuds are different from fighting for kingdoms."

Eilifr's eyes lit at Leofric's words.

"Is this how you think of it all?"

"I try not to, but yes, in the end, much of our current predicament boils down to a family feud. Cnut, for all that I respected him as our King and the Emperor of the North that he hoped to be, should have done more for all of his sons, and those of his wife's sons. Much of this…mess, could have been avoided had he done so. He once promised to divide his Empire among his sons. He should have followed through with that ideal. Brothers will not easily be subjected to each other."

"I suspect the King thought there would be more time."

"I do as well, but in the end, he was, and it pains me to say it, a coward. He should have stood up to his wife, and to Earl Godwine, and even to Harthacnut. He made Swein King of Norway, he made Harthacnut King of Denmark, it seems only right that Harald had his own kingdom, as Cnut had promised him."

"Hah," Eilifr barked. "You've always had clarity for distilling problems that others fail to grasp. I wish you well, Earl Leofric." With that Eilifr allowed himself to be swept away with the dwindling crowd of people dispersing from the church. Leofric spared him a further thought, before meeting the arresting gaze of Lady Gunnhildr.

He bowed toward her, but only hard eyes returned his greeting, and so he turned away, only for her to speak his name.

"Lord Leofric, it is, as ever a pleasure to see you. Where is your wonderful wife?"

Leofric suppressed a grimace at her words. His wife was no fan of

Lady Gunnhildr. At her side, he noticed a young woman, not much older than her own son, who he took to be her daughter.

"She's gone on, with my brother, Lord Eadwine. She doesn't much like the cold."

"Ah well, the weather is always a concern for you English," Gunnhildr growled, and Leofric felt his eyebrows rise in surprise. The Danish nobility was fond of reminding the English of what 'true' winter felt like in the dark lands of the far north.

"Is this your daughter?" he asked, trying to turn the conversation away from any further slights, and the girl looked pleased to be mentioned until Gunnhildr pinched her arm and tried to shield her with her own body.

"She'll marry a good Danish man," Gunnhildr spat, and all traces of her reason for singling out Leofric seemed to disappear from her mind as she marched her daughter away. Leofric laughed at the small scene. He wasn't looking for a wife for his son. He thought his son might just have found one for himself, or so his wife had warned him.

"I'd thank you not to laugh at my wife," a large man said, standing too close to Leofric for comfort. Leofric looked into the smirking face of Harold, son of Earl Thorkell.

"Harold, well met," Leofric said, holding his arm out to clasp the other man's forearm. The son of Earl Thorkell shared few of his father's characteristics, but the size was one of them. He towered over many of the men, and Leofric had to strain to meet his eyes.

"A strange business," Harold continued. "My wife is adamant her daughter will marry a Dane. I don't see the problem myself, with a good English boy, but then, I'm not the girl's father, and so I've learned to hold my tongue."

"I don't blame you," Leofric consoled. "I didn't even mention it, and she took great umbrage."

"Ah, she will. She thinks this war with Denmark, or rather with Harthacnut, has been dreamt up just to delay her plans to find the girl a husband."

"Would she not even accept the king?" Leofric asked, more by way of a joke than anything, but Harold's face immediately soured.

"Certainly not the king. She predicts that Harthacnut will launch an invasion on England and that Harald will only have a short-lived kingship."

"And what do you think?" Leofric asked, sobering at the bluntly spoken words.

"I think Cnut should have been more careful where he put his cock," the large man laughed at his crass humour. "Fewer sons, and certainly, fewer wives, would have made Cnut a man with a more lasting legacy. I fear that King Harald will face many trials, and I've no idea if he'll survive or not. In the meantime, I confess, I've made some enquiries about returning to Denmark. It might be safer for a Danish man to live in his home country than in England, should war come."

"You'd leave England?"

"I would prolong my life. My father's name means a great deal more to the Danish and the Norwegians than it does to the English."

As they spoke, they'd begun to drift with the very tail-end of the congregation from the Church, but Leofric still occasionally glanced behind him, and so he saw Lady Ælfgifu leave the church, her surviving brother at her side, Wulfhead, and also another woman, who Leofric squinted to recognise. Beside them all a pretty woman walked, her face pinched with cold, her hands beneath her cloak, where Leofric thought she must hug herself for warmth.

The group walked quickly and were soon past Leofric and Harold, who now spoke of small matters of Mercia rather than kingdoms and family feuds.

"Who's that woman?" Leofric asked, and Harold craned to look.

"That's Lady Eadgyth."

"Ah," Leofric muttered, he was right to think the girl was who he thought she was. But he would wait. At some point, his son would need to speak to him of his intentions. When he did, he could see no value in denying the marriage. It would be a good one between his son and Ælfgifu, daughter of Morcar, the thegn killed by Earl Eadric on King Æthelred's orders so many years ago.

How muddled the world of politics could become.

As he'd expected, his king called him to his side during the coronation feast. When all were drinking and eating, and a festive atmosphere had reduced the inhibitions of all, Leofric made his way to Harald's side.

Harald was grinning from ear to ear, a delicate wine goblet in one hand sloshing its contents all over the floor. The hall was lit with hundreds upon hundreds of candles, and the smell of wine, mead, ale and meat hung heavy in the air, all combining to give Leofric a headache.

The days of his boyhood overindulgence were long gone. He much preferred to sip a small quantity of wine and watch. His wife had long left his side, to mingle with Lady Ælfgifu and toast her triumph. Leofric had been quietly speaking with Orkning and, earlier in the evening, Earl Siward. He could see that many others wished to bend his ear, but he was determined to do as little politicking as possible until he'd had the opportunity to speak to King Harald.

It was somewhat of a relief to mount the short wooden stairs and settle beside Harald. The king had been eating with his mother, and his remaining uncle, but now they had left him so that he could disperse his patronage on those he most favoured.

"Ah, Earl Leofric," Harald called, his face flushed and his eyes struggling to focus. "My ally and conscience, all rolled into one, and that's before I mention foster-father," Leofric winced at the harsh tone, and was determined to brazen out any unhappiness his new king might wish to fling his way.

"My mother is most unhappy with you," Harald continued, "but then, she's disappointed with all men, blaming them for every ill that befalls the world." He paused to drink more wine and then swayed his goblet in front of his own face.

"Uncle Ufegat died, you know."

"I heard, My Lord King. My sorrow for your loss."

The king hiccupped as he laughed. "My thanks, but it was for the best. He was a sour old devil, who found no enjoyment in anything as he aged. We were once close, but he placed too many demands upon me."

"Then my apologies for reminding you of him," Leofric mollified. It seemed his new king was already keen to distance himself from the Uncle responsible for the wounds inflicted upon Lord Alfred. Leofric held his disdain in check. He'd instead respect a man who admitted to his shortcomings.

"Indeed," Harald said, sobering as he leant forward on his knees, and faced Leofric squarely.

"I'd thank you for supporting me, for doing all you have for my Regency and my kingship, but I don't understand your need to interfere in the matter of Lord Alfred. Explain it to me. I would understand why my foster-father interfered."

Leofric had been expecting the question for a long time. He thought Harald already knew the answer, after all, he'd greeted him by calling him his 'conscience'.

"Your father's reign began in blood and the loss of life – my own brother was a victim of your father's insecurities. I'd rather you weren't tainted in the same way."

"But my father was a great King of England, Emperor of the Northern Empire no less."

"Yes, he became just that. But it seems to me his reign was always cursed because of it."

"Cursed, in what way?"

"Look at his empire now, Harald. Where is it? It's fallen to pieces. None shall resurrect it, not now, and not when you and your brothers can't be allies or even friends. No, I don't wish your reign to begin with the same taint as your father's, and so I intervened or at least tried to. Earl Godwine isn't to be trusted, even your father didn't trust him in the end. The Queen Dowager is not to be trusted, and whether you are to be trusted remains to be seen."

Harald's eyes widened at the slight, but then he smiled, a lazy thing that slipped across his ale slack face.

"You speak your mind. I like that."

"It is always better to be honest," Leofric retorted, thinking of the times he'd despaired of his father's blunt honesty when dealing with men of politics, and also of the times he'd berated Harald and Ælfgar when they'd both lived under his roof.

"It may be. But some kings prefer men who pander to them," Harald continued.

"Those are the kings who are weak like King Æthelred was. He liked men who only ever agreed with him. It's better to have at least one voice that will question you. It makes more honest men of us all. I hoped I'd taught you that."

"And you have that voice?" Harald goaded, perhaps stung by the possible comparison with Æthelred, the man who'd killed his grandfather, blinded his Uncles and made his mother bitter.

"I've always had men who speak to me as they see fit. It's not dishonourable of them to do so. I'd sooner men told me I was a fool than waited for me to become a fool and then say, 'I told you so.'"

Harald furrowed his brow.

"You think me a fool?"

"Of course not," Leofric allowed a small smile onto his face. "I think you're wise enough to know that you must have those who speak against you. I believe that's why you've given me my voice to use as I must, to protect Lord Alfred."

"You flatter me now," Harald jibbed angrily, but Leofric shook his head.

"I never flatter, My Lord King. I speak when I must and hold my tongue only rarely. Surely you know that. You lived with me for four years!" Leofric allowed incredulity to flood his voice. He looked at the young man before him, seeing the angry, and often violent youth who'd been thrust into his hands by his overly ambitious mother and father.

He'd pitied Harald then, and sometimes he still did. He'd never had the sort of childhood that Leofric prided himself on giving Ælfgar, and the four years they'd had together had been turbulent, and too short to undo the harm done by Ælfgifu and Cnut. But that hadn't stopped him from trying.

He prided himself now on helping Harald see the way a man should act, and worried when Harald reverted to his former self. His foster-son was fiercely loyal to his mother and his Uncles, and that sometimes extended beyond the range of his family, but not always. Not that he always liked his family. Loyalty and affection were two different things for Harald.

Harald sighed heavily, rubbing his face in his left hand as he did so.

"We must reach some sort of agreement about Lord Alfred. About how we present your meddling in the matter."

"There's no need, provided he lives. It is if he dies that I worry."

"He might die?" Harald winced, looking up quickly and gazing into Leofric's face as though hoping he lied.

Now Leofric sighed heavily. "The news is poor. There is an infection that won't heal. Every day I expect to hear the news that he's dead."

"From where?" Harald jibbed, but Leofric shook his head. There were some secrets that he'd never share with his foster-son. Not while the relationship was so rocky.

"From where he feels safe," Leofric admonished softly, and Harald nodded again, and swallowed thickly.

"I always loved my Uncle Ufegat. I owed him a debt, and I tried to pay it."

"Yes, but you shouldn't have done. I think you know that now. It takes a brave man to admit he's been wrong," Leofric cautioned, holding his hands up to ward off the fury that had briefly sheeted his king's face.

"I would send funds to the monastery, make reparations," Harald said, his rage controlled by pure force of will.

"All in good time," Leofric argued. "Too soon and it will be interpreted badly. We must simply wait, see what happens. Not that I think we will need to wait too long."

"And the Queen Dowager?" Harald grumbled. "What should be done with her?"

"I think no one would argue with banishment. It's actually Earl Godwine who's the more problematic."

"Ah, Earl Godwine is obedient," Harald said, waving his hand and dismissing the topic too quickly for Leofric's liking. "I have him by the balls. He needs to do as I command or he knows he'll lose all."

"Yes, but your father had the same relationship with him, and look how that ended."

"My father relied on Earl Godwine. I don't. He relies on me. A subtle distinction, I know, but one my father never truly understood. The Danish earls, Hakon, Hrani, Eilifr, even bloody Ulfr, knew their advancements relied exclusively on my father's goodwill. Godwine has always been far more devious."

Leofric held his tongue, impressed by Harald's insight.

"So you believe you have him contained?"

"For now I do. Time, as you said about Lord Alfred, will reveal the truth of the matter."

Leofric was about to say more, but he saw his son in the crowd, trying to catch his attention, and behind him, he saw the figure of Orkning, and his heart sank.

He swallowed thickly, as Harald peered into the crowded hall to see what arrested their conversation.

"Ah," was all Harald said. "It seems that time has run out for Lord Alfred." He winced as he spoke, his face devoid of all the rosiness the alcohol had placed there.

"Go," Harald said, "inform the Queen Dowager, banish her, but," and here Harald paused and considered his next words and Leofric thought they might well be consolidatory, but he was wrong to hope.

Harald's voice was hard when he spoke again, anger replacing any temporary sorrow. "Tell her she's never to return to England while I rule. And tell her, it was all Earl Godwine. He acted on his own initiative. I'll not be blamed for what's happened. Now go," he grumbled, and Leofric bowed himself away from his foster-son, sorrow guiding his steps as he sought our Ælfgar and Orkning.

Just for a moment, he'd thought Harald the man he'd long hoped he'd be, able to accept his own flaws and mistakes, to make reparations for actions that were impossible to change.

It seemed he'd been wrong.

He sighed. He knew his father's constant sorrow then.

# 17
## AD 1037

His heart was heavy, but he knew his duty.

Dismounting from his fine mount, he trod a path toward the Queen Dowager's home. It was a pleasant enough building, he decided, but it would not be hers after their meeting.

He'd come to inform, but also to warn, and he prayed that the woman who'd variously hated him and relied on him for much of the last few years, had the intelligence to understand his words, and to heed them.

Leofric had told himself not to pity her. But it was impossible.

He might have managed to gain from Harald's promotion to the kingship of England, but the cost had been too high for him, the price of Lord Alfred's life far too much, the Queen Dowager too ambitious for her own good.

The Queen Dowager had been abandoned, by almost everyone. She was alone, without a single friend within England, and only his sense of deep-seated duty to his father's memory guided his steps now, that and the knowledge that in a similar situation he would have hoped someone would have had the honour to do as he did now.

His presence so far had gone without notice, but he was unsurprised. He'd insisted on coming alone, and why would the sound of one horse make the Queen Dowager jump from whatever task currently consumed her attention?

Lifting his arm, he rapped on the smooth wooden doorway, turning away as he did so. He wanted to be recognised first so that he'd not have to witness the dawning realisation on her face.

He wasn't a coward, but this he couldn't face seeing.

A scurry of movement at his back, and a sharp inhalation heard on the crisp morning air, told him all he needed to know. Turning he caught sight of the Queen Dowager standing behind the servant who'd actually opened the door, and he bowed his head.

Her eyes were frantic, the understanding clear to see, and yet shock kept her rooted to the spot.

"May I enter?" he asked. "I'm Earl Leofric," he added for the servant's benefit, although it seemed hardly necessary.

The servant moved away from the door so that he could slide inside, but Lady Emma hadn't even blinked. Sorrow swamped him.

He'd never lost a child, only a brother, a mother and a father, and he knew the grief would be intense. Without hesitating, he dropped to his knee, his head bowed before a woman he'd always known as queen, aside from the last two years, and even then, it was an effort to remember to call her queen dowager.

She was owed his respect even though he brought terrible news.

He stayed in position, waiting for her to acknowledge him, aware of a flurry of activity around him. The Queen Dowager may not have moved, but her few servants had. Still, he waited. He could not offer his respect and then snatch it back just because she made him wait an overly long amount of time.

Eventually, he felt a hand on the crown of his head and knew to stand.

Her face held understanding, even acceptance, but he wasn't sure for which of the two messages he carried. She might think him on an errand for King Harald. She might, for all he knew, know the truth of the matter already. He suspected that she knew. She wasn't stupid.

"Earl Leofric," she managed to stutter.

"Queen Dowager," he replied, offering her title for one final time.

She winced at his words, and he regretted them but couldn't retract them.

"You're an errand boy now for King Harald?" she scorned, and he swallowed his immediate angry retort. She wasn't to know what he'd endured to be here now.

"I come from King Harald, yes, but there's also more."

"The King would banish me?" she asked, turning away from Leofric so that he was forced to trail her to the seat before the hearth where she and her women had been stitching and repairing clothing. He found the mundanity of the task both jarring and comforting. He'd come to speak to the Queen Dowager, but he'd demanded the role because she was also a woman and a mother, and for that, she deserved the respect he would have accorded his own mother.

The fact that she spoke of the King before she did her son was more telling than anything else. Whatever Leofric had come to tell her about her son, it seemed she would rather put off the news, concern herself instead with King Harald's plans for her.

"The King requests that you cease your meddling," Leofric confirmed, standing before the gaggle of women, and wishing they'd move away. "Banishment is too strong a word. You should think of yourself more as exiled, for your own safety. Perhaps you could seek out Edward, in Normandy." He managed to refrain from adding, 'your only surviving son from your marriage to Æthelred.' It was a harshness she might have deserved, but he was not cruel.

"I must hold the kingdom for Harthacnut," she countered weakly, and once more he felt compelled to take to his knees, and so he did so. He must convince her of the peril.

"Harthacnut is not coming. He was never coming. Magnus of Norway is too great a threat. Harthacnut, alas, is not his father, and conditions have changed. It no longer takes a warrior to keep England safe and secure, and she now has a new king."

Manic laughter burst from her mouth as he spoke, and he watched in shock as her laughter quickly descended to tears.

"Tell me the rest," she demanded softly, and he nodded. She was brave. She always had been.

"Ætheling Alfred is dead. I have," he hesitated, fearful of uttering the next words, "brought his body to you for burial."

At those words, the Queen Dowager screeched a terrible noise that reflected all her lost dreams and hopes, the trauma of birthing a son she'd seen so little of since his father's death, and who she could blame no one but herself for his capture. Her eyes fluttered in her head, and Leofric jumped forward to catch her limp body as she slid down the wooden chair back she was sitting in.

Her women, with reactions far slower, fluttered like disturbed hens, and Leofric spoke sharply.

"Show me to her chamber. She'll need to lie down. Come, quickly." He bent and scooped her into his arms, surprised by her lightness and the pleasant scent of soap that enveloped him.

He cursed her frailty, something he'd never witnessed before, as he followed one of the more astute women to an area curtained off from the main room, and behind which a regal bed lay waiting for its occupant. He put her on the bed, as the woman fussed around her, and then he withdrew just as quickly. His place was to be waiting when she was once more sensible of her surroundings.

Outside he could hear the rest of his party arriving, and he made the snap decision to return to his men. The Queen Dowager's women, few as they were, watched him with haunted eyes. They understood the implication of his news, and he felt it was only right to allow them their final moments within the house at Winchester that the Queen Dowager had made her home since Harald had attacked the royal treasury.

Quickly, he strode to the door and then outside. His own men, under the instructions of his son, were gingerly bringing the cart animals to a stop. The coffin of poor Lord Alfred nestled upon it, covered by a black cloth. Seeing it once more, Leofric felt his anger and disappointment rekindle.

He was beginning to understand his father's sadness in those he thought above such petty acts.

His son came to him, a question in his eyes.

"She fainted," he whispered, as Ælfgar's own eyes reflected his sorrow for their journey, but he said nothing more.

Leofric watched as he went back to organise the men. Any of them could have refused this duty. Leofric hadn't commanded any of them to escort the coffin of the ætheling, but his nephews hadn't shrunk from the task, and neither had his brothers. Together they hoped to do Alfred the honour he'd been denied in life.

It had taken all of his guile to prevent his nephew from the Abbey at Peterborough from accompanying the body of the man he'd come to know as a friend. But, or so Leofric had reasoned with his namesake if they'd managed to keep the news of those who'd sheltered Alfred from general knowledge it was necessary to continue the charade. It would go poorly if King Harald discovered Peterborough had harboured Alfred.

Anger still turned Leofric's stomach when he considered what had happened to the man, hardly given a chance at life. Alfred had been exiled when little more than a child and his father's restoration to the kingdom of England had been short-lived and ended in death. Neither, it seemed, had he been accorded a tremendous amount of respect from his Uncle in Normandy. Instead, he'd found comfort and support from his sister and her husband and would no doubt have been content if his mother hadn't summoned him to England.

He cursed himself for not realising how desperate the Queen Dowager had become, or even, how desperate Earl Godwine had been to build his broken relationship with the King.

If he'd known.

If he'd acted.

He grumbled under his breath.

He'd done what he could, but it had all been too late, and this was the only honour he could now offer ætheling Alfred.

He had no children, no heirs, no one to remember him apart from his mother, and perhaps, his half-brother and remaining full brother. He was curious to see how Harthacnut, should he ever come to England, would react to what had befallen his mother's other son. He hoped that whatever message Alfred had sent to Harthacnut, it hadn't implicated the whole of the English race. He also hoped that Alfred had contacted his full blood brother, Edward, and let him know that while he'd been tortured, it had only been by one man, not the whole of England.

The ground was crisp underfoot as he wondered around outside Emma's home. The winter had been harsh but bearable. There had been storms and snow, but nothing that prevented the early burgeoning of green shoots and small flowers. The world was waking up, but not Alfred, who was dead to it all.

Behind him, he became aware of a door opening and turned to see that he was being beckoned back inside. He went with heavy feet. Now that Lady Emma was sensible, there would be difficult questions to answer, and an even more imperative instruction to give.

He ducked his head as he walked back into the small hall. Lady Emma was still in her bed, and he was escorted to her side. She sat on the side of the bed, composed but paler than Alfred's corpse had been when Leofric had claimed it.

"Tell me," she demanded, her voice a flutter of wings, and Leofric swallowed his distaste at what he must say.

"He died from his wounds. The monks did all they could for him, and there was a belief that he'd recover, but infection struck one of his injuries, and it wouldn't heal. There was little more they could do for him, but ease his end."

He hoped to avoid explaining the extent of Alfred's injuries, but Emma glared at him.

"He was beaten and blinded," he offered, his words falling like daggers onto a metalled road. Each word made Lady Emma flinch, and he wished he'd been less harsh.

"Who?" she asked, and it was his turn to flinch. She would have guessed already. He was sure of it.

"Earl Godwine took him hostage and handed him to Harald or rather Lord Ufegat, his Uncle. I took command of Alfred as soon as I knew of his presence in Mercia, but many, many months had passed, as you know. I wish I could have done more to intervene, but I met only a wall of silence. Alfred was too weak to move once I found him, and King Harald wouldn't have let you venture so far into Mercia, and I had to keep his whereabouts a secret. I'm sincerely sorry, Lady Emma." He tried not to make excuses for himself, or lay the blame at the feet of others, but he hadn't created the mess.

"Why have you come?" she cried angrily, "to gloat? To berate? And why you?" Her final words were almost a howl of denial, and Leofric winced in the face of her grief and sorrow.

"I came to honour you and your son. This was badly done. Neither of you deserved it."

"A fine time for your honour to reassert itself, Earl Leofric." Her tone had turned spiteful, and her face had gone from dead white to hectic magenta. He ignored the change.

"You should not question the honour of another when others have also shown a lack in that regard." He couldn't wound her again by blaming her for Alfred's death. He was sure she'd blame herself anyway. How could she not?

"The King wished to send his household troop to inform you, and to escort you from England. I thought you'd prefer a friendlier face, but perhaps not." He tried to keep the rancour from his voice. After all, the woman was traumatised, but he scowled with the sourness of his tone.

She choked as he spoke, her face once more draining of colour.

"I must leave?" she said. Leofric nodded.

"The King doesn't trust you in England. He's banished you."

"But it's my home. It has been for over thirty years."

"I know that. You should perhaps have remembered that before you reached out to your older children. The King could have tolerated you if you'd posed less of a threat."

At his words, her face crumbled, and her shoulders heaved with sobs. He swallowed down his own sorrow. Suddenly, it all felt like petty revenge from his king. Harald had won. Could he not have been content with that? But now, even Leofric knew that the Queen Dowager was too much of a temptation for the erstwhile Earl Godwine. Either Emma or Godwine had to go, and at the moment, as weak and abandoned as she was, Emma made the easiest victim.

"You have allies, My Lady," he tried to console, but she couldn't hear him over the noise of her wailing sobs. He shifted uncomfortably on his feet. He still needed to speak to her about Alfred's body. He went to turn away, to leave her once more, but she reached out and grabbed his arm.

"Alfred should be buried with his father," she moaned, but he shook his head.

"The King will not allow you anywhere near London. He counts it as his capital and more important than Winchester. Alfred should be interred within the Old or the New Minster. You must decide so that arrangements can be made, and carried out in your absence."

"The King will not allow me time to bury my own son?" she exclaimed, and Leofric shook his head.

"The king wants you gone, immediately. The death of Alfred doesn't concern him. It's not that which has caused your banishment. It's just one of those strange coincidences that the two events have occurred so close together."

The Queen Dowager paused, as though to consider her next words, and then she made a snap decision.

"My son will be buried at Shaftesbury Abbey, along with another murdered by his own family. You'll escort us there, and remain until he's buried, and only then will I leave England."

Leofric sighed at her stubbornness.

"You'd have me escort you through the lands controlled by Earl

Godwine? I understood that you and he were not allies." A shadow fell across her face at his words, and he hated himself for prodding her already bleeding wounds.

"You'll protect me," she stated, and in those words, Leofric heard a queen speaking and bowed his head in submission. He'd sworn to do this last act for the Queen Dowager. There was no other who would have taken the risk, and been assured of retaining the king's trust and support. What did it matter if it took him longer than he'd at first envisaged?

# 18
## AD1037

The journey to Shaftesbury was accomplished far more easily than Leofric could have imagined. He'd have thought the Queen Dowager would have wanted to dally and recover her strength, but she demanded they leave the day after his arrival in Winchester, and so the ætheling Alfred was interred at Shaftesbury even more quickly than Leofric thought he could have arranged the same in Winchester.

Lady Emma had wept on seeing her son's coffin, but Leofric had refused to follow her command to open it so that she could see his face one more time. The monks had embalmed the body, but that had only served to highlight his terrible wounds, and Leofric felt he owed it to Cnut to spare his wife the horrific knowledge of just what her ambitions had done to her son.

Instead, he'd allowed her and her women to weep and wail all the way from Winchester to Shaftesbury, cautioning his men to hold their reserve and keep ever vigilant. Earl Godwine was only just in the favour of the new king. Leofric would not put it past him to apprehend the Queen Dowager and the coffin and cast them both into oblivion. Leofric's honour wouldn't allow that to happen. And he'd have hoped King Harald wouldn't have either, but a faint worry remained.

Now at Shaftesbury, he found himself waiting for Lady Emma to announce that she was ready to begin her exile, and it was here that he encountered problems.

"There is time aplenty, Earl Leofric," she cautioned him, her face aged beyond her years and her tone subdued and sad.

"There is not, My Lady. The King demands your departure. I've already given you more time than he'd have liked, and I've no problem with that, but you must leave with all haste."

"Why?" she barked, "will the King kill me too?"

"The King didn't kill your son," Leofric temporised, but she laughed wildly.

"I know who killed my son, and I know your worries, but I'd face Earl Godwine one more time. I've sent for him. It remains to be seen whether he'll come or not, but I'm content to wait."

"My Lady," Leofric groaned. "Earl Godwine is in a precarious position. He can't come to you without incurring the King's wrath. If he does come, he might even try and imprison you as well."

"Don't think that I fear Earl Godwine," she hissed. "He must account for his actions before I leave England, forever."

"Why must he? Surely you must have realised he'd have no love for your children with Æthelred."

"How can he blame my children for their father's actions?" she countered, her face hectic.

"How can't he? He owes his wealth and position to Cnut, and to retain it he needed Harthacnut, and you. You put him in a position where he couldn't win either way. Either he supported the other son of Cnut or the son of Æthelred. My Lady, you compromised Earl Godwine, and he reacted, badly. Very badly."

"He can't blame me for events of so long ago?"

"What, just as you won't blame the King in thirty years' time for the death of your son?" he countered.

"It's not the same thing," she reacted immediately, and he shook his head.

"Of course it's the same thing. He lost his position and his wealth when his father was forced to leave England on King Æthelred's order. Just as you have now. And you're more fortunate than Earl Godwine ever was. You've powerful family and allies on the Continent, you have Harthacnut as King of Denmark, a nephew in Normandy, a great-grandson in the Vexin. You aren't alone."

"So now you stick up for Earl Godwine?" she mocked, but he held his tongue. Now was not the time to reason with her.

"We leave for the coast tomorrow," he announced. "If you're not ready, my men will use force. I'd suggest you accept the inevitable, My Lady." With that, he stalked from her presence within the Abbey itself and strode to the stables.

His men were there, his family as well. He craved the company of their clear thinking, that desire to follow his every command that was missing in Lady Emma, despite his hopes of helping her.

The sound of approaching horses pulled at his scattered attention. He groaned. He hoped Earl Godwine hadn't heeded the Queen Dowager's request. In that, he was to be disappointed.

Rounding the stable building, he was met by a handful of mounted men, Earl Godwine at their fore. He was accompanied by one of his sons, although Leofric couldn't have said which one. The young men were all too similar, and he barely knew them by sight, let alone by name.

"Earl Godwine, this is an unfortunate meeting," Leofric called to him when he was within hailing distance. Godwine looked at him with a flicker of worry on his face.

"I," he stuttered, and Leofric held his eyes for a long moment.

"I know why you're here. Do you think this is wise? The King is hardly charmed with you."

Earl Godwine slid from his horse's back as Leofric spoke. When the other man turned, Leofric was surprised to see the sorrow etched into his face.

"Lady Emma summoned me. I owe her an explanation," Godwine countered, but Leofric shook his head.

"She's grieving, and she's banished from her home of over thirty years, what good would your self-serving explanation do for her?"

Expecting a testy response from his erstwhile enemy, Leofric was surprised by the weariness in Godwine's voice.

"We all make mistakes, Leofric. Well, all of us apart from you and your father. I would speak to her. I can even escort her to the coast if you wish to be rid of her." He ended his words with an animal growl, but Leofric refused to be drawn into any sort of argument that would allow Earl Godwine to lash out at him.

"I've sworn an oath to the King that I'll escort Lady Emma. If you wish to see her, be my guest, but I warn you against it."

"Your concern is ill-founded, but I thank you for it. But excuse me. I came to speak to my dead friend's wife, not argue with you." Godwine stalked from his presence then, and Leofric watched him go pensively.

By then his son was at his side, and he solved the riddle of Earl Godwine's son.

"Well met, Harold," his son called as the remaining horsemen milled around.

"Come, dismount, have food and ale," he continued, and Harold looked as though he wanted to agree but was hesitant. "I'm sure your father and the Queen Dowager have much to discuss, and there's no threat here," Ælfgar assured, and Leofric was proud of his son. He also trusted him enough to walk away and leave the two younger men to talk. His concerns were more with Earl Godwine's reason for being here.

He couldn't believe the audacity of the man. Leofric had the King's express permission to escort Emma from England. While he might have been a little lenient with his interpretation of that permission, he knew the King wouldn't object to his actions. But then, Harald trusted him as implicitly as he would a father. The same couldn't be said for Earl Godwine.

Did he and the Queen Dowager plot within the abbey grounds? Or did he genuinely come to offer his apologies and sympathies? Leofric couldn't be sure of either of those options. Perhaps he came to do both. But would the Queen Dowager allow herself to ally with Earl Godwine once more? He rubbed his head as he ambled back to the stables and his men. He'd thought Emma's exile from England would bring an end to his worries, now he was unsure.

And in the background, Harthacnut still hovered. Leofric was convinced that Earl Godwine was sending money to support Magnus' attack on Denmark, content to do anything that would keep Harthacnut away from England.

None of Cnut's children, not even Harthacnut, had inherited their father's prowess in battle. They suffered because their reputation was not one of warrior men. Instead, they had taken to guile and persuasion, gaining the upper hand, no matter the cost. Leofric thought it reminiscent of the way Æthelred had once tried to govern England – another man who'd been no warrior.

A flurry of ragged voices and Leofric found his feet rushing him back to where Earl Godwine's horses waited for their lord. Harold and Ælfgar had reached an agreement whereby food and ale were brought to the men while they remained on horseback, or so Leofric surmised from the hastily discarded cups and plates, as Earl Godwine rushed back to his horse.

His anger was evident on every part of his body, from his tense shoulders to flushed face, and gesticulating arms.

It seemed the meeting with the Queen Dowager had gone poorly. 'How could either of them have expected anything else?' Leofric thought to himself, a wry expression on his face.

'She's a mad bitch," Earl Godwine was shouting as he neared his horse, and Leofric shook his head to hear him speak so about the widow of a man he'd always called a friend, or so he'd just chastised Leofric.

"Get her from England," he called to Leofric, hastily mounting his horse as he shouted, and turning to meet Leofric's surprised expression.

"Get that mad bitch from England's shores. She means to undo us all." With a roar of anger, he kneed his steed forward, and Leofric watched the party go with trepidation.

Had he just witnessed the next stage in the combined efforts of Earl Godwine and Lady Emma to secure the English throne for Harthacnut? Or was his anger real? Neither would surprise him.

Later that same day, Leofric rode towards the English coastline. After her meeting with Earl Godwine, Lady Emma had quickly sent word that she was ready to leave. There had been tearful departures between Emma and three of her women, unable or unwilling to follow the former queen into exile. Leofric had despatched two of his men to escort the women back to Winchester, while he and the Queen Dowager and the rest of the men made their way to Exeter. He'd been hoping to persuade Emma to depart from Southampton, but she'd refused to head back into the heart of Wessex land under the control of Earl Godwine. Leofric knew she had long-standing connections with Exeter, so understood her choice while cursing it at the same time.

He was keen to be done with his duty, and back in London or Oxford with King Harald. There was still much that remained to be done to secure England, and he was only too pleased that few decisions could be reached if both he and Earl Godwine were absent from the King's Court.

Emma was near silent on her horse, a small cart following them, filled with a few possessions she'd insisted on bringing with her. Leofric thought what a pitiful sight it made for a woman who'd been a queen for nearly thirty years, but he kept his thoughts to himself.

It was a cold day, and they'd not reach their destination without an overnight stop. He hoped they got as far as Dorchester and weren't forced to seek shelter wherever they could, a cow barn or some such low place. He already felt as though he snuck Lady Emma out of England, just as his father had once told him about sneaking her into England, out of sight of the determined opposition of Swein of Denmark who'd wanted to capture her for himself, and another disgruntled earl, who'd wanted to get his revenge on King Æthelred.

Ælfgar had taken him to one side as soon as their journey had begun and told him about his conversation with Harold Godwinesson.

"He knows little. His father doesn't let him into his confidences, or so he says. I doubt that's true, but I also know that fathers do keep secrets," his son chided him, and Leofric laughed.

"Just as sons do," he retorted with a smile, the first such to cross his face since he'd encountered Lady Emma.

"He says his father is keen to make any further amends that King Harald deems necessary and that the people of Wessex and Hampshire are pleased that he remains as their earl."

"And what do you think?" he pressed his son. Ælfgar was as astute as Leofric's own father had been. He talked, and he listened, but he heard much more than the average person.

"I think Harold is scared for the future and doesn't understand why his father agreed to Lady Emma's summons. He seemed worried by his father's plans."

"And what of his feelings toward the King?"

"He seemed to have no real interest in the King. Both a bad and a good sign," his son continued, and Leofric nodded.

"The king will need to decide whether to engage with Godwine's sons or whether he means to cast them aside. After all, Earl Godwine is no longer a young man. One day he'll need a replacement, and the King may not think that one of his sons should fill the position."

"Really?" his son's eyes bulged at the thought. "I can't imagine that would please many people," he said, laughing at the understatement.

"You still don't like Harold or his brothers?" Leofric pressed.

"I'm no longer scared of them," Ælfgar reassured. "There might be hundreds of them, and new ones being born every day, but without the ear of the King, they'll struggle to advance."

Leofric nodded at his son, and rode away from him, back toward the Queen Dowager.

She sat proudly on her horse, her back rigid, her eyes only on the way forward, as her horse, one of Leofric's favourites, carefully placed each hoof before putting its full weight on it. He admired both the horse and the woman.

She spoke to no one, and Leofric considered how he'd be reacting should the position be reversed. He doubted he'd be as calm, or self-assured.

"Earl Leofric," she called to him, and he trotted his horse to ride beside her.

"My Lady?" he quizzed watching her face, but she kept her eyes firmly forward.

"Earl Godwine should never be trusted," she said, adding nothing further. Leofric contained a smug smile at those words. He'd never trusted Earl Godwine. There'd never been any need to, and yet he found her words unsettling. Was this just another part of whatever plan they'd decided upon while they spoke alone. He couldn't dismiss the notion that Earl Godwine had been acting when he left Shaftesbury Abbey, and not very well at that.

Either it had been an act, or he'd been genuinely angry beyond coherent words and thoughts.

Lady Emma said nothing else, and so he kneed his horse forward, wanting to ride at the front of their strange little procession. He'd be pleased when he saw the sea and could arrange passage overseas for Cnut's widow.

Earl Godwine had once held a significant threat over the Queen Dowager. He'd gained from her desire to keep the secrets he'd known, and for all that the King had eventually been made aware, the damage was done. Or had it? The Queen Dowager still seemed much in his awe.

Only as the day was nearing its end did he get his wish of seeing the sea, and then he reined in and gazed at the splendour of the view before him. Spending so much of his time within Mercia, he rarely glimpsed the sea and was always stunned by its vastness. How could the Viking raiders of yesteryear have found England when there was just so much else out there? Perhaps, after all, it had been as punishment for the sinful English, or so the holy men and women usually said.

"We'll find lodgings within Dorchester," he confirmed, and Lady Emma nodded but didn't speak, and neither did she all night, as they rested within the home of the local reeve, almost beside himself at the strange honour done to him. He provided excellent food and wine, but his desire for conversation had to be met by Ælfgar and Leofric's brothers. Neither Lady Emma nor Leofric himself were to be tempted to gossip.

Leofric arranged for a messenger to be sent to Exeter, to the reeve there, so that transport could be arranged for Lady Emma to travel to Normandy or wherever she chose to go. He didn't wish to spend too much time in the settlement. He knew that there was a lingering fondness for Lady Emma there, and he wouldn't have been surprised if some chose to rise up against her exile from England.

It would be best if her time within Exeter were as short as possible.

And indeed, so it proved. On nearing Exeter the following day, the Reeve himself rode out to meet the strange convoy.

"Lord Leofric," the man called. "I'm Gospatric, Reeve of Exeter. I've arranged for a ship for Lady Emma," he spoke to Leofric, perhaps not wishing to meet the eyes of the woman he talked about. Idly Leofric wondered if they'd been allies, or if the man simply knew of Lady Emma, and not actually her.

Gospatric was a slight man, who rode a delicate horse. He was no warrior. No doubt he spent his days indoors counting the King's taxes.

"It'll leave today, on the high tide, provided we arrive in time."

He offered that as he noted how slowly the horses moved, glancing anxiously back the way he'd just come.

Leofric took in the gait of the horses, and the dejected figure of Lady Emma. Was she keen to be gone? Or was she dawdling on purpose?

"I'll consult the Queen Dowager," he replied, ensuring Emma had her correct title. Despite her perilous position, he couldn't think that it was right to have those who looked up to her doubting their previous allegiances.

Gospatric perked up at his use of the title, as Leofric had surmised, and some of the anxiousness drained from his face.

"Will the ship wait, should its passenger be delayed?" Leofric thought to ask, and Gospatric nodded enthusiastically.

"Of course, the captain and I have reached an agreement. If he's forced to remain, then I'll offset any loses he might make, and pay for food for his men."

"Excellent. Well done," he said to the man, before kneeing his steed close to Lady Emma.

She watched him come with vacant eyes, and he swallowed his unease. With each passing step, it seemed as though her previous pride and belief in herself drained away. He envisaged arriving in Exeter to find she no longer believed she'd ever been a queen. It unsettled him.

"My Lady," he called, and she nodded.

"The ship can leave today, but we'd need to hurry, or we can tarry, and it'll take you tomorrow."

Piercing eyes met his own, and he was pleased to see she was recalled to herself and dismayed to see the tears that leaked from her eyes.

"I would go today, if possible," she announced. "I'm no longer needed here. I'd prefer to be gone."

"As you wish, My Lady. I'll have the Reeve set the pace to ensure we arrive in time."

"My thanks, Earl Leofric," she said demurely, before reaching out to clasp the reins on his horse and arrest his return to Gospatric.

"I'd thank you for your honour and respect. I once berated you for being a lesser man than your father, I wish to retract that statement. You and he lived in different times, with different men," she smiled bitterly. "I'll never forget this, and neither will my sons."

As she spoke Leofric felt a fierce gust of wind unsettle his cloak, and he turned, surprised by it. When he looked back, Lady Emma was smiling.

"Your time is not yet done, and neither is mine."

With that, she kicked her mount to action, and the animal leapt to her commands. Leofric rushed to follow, beckoning for Gospatric to take the lead. As he rode, the weight of an unknown future settled around him, and he considered his actions and his place.

No matter what, he'd fulfilled oaths pressed on him by men in positions of power, and he'd never acted in anger or rage.

He was proud of himself, and of his family.

Whatever the future might bring, he'd accept it with good grace.

As he watched the ship being loaded with Lady Emma's belongings, she sought him out once again. She was well-dressed for the short journey at sea, with a thick cloak around her shoulders, and warm boots on her feet.

He was pleased with Gospatric's choice of commander and ship. It was a smart vessel, freshly caulked from a winter on land, and the man was burly but business-like. He carried trade goods of high value and had a rigid control of his crew, who worked quickly to escort Lady Emma's few companions on board, with little conversation and no coarse comments.

Her hand rested on his forearm, and he startled at her touch.

"We'll meet again, Earl Leofric," she said, before turning away and he found himself speaking without realising.

"I hope so, My Lady Emma. I really hope so."

# THE ANGLO SAXON CHRONICLE ENTRY FOR 1037

This year was Harold chosen king over all, and Hardecanute (Harthacnut) forsaken, because he stayed too long in Denmark; and then they drove out his mother (Lady Emma) Elfgive, the queen, without any kind of mercy, against the stormy winter.

# CAST OF CHARACTERS

## THE HOUSE OF LEOFWINE

**Leofric**, born 998

    Marries the **Lady Godgifu** in 1018

    **Ælfgar**, son, born in 1018

    **Ealdgyth**, his sister born 1000

    Marries **Olaf** son of **Horic** (this is not historically attested, but neither is Ealdorman Leofwine's daughter – just the vague understanding that he had five children, one of whom is unnamed.)

    **Godwine**, his younger brother born 1002

    **Eadwine**, his younger brother born 1006

    **Hund**, Leofric's hound

    **Leofwine**, father of Leofric and his brothers and sister, Ealdorman of the Hwicce/Earl of Mercia under Cnut although difficult to pinpoint where his power was based (dies 1023). Son of Ælfwine who dies at the Battle of Maldon in 991.

    **Æthelflæd**, Leofwine's wife (Leofric's mother – and mother to all of Leofwine's children)

**Northman**, Leofwine's oldest son born 996, executed 1017 on the orders of Cnut

Marries **Mildryth** in 1011 – two sons born 1012 – **Wulfstan** and 1014 – **Ælfwine** (not historically attested)

**Leofric's Household**

**Wulfstan** (commended man and war leader of Leofwine/dies 1012)

**Horic** (commended man and second in command, originally a member of Olaf Tryggvason's warband) his wife, **Agata**, dies 1016.

**Orkning** (his son)

**Olaf** (his son), married Ealdgyth, Leofric's sister

**Oscetel** (part of the warband/household troop/ Leofwine's commander/dies in 1031)

**Godwulf,** member of Leofric's household troop

## KINGS/PRINCES

**Jakob Anund**, King of Sweden, Olof Skotkonung's son. Reigns until 1050.

**Olaf Haraldson**, King of Norway (Olaf of Norway/St Olaf), exiled in 1028, dies in 1030 at the Battle of Seiklestad.

**Magnus**, his illegitimate son, becomes King of Norway in 1035, following Swein Cnutsson's exile, and with the support of two regents,

**Æthelred II** of England (dies 1016), Emma's first husband

**Swein** of Denmark (dies 1014)

**Cnut** (son) of England (from 1016 with Edmund/1017 sole ruler of England) and Denmark (from 1018).

His children with **Lady Ælfgifu** – **Swein**, King of Norway (1030-35)

**Harald**, Regent/King of England (1035-

His children with **Lady Emma** – **Harthacnut**, King of Denmark 1035-

**Gunnhilda**, married to **Henry**, son of **Conrad II**, Holy Roman Emperor

**Harald of Denmark** (from 1014 when his father, Swein, dies in England until 1018 when he dies and Cnut becomes King of Denmark as well).

**Lady Estrid**, daughter of Swein Forkbeard, wife of Earl Ulfr, with whom she has two children **Sweyn/Svein Estridsson** (take their mother's patronym, not their father's who is killed for treason in about 1026.)

**Beorn Estridsson**

**Olaf Tryggvason**, King of Norway, dies 1000 at the Battle of Svølder (ties with the House of Leofwine)

**Donnchaid Mac Crinain**, King of Scotland (Duncan in Macbeth)

**Conrad II**, Holy Roman Emperor,

his son, who would be **Henry III marries Lady Gunnhilda** (Cnut and Emma's daughter)

**Duke Robert of Normandy,** Emma's nephew. Left one illegitimate son, who would become **William the Conqueror**.

**Godgifu**, Countess of Boulogne, daughter of **Lady Emma** and **Æthelred II**

**Walter**, her son with first husband, Count of Vexin

**Lord Edward**, son of **Lady Emma** and **Æthelred II**, in exile in Normandy

**Lord Alfred**, son of **Lady Emma** and **Æthelred II,** in exile in Normandy

## CNUT'S WIVES

**Lady Emma, Queen Dowager** (King Æthelred's second wife – renamed from Ælfgifu – mother of Edward and Alfred) (King Cnut's wife from Summer 1017 – mother of Harthacnut (son) and Gunnhilda (daughter))

**Lady Ælfgifu** (King Cnut's first wife, even though also married to Emma – sons Harald and Swein.)

Her brothers are **Ufegat** and **Wulfhead** who were blinded by **Æthelred II** when their father was murdered, the Ealdorman of Northumbria, **Ælfhelm**, by **Eadric** in the early 1000's.

## EALDORMEN

**(may have already died but important to know who they are/were) The title of Ealdorman was replaced by the Danish Earl (Jarl) under Cnut. Actually has a different meaning to current day earl – they ruled land for their king without necessary owning it, and often had allegiances elsewhere**

**Ælfric** (of Hampshire – Kent, Sussex, Surrey and Berkshire and Wiltshire) Dead

**Leofwine** (of the Hwicce) Dead

**Eadric** (of the Mercians, executed 1017)

**Ulfcytel** (of the East Angles from 1004 marries Wulfhilda – King Æthelred's daughter) Killed in battle 1016

**Uhtred** (of Northumbria marries King Æthelred's daughter). Killed in battle 1016

**Æthelmær** of the Western Provinces dies 1015

**Godric** – reappears under Harald

## EARLS

**Earl Thorkell** (East Anglia) – married to Wulfhilda (second marriage) (widowed wife of Ulfcytel, Ealdorman of the East Anglians and the daughter of Æthelred) dies c.1023-25

**Earl Erik** (Northumbria) dies c.1023-25

**Earl Hakon** (Worcester) son of Erik of Northumbria (Swein and Cnut's ally), drowned in 1030. Married to Lady Gunnhildr, who later remarries Earl Thorkell's son, Harold

**Earl Hrani** (Herefordshire)
**Earl Ulfr** (Married to Cnut's sister – Estrid – father of Earl Bjorn and Swein Estrithsson – His sister marries Earl Godwine).
**Earl Eilifr** (of Gloucester) brother of Earl Ulfr
**Earl Godwine** (of Kent and later Wessex)
Married to Lady Gytha, sister of Earls Ulfr and Eilifr
Their children,
Sweyn
Harold
Tostig
Edith
Gyth
Leofwine
Wulfnoth
Elgiva
Gunnhilda
**Earl Siward** of Northumbria
**Ealdred** (self-styled) Earl of Bamburgh

## HOLY MEN

**Bishop Lyfing** – Bishop of Worcester
    **Bishop Beorththeah** – Bishop of Winchester to AD1038
    **Archbishop Æthelnoth** – Archbishop of Canterbury
    **Archbishop Ælfric** – Archbishop of York
    **Bishop Athelstan** – Bishop of Hereford
    **Abbot Ælfsige** – of Peterborough
    **Brother Eadnoth** (fictional)
    **Brother Leofric** (Leofric's nephew – historical, although perhaps not at this time.)

## MISC

**Brothor** – member of Cnut's household troop
    **Gospatric** – Reeve of Exeter
    **Blue** – Cnut's horse
    **Coelric** – owner of house in Winchester where Leofric stays
    **Brihtric** – thegn
    **Thuri** – runs Leofric's house in Oxford

# HISTORICAL NOTES

THE ENGLISH EARL IS A LITTLE DIFFERENT TO previous Earls of Mercia books because 1) it only covers a relatively short period of time, and 2) I've skipped the final three years of King Cnut's reign, and instead provided a very brief synopsis.

This is for various reasons – 1) there is little information available for the period 1032-34, and most of that is concerned with the deaths of churchmen, and 2) because the death of King Cnut begins a period of history in England that is overlooked, often in favour of studying Æthelred II and Cnut's reign, and then the man who was king until 1066, whose death brings about the climate that 'allowed' the Norman Invasion to take place.

However, the period between Cnut and this man is one worthy of closer examination, as opposed to being overlooked. It has much the feel of the often-dismissed middle years of the Tudor Monarchy. As a student at school I studied Henry VII (yawn), Henry VIII (too much sex and religion) and my heroine, Elizabeth I (who could do no wrong in my humble opinion), somewhat out of choice, but the reigns of Edward and Mary were the 'compulsory' elements of my course – the period when great swells of change occurred quickly, and I think the period 1035-1042 is really very similar (only without the whole Protestant/Catholic thing), so excuse me for lingering here.

Events in England following Cnut's death seem to follow an almost unnerving succession that falls into place in such a way that they seem inevitable, and yet, obviously, they were not. The art of recreating this period is in teasing out the other possible 'endings', the events and acts that either didn't come to fruition or which are overlooked in favour of later events. It is in more than just the page or two accorded to the period 1035-37 in histories of the time.

Cnut's death might not have been unexpected. It seems he made provision for his death, according to historian N Higham in his book 'The Death of Anglo-Saxon England'. This makes his death even more intriguing, and, put simply, really badly 'planned', if anyone can ever plan their own death.

His son and heir, Harthacnut, had been shipped off to Denmark a number of years previously to learn to rule the kingdom there, and he issued coinage in his own name, which is a fairly clear indication that his father anticipated him inheriting his Northern Empire after his death, and certainly Denmark. Yet Cnut's death did come too soon, and a whole host of events undermined what should, perhaps, have been a smooth ride to the crown of England for Harthacnut.

It also appears that Swein, Cnut's older son with Lady Ælfgifu, was seen as King of Norway, at least by the Norwegians, if not by his father, or later, by his father's second wife, Lady Emma.

Again, I would have to stress that history is written by the victor, and in this, as time will show, Lady Emma, the Queen Dowager, did accomplish a great deal. She might very well have had much to do with the information recorded regarding the child of Cnut's that she refused to acknowledge. The clearest indication of this is the often quoted phrase in the Anglo-Saxon Chronicle, the primary source for the period, that 'many did not believe Harald was a child' of King Cnut's.

The behaviour of Earl Godwine during this period is perhaps challenging to understand, most tellingly with regard to Lady Emma's son with Æthelred II. Alfred's death was a tragedy and one that could not have been foreseen by the seemingly desperate Lady Emma. If not her son with Cnut, then her son with Æthelred could just as easily claim the throne of England. It must be wondered at her ambitious intentions during this period – but again it's worth remembering that she had been 'queen' for almost her entire life. I can't imagine she was keen to give up her hold on the throne, no matter what. Her later relationships with her surviving children are perhaps not those of a doting mother, but more a power-mad woman, desperate to claw the crown of England back under her command. But that is for future books to explore.

But back to Earl Godwine. His father had been used very poorly by the House of Wessex (events in Northman Part 1 explain this). But by now Godwine was already a very powerful man, much more likely to welcome Harthacnut as King because of his close relationship with Cnut, a relationship that had been sealed with a marriage between the Earl and one of the King's, admittedly, more distant Danish relatives, but a relative all the same. It is Earl Godwine who perhaps made the most lucrative of marriages from his relationship with Cnut. He would have looked to Denmark for his future king, and certainly not to Normandy, which sheltered the offspring of the despised King Æthelred II.

Leofric begins to be mentioned more frequently in the available source material for the period – by now he was a powerful man – perhaps more powerful than his father had ever been and yet he still had incumbent Danes on land he may have considered his own to govern – Earl Hakon might have been dead, but his widow was not, Earl Hrani reappears at this time, and so too does Earl Eilifr. It would have meant that while Leofric retained the good wishes of the King, he was in good stead, but he may have feared the return of Harthacnut, who would have rewarded family members to the detriment of Leofric himself, possibly.

As to Lady Ælfgifu – she might have lost one son, but she was still very much a player within Mercia – and the death of her husband would have accorded her more freedom than she'd had for years – freedom to finally exact her revenge on Lady Emma, the woman who stole both her husband and her kingdom, and she may have thought, her future as well.

As to Lord Harald. He was a young man at the time – born no later than 1017 when Cnut married Lady Emma. He had watched his brother gain the kingdom of Norway (and then lose it), and his half-brother was King of Denmark in all but name, while his half-sister was married to the heir of the Holy Roman Empire. He was probably within his rights to expect to be treated better by his father when he died.

This short two year period is given little space in the Anglo-Saxon Chronicle – 1035 has 7 lines, 1036 12 lines and 1037 4 lines. It's not a great deal to go on. Neither is there a body of charter evidence. Only charters issued in the name of Bishop Lyfing survive, there are none from King Harald himself. But, there is coin evidence, and the coinage was undoubtedly reminted to show Harald's image, rather than that of his father, Cnut, or his brother, Harthacnut.

Attempts might have been made to remove King Harald from the history of the period, but he was most certainly an acknowledged and respected King, and you can find images of his coins on the internet.

I would also note that the Domesday Book begins to be a helpful resource from this period onward. Its lists detailing who owns property where allows me to finally give the Earls of Mercia some geographical possessions and to determine where their loyalties lay. I once spent an entire summer trying to pinpoint a location for Ealdorman Leofwine to consider his primary residence. This was nigh on impossible and led to Deerhurst being adopted as the place, because of Leofwine and his father's affiliation with the area.

The story of the Earls of Mercia will continue in Book 8, and if you've not read the side-stories yet, Wulfstan, Swein and Cnut will keep you going until then, and might well fill in a few gaps as well. And if you're curious about events in England before the Earls of Mercia series begins, then why not try The First Queen of England trilogy, the story of Æthelred's mother.

(On another note – I make use of M Swanton's version of the Anglo-Saxon Chronicle when plotting my storylines. This edition is in copyright and so I always quote a different version within my novels taken from the Internet. However, this edition seems to have 'disappeared' from the Internet, leaving me with a much older version – apologies if it is more difficult to understand).

# ABOUT THE AUTHOR

I'm an author of historical fiction (Early English, Vikings and the British Isles as a whole before the Norman Conquest) and fantasy (Viking age/dragon-themed), born in the old Mercian kingdom at some point since AD1066. I like to write. You've been warned! Find me at mjporterauthor.com. mjporterauthor.blog and @coloursofunison on twitter. I have a monthly newsletter, which can be joined via my website. Once signed up, readers can opt into a weekly email reminder containing special offers.

- facebook.com/mjporter
- twitter.com/coloursofunison
- instagram.com/m_j_porter
- patreon.com/MJPorter
- tiktok.com/@mjporterauthor
- amazon.com/MJ-Porter/e/B006N8K6X4
- bookbub.com/authors/mj-porter

# BOOKS BY MJ PORTER (IN SERIES READING ORDER)

### Gods and Kings Series (seventh century Britain)

Pagan Warrior

Pagan King

Warrior King

### The Eagle of Mercia Chronicles

Son of Mercia

Wolf of Mercia

Warrior of Mercia

Enemy of Mercia

Protector of Mercia

### The Ninth Century

Coelwulf's Company, Tales from Before The Last King

The Last King

The Last Warrior

The Last Horse

The Last Enemy

The Last Sword

The Last Shield

The Last Seven

### The Tenth Century

The Lady of Mercia's Daughter

A Conspiracy of Kings

Kingmaker

The King's Daughters

### The Brunanburh Series

King of Kings

Kings of War

### The Mercian Brexit (can be read as a prequel to The First Queen of England)

### The First Queen of England (can be read as a prequel to The Earls of Mercia)

The First Queen of England Part 2

The First Queen of England Part 3

### The King's Mother (can be read as a sequel to The First Queen, or a prequel to The Earls of Mercia)

The Queen Dowager

Once A Queen

### The Earls of Mercia

The Earl of Mercia's Father

The Danish King's Enemy

Swein: The Danish King

Northman Part 1

Northman Part 2

Cnut: The Conqueror

Wulfstan: An Anglo-Saxon Thegn

The King's Earl

The Earl of Mercia

The English Earl

The Earl's King

Viking King

The English King

The King's Brother

Lady Estrid: A novel of Eleventh-Century Denmark (related to the Earls of Mercia series)

**Fantasy**

<u>The Dragon of Unison (fantasy based on Viking Age Iceland)</u>

Hidden Dragon

Dragon Gone

Dragon Alone

Dragon Ally

Dragon Lost

Dragon Bond

<u>As JE Porter</u>

The Innkeeper

**20<sup>th</sup> Century murder-mystery**

Cragside – a 1930s mystery

<u>The Erdington Mysteries</u>

The Custard Corpses

The Automobile Assassination

Printed in Dunstable, United Kingdom

66000741R00167